The Sword and the Passion

Yanina Stachura

Copyright © 2013 Yanina Stachura

All rights reserved.

ISBN: 1493701967
ISBN 13: 9781493701964
Library of Congress Control Number: 2013920568
CreateSpace Independent Publishing Platform
North Charleston, South Carolina

For my mother and father

Prologue

ANGELN, NORTH GERMANY, 470 AD

Icy winds tugged at the cloaks of the horsemen as they thundered through the frigid winter forest, their faces, streaked with dirt and blood, set grim. The heat of the battle they had just left was still upon them, the blood-curdling sounds of dying and wounded men still fresh in their minds. Their flaxen haired leader saw only the image of his courageous wife, big with child, who had followed him into the fray, taking her place with the other women in accordance with their custom. He slithered to a halt in a small clearing of skeletal trees, throwing snow dust clouds in his wake. Mutilated corpses lay scattered around, their blood drenching the snow. In their midst stood a bear of a man, his square-jawed face marred from cheek to jowl by a livid scar, his flame, pigtailed hair burning fiercely in the thin, watery sunlight. In his mighty, muscular arms a squalling infant, swaddled in linen, his tiny, waving fists beating the air. The blond man leapt from his horse and drew his sword, as those with him reached for their weapons. Tension cut through the air as the two warriors faced each other, they were both the same height and build, products of an age where only the strong survived.

"Stay your sword King Casto, there is no need of it here. I give you your son." The man presented him with the squirming bundle. Casto sheathed his sword and clenched the baby to him for a brief moment, his golden moustache brushing the vulnerable, crinkle soft skin.

"Who is it who has snatched my child from the jaws of death?"

"I am the Anglii chieftain Aethelstan. Although even now our tribes fight a battle, these mercenaries paid for by my own people had no right to take an innocent." He kicked over one of the lifeless bodies, revealing a gaping hole where the throat had been. "They are scum. Not worthy of the Anglii."

"Had honour not been yours my newborn son would have been at your mercy."

"Aethelstan's sword Elatha kills only warriors in the field of battle."

Their eyes met, speaking without words in the silence of the winter gripped clearing.

"Lord Aethelstan, though not tied in blood we are now bound in honour. Let this kinship be claimed between us if ever you should have need of me." Casto slipped a heavy gold ring from his finger, it was in the shape of a boar's head, the eyes glittering garnets. "This is token of a pledge before our Gods which can never be broken."

Aethelstan took the ring, clenching it in his fist.

"It is accepted King Casto. But our peoples' have long battled as they do even now, such a thing between traditional enemies must be kept close guarded."

"It is understood. This will be passed down only through our children, and all those here sworn to secrecy"

"Though we shall fight as Anglii and Frisian, from now on, Lord King, we do so with the hearts of brothers."

They grasped arms, their steel strength flowing, bowing their heads each to the other in a brief nod before Casto mounted his horse with the screaming babe and rode away, back to the battleground, through the brooding gloom of the wolf infested woods.

Chapter One

NORTHERN BRITAIN 495AD

Bright sunlight danced through the vibrant green forest foliage, smattering the boy and girl lying on their backs on the grass with flecks of light. A soft, warm breeze rustled the leaves and kissed their faces.

"It's beautiful here Edric" the girl sighed and sat up, pushing back her long red gold plait from her shoulder and breathing in the summer air, alive with birdsong.

"Hmm" her brother agreed, closing his eyes, loathe to rouse himself and ready to doze during this welcome break from collecting fruit.

The girl hugged her knees as she looked around the small clearing. "We ought to build a shrine to the goddess Hretha in this place"

"I thought our Lady Nerthus was your favoured goddess?" Edric mused sleepily.

Averil touched the chunk of rock crystal which hung from her silver necklace. It was the sacred stone of Nerthus, a birth gift from her father. Nerthus was courageous and fierce, a leader of men, she would not appreciate the serenity of this place, unlike Hretha – Averil could imagine the big-breasted fertility goddess feeling at home in this pocket of tranquil splendour in the great forest. A rogue thought darted through her mind – here would be a perfect place for the coupling which Hretha so smiled upon. Out there in the cool shade of the trees which surrounded them, lying on a yielding carpet of fern....herself and.... and whom? She didn't know, sometimes she would dream of lying with a man whom she loved above others, who was skilled in the art of pleasing a woman, and would wake up in a sweat, frustration welling up inside her. Averil knew she was not without attractions, she was considered beautiful by her fond parents, her mother never tired of telling her how lovely she was, though she felt that was because of love rather than truth. She was well of an age for marriage, and as with all women of her Anglii race, could choose her mate freely. But she had not met any man yet who aroused the slightest desire in her.... ....her brother Edric's gentle snores broke her chain of thought, she glanced at him fondly. His close cropped red hair made his look younger than his fourteen years, he was the youngest of her three brothers and they were very close, sharing many adventures throughout early childhood, with the added advantage to Averil that he was the baby of the family and she could tell him what to do.

Averil stretched, her breasts, which looked larger than they were on so willowy a body, strained against the thin linen of the simple, calf-skimming dress, knotted around the waist with a leather girdle. She shook her brother into wakefulness.

"Oh Averil, can't we stay here awhile. I'm sure we have enough berries" he moaned as he sat up, rubbing his eyes.

"We can't go back until this bag is full – unless of course, you care for a whipping!" She teased him as they both stood up, brushing grass from their clothes.

"Now that is something I really do not care for sister!" they exchanged brief smiles.

"Come on Edric. The sooner we start the sooner it shall be done"

Averil picked up their half full bag of fruit and they set off into the cool undergrowth, searching for more of the berries which would be fermented into wine much favoured by their father, the Anglii chieftain Aethelstan, Ealdorman to King Ethelbert.

* * *

Horse and rider pounded through the forest at a punishing pace. Sweat poured from the panting, slavering beast as the terrified young lad astride pushed him to the limit, spurred on by the certain knowledge he was being followed. It was imperative he reach Aethelstan if he wanted to remain alive, for the message he carried from the desperately ill King Ethelbert was a weighty one, given personally by the King himself, his voice barely a whisper as he struggled to wrest more time from the once strong body which was now a weak, thin-stretched skeleton. For all the lad knew, the King his own father had served until his death in battle was now dead.........thundering hoofbeats at his back, he spurred the horse hard, fright constricting his throat, leaving him gasping for breath. From the corner of his eye he saw he was flanked by two horsemen, one of them was dressed in chainmail of iron rings sewn on a pale grey leather tunic, both wore iron helmets – the projecting nose guards gleaming ominously in the sunlight. They matched his speed, ice-cold fingers of fear rippled his spine as he realised his horse had reached the edge of endurance and he couldn't get ahead of them. A single, piercing scream ripped the air as one of the men swung his single-edged hacking sword, it glinted in a terrible beauty as he brought it down across the lad's neck, slicing off his head in one powerful blow. The blood splattered horse, mad with terror, reared up and galloped into the forest, shedding the mutilated torso which fell with a dull thud onto the soft earth.. The men pulled their mounts to a halt and cantered back, the one who had cut down the boy dismounted and began to search the body, pulling out a folded piece of parchment which he lifted for his companion to see before dragging the corpse into the undergrowth. The other man, who was clad in the chainmail, removed his helmet, revealing white blond hair tied at the nape of his neck.

"Good work Ulric" there was a shadow of a satisfied smile on the blond man's thin-lipped mouth.

"Our bird will not be singing this day Lord Girdar" the other said, squatting down to pick up a clump of grass to clean his bloodstained hands.

"It would indeed be hard for him to do so Ulric with his head so far removed from his body" their laughter rang out in the still woods.

* * *

"Averil, surely we have enough berries now!" Edric moaned, he wanted to go hawking with his brothers that very afternoon and at this pace he would be lucky to be home before sunset.

"We shouldn't have dawdled so long in the clearing." Averil reminded him of his laziness "Look, there's a lot of fruit on those bushes, it should be enough."

They picked their way gingerly through the undergrowth, mindful of thorns. Edric was a little ahead, eager to get the task over and done with quickly. Suddenly, he stopped dead in his tracks as though frozen and turned to his sister, his face as pale as death.

"Averil....there's......" he didn't finish, clutching his stomach, he vomited on the spot. Horrified, Averil ran over to him.

"Edric! What is it? Are you alright?"

The boy nodded, wiping is mouth with the back of his hand. "Don't look Averil, I think it's...it's...a head...." he turned his back on her and was sick again. Averil put her arm around his quaking shoulders, her eyes irresistibly drawn to the bushes he had been facing, for a few seconds chill shock gripped as she looked upon the blood splattered head of a boy, the blue eyes wide open, glazed, the brown hair stained with.....she didn't even want to think with what. Swiftly, she dragged the retching Edric away from the gruesome sight, her mind working furiously. The blood had been fresh, there had been no chance yet for the flesh to fester, which meant the deed must have been carried out recently. It was also untouched, and a clean break from the body, making it the work of no other beast than man. Her heart raced; perhaps the perpetrators of this foul deed were still in the vicinity, and she was without her dagger! They MUST get back. She took Edric's hand and pulled him into a run. They sped through the forest as though dark demons pursued them, for in truth, both felt that they did......................

* * *

They were on the open road which wound ribbon-like to the security of their village which nestled within a gated wooden compound, running past dun-coloured cows grazing lazily on the pasture and bare chested freemen toiling on their strips of land. Averil could see thin plumes of dark smoke curling sluggishly into the heat haze as women prepared the midday meal, the thought of it threatening to make her stomach rebel as Edric's had earlier. Inside, they pushed past the clusters of bare-footed, laughing children playing noisy games, their shrieks mingling with the sound of clucking chickens which Averil shooed out of the way. They made a straight path to the timbered hall of their family and almost ran into Aethelstan as he emerged from it, flanked by his two older sons, Oswald and Ulwin.

"By all the Gods! What demon is chasing your two?" Aethelstan's broad scarred face broke into a smile as he surveyed his son and daughter, sweating and dishevelled.

"Father" Averil gasped, fighting to get her breath. Aethelstan stopped smiling as he realised they were both in distress. "We found the...the....the head of a boy in the forest. In the bushes by the path. It looked as though he had been killed only recently."

"Forgive me father. But I was sick when I saw it." Edric butted in, he had to tell the truth, even though he was deeply ashamed of his reaction.

Aethelstan ruffled his cub's hair.

"Was it the work of a beast Averil? A wolf perhaps?"

"No father. It was as if the head had been sliced from the body."

"Can you take us to it?"

Averil nodded her assent and turned to Edric, his face red with embarrassment. It had taken much to admit what he had to Aethelstan and their brothers. She put her arm protectively around his shoulders, his pride would be restored.

"We will both take you."

* * *

The rushes burned brightly in their sconces, casting glowing light on the vividly coloured bulls-hide shields and the heads of long dead animals mounted on the walls of Aethelstan's hall. A whole pig was roasting on a spit straddling a crackling fire in the centre, watched hungrily by the three hunting dogs lying at the feet of their master, who sat in the central seat at the long table.

"The boy must have been set upon by robbers" It was Oswald speaking, as a slave served him a large piece of roast meat.

"But why didn't they take his garments? They were of very fine linen and not so bloody that the stains could not be erased." Ulwin challenged his brother's assessment.

Aethelstan drained his amber glass goblet of mead and wiped his bearded mouth with the back of his hand.

"This boy was no freeman or slave – his dress denotes one of some rank. It is possible he was set upon by cutthroats, although it is strange the jackals did not strip him naked"

"A vendetta perhaps?" Ulwin ventured, aware that it could be a perfect explanation, the vendetta was common among their people and could carry on for many generations.

"Perhaps....." Aethelstan's voice trailed off, they had found the body not too far away from the head, and, on the path beyond, a trail which indicated two horsemen – two men striking down an obviously defenceless lad, not must older than his own youngest son, left a very bad stench in his nostrils.

"I think we should dispel this bloody deed from our minds and talk of more happier events – my brother would probably wish to forget his lack of success at the hunt this afternoon!" Oswald slammed Ulwin good naturedly on the back, causing him to spit out some of his meat, and providing some light hearted laugher from those around.

"What say Averil sing us a fair song to lighten our mood?" Oswald asked, looking over at his sister on the women's benches.

"A good idea Oswald" Aethelstan suddenly felt the need to hear the sweet voice of his daughter. His eyes alighted on her, the red-gold hair was covered with a linen headdress tonight, embroidered lovingly by her proud mother, the Lady Edgyth, who sat by her side. His wife was still a handsome woman after all these years, aye, and able to warm his bed as no other had done. He was indeed a lucky man, the Gods had blessed him greatly, three strong sons and Averil, who possessed the same delicate beauty as her mother. The kind over which battles were fought and of which songs were sung. He had also ensured that she knew how to protect that beauty – he smiled fondly with pride at how skilled his lovely daughter was with the dagger.

"Averil!" his voice was a good natured roar across the hall. "Come sing to us."

Averil smiled and nodded her consent, bowing briefly to her mother before leaving the table to pick up a small maple-framed lyre leant against the wall nearby. Aethelstan brought his fist hard down on the table, demanding silence while his daughter entertained them. She plucked the strings with a light, skilful touch and was soon lost in the song, a legend of a brave and honourable warrior who fought and defeated a ferocious beast to serve his king. The heroic tale had reached its final chord when the door burst open, a gust of wind tugged at the torch flames, momentarily dimming the light. Averil turned to see a spear carrying sentry and three men – one of whom was being carried in the arms of his companion – silhouetted against the night sky. They strode inside, Averil's eyes drawn to the unconscious man, his dress, of leather chainmail, which denoted high rank, was smeared with dried dark red blood. A cold shiver crept along her spine as the strangers moved closer and she had a better look at the wounded man. His long, pigtailed hair was white blond, a colour she had never before seen but had sung of many times – when describing the demon who had defiled and murdered the wood nymph Triona – daughter of the goddess Hretha.

"My Lord" it was the sentry speaking "These men claim to be messengers from the king."

Murmurs rippled through the hall as Aethelstan surveyed his unexpected visitors with suspicious eyes.

"What is your business in this part of the kingdom? And how is it one of your party is wounded?" Aethelstan demanded.

"We are of King Ethelbert's retinue, sent ahead to inform Ealdorman Aethelstan of the arrival of his liege on a new progress in the next few weeks."

There was a palpable silence as Aethelstan waited for them to continue.

"Our Lord, Girdar, son of Ealdorman Leofric, has been sorely wounded by a band of robbers – we killed all those who set upon us, our master was struck down in the fight."

The one who was without the burden of his Lord moved forward, and took out a folded piece of parchment from the breast of his tunic.

"Here is a token from the king" he placed it on the table in front of Aethelstan. A wax seal bearing the initial E held the parchment fast; it opened to reveal a small, exquisite brooch of polished garnets. Satisfied, Aethelstan gave his unexpected visitors a smile of welcome.

"Take your Lord to sleeping quarters for our guests. My eldest son Ulric shall lead the way. Your Lord's wounds will be attended to."

Ulric moved immediately on the command to extend hospitality to those sent by the King, leading the group out through the back door of the hall.

"Father, the robbers who wounded this Lord must surely be those who cut down the boy." Oswald spoke, following the logical explanation for the mutilated corpse as eating and drinking resumed once more.

"Hah! I am getting old my son" Aethelstan shrugged. "I am beset by strange humour. Averil. Come on girl. Sing us a sweet song of warriors on the battlefield!"

* * *

Averil sat at a wooden table in her bower, surveying her face in the bronze hand mirror as her British slave Ebba combed the wavy mass of her hair. Her stomach felt knotted with an inexplicable feeling of foreboding which had been with her since the grisly discovery in the forest and had magnified since the appearance of the white haired Lord.

"Averil. Are you not abed yet?" her mother's voice made her jump. Ebba put down the comb and went over to the oak chest to fold her mistress's clothes away as Lady Edgyth entered her daughter's bower.

"Mother, has Lord Girdar's wound been attended to?"

"I made up a salve from herbs myself for it but his men refused me entry to their Lord, taking it from me and saying they would attend to him themselves. "

"Do you not think that is odd?"

"Odd? Why no daughter. Remember he is their Lord and has been attacked. It is natural they would want to tend to him."

Averil could find no suitable reply, unable to voice her fears to her sensible, down-to-earth mother, what could she say? She felt something wasn't quite right? She would sound crazed.

"It is good news that the King is to visit."

"How so mother?"

"Well, perhaps you might find someone in his retinue you desire at last" Edyth kissed her daughter's cheek. "I wish you good sleep my dear one."

.Before Averil could even think of a reply her mother was gone, leaving her with fresh thoughts to stifle those which so disturbed.

Chapter Two

Averil was sinking into a stormy, ice-cold sea, fighting for breath as she struggled to break through to the surface, screams and cries assailing her from all directions.

"Lady Averil" the voice, urgent, fearful, called clearly above the others over and over again, Averil tossed in the foam-flecked angry ocean, gasping for air.....she awoke, sitting up abruptly to see Ebba standing by the bed, her face terror stricken.

"Ebba? What is it?"

"Oh Lady!" Ebba wailed her distress "Something terrible is happening!"

Averil suddenly realised she could still hear the noises of her dream and see Ebba quite clearly....the room was lit up, shadows of flame tongues danced grotesquely on the wooden walls....fire!

"What?!" she jumped up and dashed to the window, her parents bower and the cluster of sleeping quarters were burning fiercely, in the eye-dazzling light she could see bodies strewn on the ground, men were fighting everywhere, some hand to hand, others with swords and axes. Was this a nightmare still – would she wake from this mayhem? What had happened? Where were her family? As the questions tumbled against each other, instinct screeched replies. Her kinsmen had been attacked, her father and brothers were strong warriors with many men and they would win this fight, they would protect her mother and little brother, but should she be caught before they repelled the enemy she would be raped and probably murdered. She closed her eyes momentarily, willing control. Heart hammering, she ran to the chest and retrieved a jewel encrusted dagger and two thick cloaks, throwing one to Ebba and giving her slave one of her own amber studded brooches to fasten it with.

"Come on Ebba....quickly! "They ran to the heavy wooden door of the hut, stopping to listen, making sure no-one was there before darting outside, Averil feeling the searing heat of the blazing buildings against her face as she and Ebba disappeared into the dark shadows behind the bower. The wooden wall of the compound was straight behind them; Averil thanked the goddess Nerthus for its proximity. It was roughly hewn and could be climbed. The girls ripped and bloodied their hands but hardly noticed the pain in their desperation to escape, half way down the other side they jumped, thudding to the ground. Not wasting a second, Averil was swiftly up and grabbing hold of Ebba's hand, dragging her slave into the brooding darkness of the woods, further and further in, away from the horrific sounds of violence and death which filled the air, catching their garments on thorn and bramble bushes which tore at their bare legs and feet, neither noticing as they were swallowed up by the trees which offered them safety....for a while.

* * *

Blood splattered the hunting trophies which hung in the main hall, littered with the broken bodies of dead warriors.

Aethelstan's three proud hunting dogs cowered and whimpered in the corner as the tall, white blond haired man stepped through the carnage, flanked by two of his men, kicking the corpses aside which blocked his way.

"I want them piled up and burnt with the remains of their Lord and his kinsmen. See to it." Girdar gave the order to one of the men beside him, who quickly left the hall to carry them out.

"A good morning's work Ulric. We would have lost more warriors had not Aethelstan and his sons not been already cold in their beds with slit throats." His eyes glinted as he savoured the words. "You did cut off the heads of Aethelstan and all his kin as I instructed?"

Ulric nodded, that was something he would not forget to do, decapitation prevented the dead from walking, he did not want to be haunted by the shades of those he had helped murder.

Girdar left the hall and stepped into the bright morning sunlight, surveying the blackened shell which was all that remained of Aethelstan's sleeping quarters.

"It's a pity most of the women were lost in the fire with Aethelstan's Lady.....still, there should be enough to go around for our celebrations." Girdar turned an ice blue gaze on his faithful retainer. "Which brings me to the matter of the traitor's daughter..." he clicked his fingers for a reminder of the name.

"Averil, Lord."

"Ah yes. Averil. Whose beauty is said to be beyond compare." His laughter was not pleasant; Ulric steeled himself for the attack which he knew was the come.

"It seems that her skill at escaping my finest warriors is also beyond compare! I want her found Ulric. She can't have got far. Search the woods beyond her bower."

Ulric saluted his Lord with his fist on his heart and stalked off, calling for a group of men to join the search.

* * *

An early morning mist hung in the crisp, damp air of the wakening forest as the two cloaked figures picked their way through the undergrowth of dew-covered fern. The girls' movement was slow, for exhaustion was now threatening to overtake them. Fear had spurred them to physical exertion they would never have thought themselves capable of and Averil and Ebba had covered more miles than they knew.

"Lady. We must rest."

Averil looked at the girl and blinked, almost as if she were seeing her for the first time. The events of just a few short hours ago had dogged her every step, every scream and cry haunting until her shocked mind was a seething cauldron of horror. Tears had fallen unchecked down her face as they had raced through the forest, for she knew only too well what fate awaited her kin should they not triumph over...over whom? The answer was plain – the Lord with the white blond hair, a mark of evil in legend and now she knew for certain, evil in reality. Girdar. To say his name was to speak the word death. It was so. She pulled the cloak more tightly around her as she shivered at the quicksilver thought, the question of why this Lord should attack her family reverberating without an answer.

"Lady Averil...." Ebba pressed.

"I heard you Ebba. And you are right. Come."

Ebba followed Averil towards an expanse of thigh-high fern.

"If we lay in the middle of this we should be able to sleep unseen. Be careful not to crush the fern too much, we must cover our tracks through it in case...."she did not finish. Her father was a brave, highly skilled warrior; he would win through over the enemy! This was only a precaution – they made their way through the plants, covering their path as best they could until they reached what was roughly the centre and fell into the springy softness. Everything was still and silent, as though the Gods themselves were sleeping.

"Ebba."

The girl turned her tired face to Averil.

"My father WILL have defeated his attackers."

Ebba surveyed the mistress who had always treated her with kindness. Lady Averil's eyes were wild, denying the outward calm.

"I shall pray to the one God that your victorious kin have been unharmed Lady." She rose onto her knees, closing her hands tightly and pressing her hands together. Averil was too exhausted to be curious at the different ways of worship of Ebba's people and herself muttered incantations to the mighty Tiw, God of War. Her lips were still moving in prayer as she fell into the merciful blackness of an exhausted sleep.

* * *

The four horsemen fanned out in a line, trotting their horses through the forest, eyes to the ground in search of a trail. They had already found pieces of torn linen on a bramble thicket and knew they were on their way to netting their prey. The sun had risen high in the sky when they saw the girl picking berries. She turned as the fearsome warriors galloped towards her, pure terror easy to read on her small features. Ulric reached her first, pulling up his horse – taking in her appearance, scrawny indeed, breasts no bigger than those of a lad! Straggly hair....surely.....his eyes alighted on the beautiful, cruciform brooch glinting on her cloak.

"The fair daughter of Aethelstan! You have led us a chase this day" he and his men dismounted, laughing as she backed away.

"I think we could celebrate our victory early Ulric" one of the horsemen smiled salaciously at the girl, she was a little skinny and young perhaps, but who cared?

Ulric grabbed the girl's arm in a rough grip.

"No. Lord Girdar wants this untouched. She is the last of them."

Averil pressed against the thick bark of a mighty oak. They had been picking fruit when the horsemen came, Ebba had been unable to hide in time..........these men in the forest looking for her meant only one thing........her father and brothers must be dead...... but her mother? Edric? Averil closed her eyes, the warrior's words pounding through her brain.......No. They were all dead. She gulped for breath, her heart hammering, not willing or able to accept the horrific truth..... ....Sweet Nerthus it cannot be so!...it cannot!......... sorrow washed over her.....she felt her legs would give way beneath her and she would fall to the ground in a quivering heap.........tears streamed unchecked down her face as the ribald laughter of the men cut through her shocked mind......knowing what they were thinking....if she stayed hidden, Ebba would be their victim, she would be safe while her poor slave was abused by these warriors....she would..........the voice within screamed disgust...was this snivelling coward shivering behind a tree the daughter of a mighty warrior Lord whose noble blood flowed in her veins? Yes! It was, and she didn't care! Her family were all dead! It were as though she could not function....the grief was too much to bear.....she would go mad with it! Averil grabbed the rock crystal at her throat and prayed to Nerthus to help her. She was the only one left to act for her father's noble house. The honour of the family was in her hands, and, despite what had happened, she was still Lady Averil, daughter of Aethelstan. She could hide away from this now, but never from herself. To have abandoned honour, to disgrace her family, was to be worse than dead. Whatever her fate she would not, could not, disgrace her bloodline. She felt her dagger in a hidden pocket of her cloak as if for reassurance

"You will release that which is my property" the clear voice rang out through the woods, each word perfectly pronounced with cool authority.

The warriors looked beyond the slave – at that moment a dazzling shaft of sunlight pierced the trees, lighting up the tall, willowy figure walking through the ankle high mist towards them, turning her mass of wavy, knee length red-gold hair into a halo of burnished copper, giving her pale, unblemished skin a ghostly translucency. A superstitious fear pulsed palpably around the men – Ulric found himself swallowing hard – it was as had been said, more so, the girl was beyond compare in beauty, he had never seen her like, only heard of it in legends. She emerged as a wood sprite in full glory, a child of the Gods who now lit the path for her. A strong breeze rustled the leaves of the trees all around, to a man they looked at the quivering foliage, all knowing the mighty trees protected the nymphs of their dominions. Averil prayed silently to Nerthus to keep giving her courage as she walked towards the men, reminding herself over and over again what her bloodline demanded...her dear mother and father would be proud to see her thus....... As she stopped before them Ebba fell at her feet, grabbing her cloak and kissing it in gratitude, the action magnifying the impression Averil had already made on her captors. She stood statue still, Ulric saw her eyes were a deep, emerald green, as of the forest, and around her slender neck was a silver pendant of mystical rock crystal, used, Ulric knew, in incantations when summoning divine powers. He fought the urge to bow. Averil looked at the unspeaking company, sensing their uneasiness, seeing uncertainly in their eyes, not knowing why this was so but thanking

Nerthus and the forest gods for it, for it gave the strength of tenuous hope, perhaps they would not be harmed, at least for now....she gambled.

"I am Averil, daughter of the House of Aethelstan. I believe it is I whom you seek. You will take myself and my slave unmolested to your master Lord Girdar."

Ulric unwittingly took a step back, Averil had spoken the truth arrived at logically – a quality these superstitious men did not possess in abundance. How did she know it was their Lord who had taken Aethelstan's hall? There was magic here, danger lurking in the darkness of the trees – they must get away from this place and quickly.

"Grimwald! Take the slave!" Ulric barked his order as he watched Averil. "You will ride with me...Lady." It would be well to give her respect in this place.

* * *

They emerged from the shady woods into piercing sunlight. Averil surveyed the scene, empty fields, livestock wandering from their allotted pastures without herdsmen to stop them, palls of black smoke rising ominously from the compound. Ulric slowed down the pace now they were away from the sinister forest and they trotted along the path. Pain seared Averil as she remembered how she and her young brother had trodden it just yesterday, light of heart, on their way to collect berries – and now.....tears filled her eyes, she fought to stem them, battling within against the girl who had thrived carefree under the fond protection of her kin, now lost forever, willing in her place, a strong, fearless woman grown. For there must be no display of weakness – she must not disgrace her family.

The compound was unnaturally quiet, only broken by the muffled sounds of weeping. Unattended geese and chickens ran amok, the blacksmith's workshop was silent, the furnace unlit and the anvil unattended. Averil tasted the bitter misery of the people, how many had been killed or maimed? How many of the women abused? She knew the answer - just enough. Enough to let the people know Girdar had defeated their master, enough so that once more the fields could be worked, livestock attended, implements made, wool spun. Averil knew the economics of ruling, to murder all was wasteful, pruning ranks to ensure future productiveness was sufficient. Her mind span as she searched for the reason for Lord Girdar's attack – vendetta? They rode into a courtyard alive with activity, bearded, wild haired warriors cleaned their weapons, some sat in groups laughing and joking, others were testing their skills with throwing axes and some were playing noisy games of dice. Ulric dismounted outside the hall and lifted Averil down onto the hard-baked earth, refusing to meet her eyes. She followed him into the building where she had shared laughter, joy and love with her parents and brothers, now it was empty, only echoes of that past remaining, sorrow struck her as a physical blow.

"Well? Where is the daughter of Aethelstan?" the demand was barely uttered before Averil stepped out from behind the large figure of Ulric to face Lord Girdar. He sat in her father's wooden seat decorated with grinning wolf heads, toying with Aethelstans' gaming pieces made from the knuckle bones of sheep. His legs were on the long table and were bare underneath the cross garters from his leather shoes. The chainmail he wore had no traces of the caked blood so visible the night before. His face was naked of hair, marking more clearly the hard, strikingly handsome features, the eyes which met hers were a startling blue and as cold as the gleaming scales of a dead fish as they swept every inch of her, mentally removing the cloak and ripping off the torn white linen nightgown beneath. Here was a rich reward indeed! By the Gods, this one had a loveliness worth killing for!

Averil read the raw sexual desire in his look and felt her stomach heave, she was in great danger of being sick. But she must do what now had to be done.

"Lord Girdar." Averil's voice betrayed her, shaking as it resounded in the emptiness of the hall, giving Girdar much satisfaction, for it pleased him greatly to see this luscious creature afraid.

Averil closed her eyes for an instant, touching the stone around her neck for courage as she had done in the forest, feeling rather than seeing Ulric step back as she did so.

This time her tone was steady, calm, authoritative. "Since all my kin now break meat with the gods, under our law I am the mistress of this hall until I have performed the sacred duty of burning the earthy remains of my great father and brave brothers as befitting warriors."

There was a silence, the statement had wiped the smugness from Girdar's face. She whom he had believed completely cowed was far from being so. Safe in her precious honour. Mindful of the law! He was on his feet and before her in a few strides – he could snap that slim white neck with just a casual squeeze of his hand....

"But warriors die in battle do they not?" he circled her as he asked the question. Averil held her head high, refusing to be intimidated outwardly though her insides churned. His next words were a hiss in her ear "And your kinsmen died in the soft comfort of their beds."

Averil's breath caught as the words hammered into her consciousness."You .....you murdered them!" she whirled around to confront him. "You denied my father and brothers death with honour!"

Girdar's face twisted into a travesty of a smile. "Honour! How freely the daughter of a traitor speaks of it! Your father was a threat to the rightful master of this territory – Ealdorman Oswin, descendent of Woden and now the king. Even as we speak others who would deny him his inheritance are being cut down. The bodies of your kinsmen have been decapitated and burnt as befitting traitors. I now lay claim to this hall on behalf of King Oswin, YOU are subject to my will."

Averil could barely take in what he was saying.....her mind was spinning......her father.....brothers....murdered! It could not be so....he was speaking once more.....as if from a distance as she struggled to come to terms with this new horror.....he had committed the most unspeakable crime of their race which the man price, wergild, could never repay.

"I think that you must learn the first lesson of your new life in my service – which is obedience. Ulric, take my new slave to one of the storage huts. Guard her there and let no-one give her food or drink until I command it."

Anger seethed within Girdar as he watched Ulric drag Averil out. He would wipe that proud, superior look from that bitch's face, she would bow to him soon, what did she understand of the politics of power? Her father's time was gone. His was just beginning.

Chapter Three

Evening's dark fingers clutched at the pale blue sky. The women were still busying themselves in the kitchens where they had already spent many hours up to their arms in blood and bones, preparing the meat to be roasted for the pleasure of the triumphant warriors. It was to be a great feast, they had already been into the storerooms and rolled out the heavy wooden barrels of ale, mead and heady rich wine so beloved of their former master. Wooden plates were being stacked, ready to be carried to the long tables of the hall in which half a side of beef was already cooking over the central fire. They all knew that few would get through the night unmolested, some had already chosen which men they would give their favours to, in that way lay a kind of safety, better one than many, and besides, some of them would be capable of little if they kept plying them with drink – especially the wine. Ebba was leaning against the wall, wiping her sweating, smoke stained face with a cloth. She was exhausted, her thin arms ached from all the lifting and carrying and her mind was in worst pain every time she pondered on the fate of her Lady, who had saved her from the clutches of Girdar's men by giving herself up to them. She had heard the women talk in hushed, fear-laced tones about Averil. Her Lady's wrists had been chained by the reluctant blacksmith Master Leif and she had been imprisoned in a small hut where firewood was kept.

Mona, the only one of Lady Edyth's attendants left alive, had been ordered to give her a rough tunic to wear as befitting a slave and had been threatened with death if she brought her food and water. It was the pale haired Lord's orders – she was to have no sustenance until he gave the word. It had been many hours since their flight from the hall, Averil had only eaten a handful of berries since then and drunk nothing. Ebba's eyes alighted on a small wooden pitcher of water, she had decided on her course of action. There was a huge leg of pork on one of the platters, some of it had already been carved, as the women flitted around like fluttering birds she slipped some pieces off and clutched them tightly, then she picked up the pitcher and melted away wraith-like into the crisp night air, moving stealthily between the huts.

* * *

All Averil's pent up grief had been spent, she longed for the sweet gentleness of her mother, ached for the warmth of her arms. She comforted herself knowing that Edric and her mother had been spared all this and were now safe and happy in the serene realm of the beauteous goddess Frig, mother of all men and gods. But what of her noble father and dear brothers? It was their fate that tormented her. They had not died fighting and perhaps Great Woden, he who had struck the serpent of evil into nine parts, supreme God in knowledge and wisdom, may not have allowed them to join their ancestors in his halls. She told herself over and over again that this would not be so, that Woden would welcome them in the knowledge they were brave warriors, tried and tested in many battles. It had never occurred to her that they would have been denied the noble death which was their right. In her naivety she had thought all noblemen had honour. What a child she had been! It were as though she were trapped in a nightmare.She turned fitfully on the straw-strewn floor, licking her cracked dried lips as she suffered from a thirst almost akin to physical pain. There was hunger too, but the need for a drink was much harder to bear than an empty, grumbling belly. There was a small, high window without glass, covered with sacking, the moon shone palely through it just as it always had, as though nothing had happened.

"Lady!" it was the same urgent voice which had woken her from a bad dream into a living nightmare.Ebba.

A wooden pitcher of water was handed over, she took it eagerly, putting it to her lips and taking great gulps, giving herself indigestion but not caring as the water quenched her parched throat. A shadowy hand gave her some slices of meat.

"I will be back with more when I can" then nothing, Ebba had slipped away.

Averil fell onto the straw and ate the meat, savouring every last morsel before drinking the water, slowly this time....it tasted like nectar. She splashed a few precious drops onto her face and felt refreshed, seconds ago she had been wretched, now the kindness and bravery of a slave girl had given her fresh will. What had she been thinking! She was Aethelstan's daughter! The daughter of a great warrior of a noble house! No-one could ever take that away from her whatever happened – especially not that bastard Girdar! She knew not how, but she would find a way to right this wrong. To restore the honour of her house. The Goddess Nerthus would protect and guide her. She took off her cloak and placed it near the firewood pile, the hidden dagger was still inside it and must stay out of sight, she was fortunate that the cloak had not been taken from her when she was thrown into the hut. She had a weapon and when the time came she would work out the best way to put it to use.

* * *

The feast was going well, there was more than enough meat and drink to go around, and enough women to share should the warriors fancy to take anyone later on. The communal drinking horn, embossed with animal designs in glittering silver, was passed around while the wooden goblets were refilled swiftly by the serving women. Girdar presided over it all, watching rather than taking part in the celebration, sitting with his elbow resting on the arm of Aethelstan's chair, rubbing his chin thoughtfully. He turned to a whipcord thin retainer who stood behind him

"Egforth. Bring me my captive. I wish her to serve me."

The man's seamed face split into a wide, yellow-toothed grin as he bowed.

"And don't touch her! She is the sole property of your master."

Egforth scuttled away, unhappy with the turn of events but willing to wait his turn should the time come.

The light of the hall hurt Averil's eyes after the darkness of her imprisonment. Egforth pushed her to the front of the long table and jabbed her in the small of the back, causing her to fall on her knees before Girdar. She struggled up, hampered by the chain linking her wrists, only to receive a second blow which brought her down again, to the general delight of everyone. Averil battled to control a grimace of pain as she got to her feet once more.

"You may let her stand. Come here." It was the way you would speak to the lowliest animal and it damaged Averil far more than the shooting pain along her spine. Egforth dragged the chain to bring her to Girdar's side.

"Since you call yourself the mistress of this hall you will do your duty and serve your new Lord. Cut my meat and feed me."

More laughter and nudges, tightly pressed lips and closed faces among the serving women who feared for their distressed Lady, whose kin had been badly wronged.

Averil's reply echoed through the hall. "A dog tears his own food. He needs none to do the task for him."

Sweet Christ! Ebba dropped the plate she was carrying as she heard the ringing tones from where she was serving at the end of the hall – he will kill her!

Girdar sprang from the chair, grabbing a handful of the soft copper hair, tugging at it with a relished viciousness.

"You go too far! Would you like me to cut off the fair hands which refuse to serve their master?"

If he'd threatened to kill her she would have been ready – but mutilation! Reserved for thieves and cut-throats! The dreadful idea of it hit its mark, a glimmer of fear marred her face for just a split second, giving Girdar very much what he wanted to see.

"Perhaps if I took away one hand, as a reminder to the other to obey?" her breasts brushed his chest as he pulled her to him, he felt excited by the thought of the exquisite, unmarked body which he knew was beneath the rough tunic. No, he would not cut it just yet.....he threw her onto the floor. Suddenly, the dogs, who had been sleeping full-bellied by the fire, began to bark as the main door swung open, a whisper of night air invaded the oppressive warmth, men stood up, their weapons at the ready. A lone, dark cloaked figure strode inside. Averil felt her throat tighten as the stranger came into the light. He was the mirror image of Girdar, but they were as night and day. The other's long, pigtailed hair was as black as a raven's wing, one side of his clean-shaven face marked by an angry jagged slash of a scar clearly outlined against the bronzed skin. Two magnificent cruciform brooches studded with blood-red garnets glittered at his shoulder, she saw he wore chainmail underneath the cloak, the iron rings sewn onto a dark tunic of deep brown leather. His sword was in a wooden scabbard lined with fleece, the bronze handle glinting in the firelight. He came to a halt in front of the main table and gave Girdar something akin to a smile – it didn't warm the coldness of his eyes.

"So Girdar, you are to be congratulated on capturing the hall of the mighty Aethelstan."

"You are not the only one of our brood who can triumph in battle over a worthy opponent Ranulph."

The declaration branded itself on Averil's consciousness – what lies were these? Every nerve within her rose in rebellion, the fear which had been so real seconds ago was obliterated by a white hot anger.

"This Lord did not triumph in battle!" the words filled the hall as Averil emerged from the shadows, walking around the table to face Ranulph. "He cut down my father Aethlestan and my brothers as they slept in their beds!"

Ranulph saw a magnificent, fiery haired girl in chains before him.

"Your kinsman denied mine the right to die in honour. I, Lady Averil, daughter of Aethelstan, demand blood feud. It is my right!"

There was a clamour of voices . Blood feud. A vendetta which could carry on a murderous path for generations and ended only by the death of the accused or the acceptance of wergild – man-price – in recompense.

"Your wits are addled! I acted in defence of my liege King Oswin. Blood feud is not an issue." Girdar's expression was pure malice as he stepped forward to confront his accuser, but Averil didn't flinch as she faced him. Ranulph surveyed the girl, his mind working quickly, it had been a bad mistake to leave his treacherous half-brother alone to deal with Aethelstan.

"What evidence have you of this?" Ranulph demanded. Averil saw his eyes were iron-grey and as hard and uncompromising as granite.

"He boasted of it to me himself!"

It was so. He knew Girdar. That whore-spawn had besmirched the honour of their house – but it was his word against that of this girl, who obviously hadn't witnessed the deed.

"You are asking me to believe that my kinsman would commit so low and act and then tell you of it? It seems that you seek a life other than that of she who is subject to a new master. Wergild would give you this – is that not so?"

The accusation slashed at Averil's already overburdened heart. Her withering reply in clear tones came as if from someone else, not from the young woman whose grief was now at last too much to bear.

"I have been a fool to expect justice in this place. My honour is all I have left – how fitting it is that the kinsman of my father's murderer should now try to take that from me."

For a split second Ranulph was stunned, he had never seen such stupendous courage from any female before. He saw now why Girdar had chosen to murder her menfolk – he would not have stood a chance against them. Girdar's hand came down hard against Averil's cheek, knocking her to the ground, her head banged hard against a table leg and the blackness of unconsciousness engulfed her – the goddess Nerthus was sparing her from pain. For now.

* * *

The feast was in full swing, Ranulph's retainers had joined the company and there was singing, dice playing and raucous games of prowess with axes and hacking swords. Ebba pressed a dampened cloth onto the ugly blue-black bruise which marked Averil's pale cheek. She and Mona had not been prevented from rushing to Averil's aid and had dragged her away from the company to the side of the hall, resting her head on a folded cloak. The Lord with the dark hair and Girdar were eating and drinking at the main table, paying them no heed. Ebba prayed to God it would remain so while she tended her Lady.

* * *

Ranulph sat next to Girdar, watching his own contingency of men enjoying themselves – and they deserved it, they had fought long and hard against the family of Halliwell, cut down to a man along with their retainers, who, as was expected, fought on to their last breath for their Lord, even when they knew the cause to be hopeless. That was some days ago, since then word had reached him from his father Leofric that Oswin's cause was won. Their plan of campaign, hatching for months in the utmost secrecy, had been blessed by Woden, who had struck Ethelbert down with a wasting disease to help their rightful cause. Now Ethelbert was dead they had effectively wiped out any who would have opposed their choice of successor. His family now held the lands of Halliwell and Aethelstan as well as their own – and others would be given to them for their faithful service. It was well, or would have been, except for his snake of a half-brother, spawned of his despised, long-nosed stepmother Egwina.

"Who of your men helped you do the deed?" he turned emotionless eyes on Girdar.

"I told you Ranulph, the girl is mad with grief, this story is one of her own imagining."

"Do not treat me like a fool Girdar. Just tell me who they were."

"I have captured this hall as instructed by our father. It is enough." Girdar spat the words to his hated half-brother, son of a barbarian Briton who had called herself a princess, but had probably been no more than the meanest slave when his father captured her.

Ranulph laughed merrily for the benefit of the men – this would be a joke – he turned on Girdar, grabbing him by the neck of his tunic and pulling his face inches from his own.

"What you have done touches us all. You have fouled our name in such a way that it will stink in the nostrils of men."

Their eyes met, naked swords in a death duel, Girdar broke free.

"Ulric and Grimwald"

Ranulph surveyed the base coward who shared the same blood.

"I hope they can be trusted."

"What do you think?"

Ranulph drained his goblet, a buxom girl leant over the table to refill it, her ample charms clearly visible and within easy reach......it left him cold for an instant as the beautiful, noble girl filled his head. Aethelstan's daughter.

"Is the girl untouched?"

"As yet" Girdar grinned, the thought of submitting her to his will quickened his blood.

"So you have not yet added rape to her list of grievances." Ranulph remarked dryly.

"She needs to be taught a little humility first." Girdar's eyes lit up as he relished the thought of it, and then suspicion assailed him. "I hope Ranulph, you do not plan to share in my good luck."

Ranulph's laugh was deep and mellow as he surveyed the covetous expression on Girdar's face.

"Let us call her a gift. In gratitude of my stepping over the mess you have vomited over your kinsmen."

* * *

Averil dived from the blackness of unconsciousness into a different darkness – of the night. Wood smoke assailed her nostrils as cool air touched her skin. Her aching cheek was pressed against the leather tunic of a guard who was carrying her in his arms. Memory flooded painfully back. Girdar had struck her down in front of everyone, including the scar faced man whose heart was as black as his hair. A door creaked open and she was placed on the familiar straw covered floor of the storage hut. It slammed shut, leaving her alone in her dark imprisonment.

Chapter Four

Ranulph stirred on the comfortable, straw-stuffed bed, he felt the large breasts of the naked girl in his arms rub against his chest as he fully awoke from a deep, satisfying sleep for which he could largely thank his chosen bed partner – what was her name? Eglif. An accommodating girl, and skilful in what best pleased. He squeezed her bare buttocks appreciatively and then smacked them hard, causing her to squeal.

"Come on girl, get up and bring me some ale and meat." He laughed as she jumped to obey, picking up her tunic and pulling it on quickly before slipping out. He stretched his muscular body, hardened and scarred by many campaigns, and realised he stank of womanizing. No matter, he would wash later, after the hunt. The forest was rich with game, and sticking pigs was one of his favourite pastimes next to hawking, something which Girdar too excelled in, which brought his thoughts around to the younger half-brother whom he had always disliked, knowing well of his cowardice and cunning, put to use here against the fierce warrior Aethelstan, and, of course, Girdar's boastful nature, wrongly applied in his dealing with Aethelstan's undeniably beautiful daughter, a prize indeed and now his property. But the circumstances of the ownership did not rest well with Ranulph, there was no question that he would ever allow his noble father Leofric's name to be besmirched by the actions of his bastard half-brother, but nevertheless, the bloody, dishonourable deed left a very bad taste in his mouth.

"Your food Lord." It was Eglif. He took a welcome deep draught of the warm ale as he noticed the girl's nipples jutting boldly against her thin woollen tunic, the sight pushing his grim thoughts aside.. Throwing the goblet down. he pulled her onto the bed, ripping off the dress as he fell on top of her wriggling body. She giggled as his tongue explored her generous bosom and he once more took his pleasure.

* * *

The door of the hut creaked open, casting a ray of bright sunlight into the gloom. Averil sat up on the straw, squinting against the unaccustomed light as Ebba entered, carrying a large wooden tray which looked too big for her slight frame. She set her burden down and handed Averil a goblet of crystal clear water and a hunk of bread from it. The smile of thanks Averil bestowed as she accepted worth more than a thousand words.

"I don't know how it is you are come here Ebba but I am grateful for it." Averil bit into the thick chunk of warm, freshly baked bread, with a hunger she had been trying unsuccessfully to keep at bay for a long time.

"Here Lady Averil, eat some meat, it will give you strength."

Ebba deftly picked delicate breast meat from the chicken carcass she had brought and handed it to Averil before standing up.

"I have water for you to wash."

Ebba took a pitcher of water from the tray and set it down alongside two cloths – one of soft linen for Averil's body and the other of coarse wool to rub her teeth. There was also a bar of white soap Lady Edgyth had bartered with a tradesman for and then infused with the scent of crushed flowers, Averil picked it up and smelt the heady aroma which always reminded her of her mother, her heart twisted in its emptiness.

"I have brought your comb." Ebba produced a familiar delicate silver object from inside the linen cloth.

The spectre of her sweet mother disintegrated at the words, dragging Averil back to the stark reality of the present.

"Again I am grateful to you Ebba." Averil took the cleverly worked comb, feeling its cold beauty between her fingers, regarding the girl with a steady gaze. "Now tell me how it is you are able to bring such things to a prisoner?"

"You are no longer a prisoner Lady! " Ebba's smile was warm, her happiness at the news obvious.. "Well, not as before! You are still to be kept locked in this hut by night but the dark-haired Lord ordered that you work in the kitchen and that you should be fed and watered…." Ebba bit off the word hastily, its animal connotations only too clear.

Nothing was lost on Averil as an image of the scar faced man of the night before came into sharp focus in her mind's eye….he who had refused to believe her accusation about Girdar…..what turn of events was this?

"Who is this dark haired Lord?"

"His name is of the wolf's shield mistress. Ranulph. He and Girdar are half-brothers, sons to Ealdorman Leofric who serves the new king, Oswin. Come Lady. I will braid your hair."

As Ebba combed her mistress's hair as she had always done, Averil only had one thought in her mind. Ranulph. Why should he give orders on his brother's captive?

* * *

Water splashed in all directions as the horsemen pounded over the stream into the village. Coming up at the rear were the horses bearing their gory prizes – the bloody, stiff corpses of wild pigs sporting gaping spear wounds. Women and children ran from the relentless path of the men as they galloped to the hall, knocking down cooking pots and scattering excited chickens on their way. Ranulph and Girdar, side by side in the lead, reined in simultaneously outside the hall, stable boys running over immediately as the two dismounted so they could lead away the sweating, snorting beasts who had carried their masters.

"It was good sport Girdar." Ranulph beat off the dust of the ride from his dark tunic with leather gloves.

"Not bad. Although I much prefer the talons of the hawk to the sticking of a spear." They escaped from the heat of the late afternoon into the cool hall where goblets and pitchers of mead had been laid out on the main table.

"Ah yes Girdar. You would." Ranulph surveyed his half-brother dispassionately before pouring himself a drink and sitting down, Girdar always would prefer the work to be done while he took pleasure from watching.

Girdar glared at Ranulph, knowing full well what went on in his head.

"When do you plan to leave for your lands?" Girdar asked, sitting down heavily before slaking his thirst.

"What lands are these?"

"Halliwell's! You defeated him in battle so now they are yours – as Aethelstan's are mine."

Ranulph laughed and took another draught of mead.

"I wouldn't be so sure of that if I were you. It is for our king to decide what his new Ealdormen are given."

"It is right we are granted land we have fought for."

"Which is why I plan to join our father at the king's hall to make sure it is so."

"With me at your side." Their eyes met, distrust plain to read in Girdar's.

"I think not Girdar. Your taking of this hall was.....questionable, as the daughter of Aethelstan has already testified. It would be better to leave things to me."

To him? Girdar's suspicious thoughts took shape. Apart from Ranulph, Ulric and Grimwald – both of whom were sworn to serve him – only the girl knew of what had happened – and she was now the property of a brother who had little cause to love him....her accusation made on the same day as the death of her kin was lawful, but it was his word on oath against hers – nothing would come of it. Nothing. But. If Ranulph backed her, and her beauty in itself was persuasive.......he would be the legitimate target of anyone whose Lord had been Aethelstan – even the lowliest swineherd. His disgrace if wergild were paid instead of his life forfeit would have the same effect, either way Ranulph would get all the land, no king would grant it to he who had committed homicide. All Ranulph's talk about honour! Was this what the swine had in mind all along – why he had wanted her?

"Aethelstan's daughter is a problem which need not trouble us. I will have her killed."

Ranulph smiled, almost lazily, sensing fear in Girdar and knowing which path his snake mind had slithered along.

"She is no longer yours to kill Girdar – remember?"

"She's a danger to the honour of our house."

"Sweet Tiw! Tell me you do not fear a girl!" Ranulph's voice was laced with contempt. "Perhaps we shall arm her with a sword and you can fight her!"

Girdar sprang to his feet, his anger threatening to explode viciously and in bad need of an outlet other than he who was a match for him.

"Your sense of humour leaves me cold brother. I shall leave you to enjoy it on your own." He stalked out into the light, finding his target straight away, one of Aethelstan's hunting dogs, to whom he delivered a series of kicks until it fell whimpering to the ground.

* * *

Averil was working in the kitchen, swilling goblets and plates in water she had collected earlier from the stream. She almost welcomed the unaccustomed drudgery, this way, she didn't have any time at all to think.

"The Lord Ranulph has magical powers in bed." This was Eglif speaking, her ample bosom heaving and her bright blue eyes sparkling as she re-lived the work of the night and morning to Ebba. Her voice loud enough for everyone to hear.

"His body is scarred from many battles and fearsome strong....."

"Eglif!" it was Mona's authoritative voice which cut off the girl's words, much to Averil's relief. "Get me some of the warmed water."

Averil turned to see the older woman stagger into the kitchen with her heavy burden which she set down gently on the floor and knelt beside. It was the injured hunting dog, blood trickled from his mouth and his pitiful brown eyes were glazed with pain, Mona took the water from Eglif and staunched the blood, stroking the dog gently. Averil moved over to the tragic tableaux, tears stinging her eyes at the obvious distress of the poor animal.

"What happened Mona?"

"Lord Girdar kicked him. I fear his insides are smashed to pieces – it would have been kinder to kill him straight away."

Averil looked upon the poor creature whose death would be long and agonizing, it had been so when her father's favourite dog had been savaged by a wolf, then Aethelstan had plunged his sword Elatha into her heart, sparing her the misery of a slow death.

"It must be ended for him Mona. I will do it." Before anything could be said, she was gone, wiping away tears as she dashed to the hall where her father's mighty sword Elatha hung.

* * *

Balancing on a long wooden table, Averil took her father's great sword from the wall. The weapon was very heavy and cold in her hands, she touched the figures of the weird birds and reptiles skilfully worked on the silver hilt, thinking about how often her mighty father had held it as though it were as light as air in his hand. The pommel displayed a fire spewing fearsome beast, Averil traced her fingers along the outline, it appeared to move with the pressure, curious, she pressed down harder, then with all her strength as she felt it give – springing open to reveal a hollow hiding place beneath. Averil took out the object inside. It was a heavy golden ring with a boar's head insignia, the eyes glittering garnets, she saw well worked runes within its circle. It was a beautiful, barbaric object – how strange it should be so hidden, she grasped the ring firmly, gossamer recollection brushed her mind tantalizingly – and then was gone.... she replaced the top of the compartment and jumped from the table, the ring firmly in her hand.

* * *

Ranuph stood up and stretched, realising he was in sore need of a bath – but decided he would sleep first. Halfway to his quarters the thought of taking a pitcher of mead to his bed caused him to return, in time to see the bare footed girl balancing precariously on tiptoe on a table to retrieve an impressive sword from its place of honour on the wall. Even before he noted the chain attaching her wrists, he knew it was Averil, although she looked very different to the fierce eyed creature with the flowing flame hair of the night before. Curiosity held him as she appeared to examine the weapon and then jumped from the table with her burden. He stepped into the shadow of the doorway. He saw one side of her face was marred by an ugly bruise, it had always been so with Girdar, taking pleasure in harming those who were defenceless – human or animal – he watched as Averil slipped out from the back of the hall from whence she had come.

"Lady!" Mona gasped as Averil appeared with Elatha and went over quickly to the whimpering dog. She knelt down and stroked his soft fur, looking deep into his pain-wracked eyes.

"Do not fear" she spoke gently "I will release you from this pain as your own master Aethelstan would have done."

Averil got to her feet.

"The Gods know that I don't want to do this Mona. But you know that I must! " Using all her strength, she raised the sword with both hands – the gloved hand stayed the action, twisting Elatha from her grasp, sending it clanking to the ground as she almost lost her balance. The silence was deafening as the dark haired Lord picked up the sword and in one swift, expert movement, plunged the blade deep into the dog's heart, killing him instantly. Ranulph wiped the bloodstained blade on the straw before turning to Averil.

"It takes the skill of a warrior to kill cleanly. You would do well to remember it."

"You do not have to tell the daughter of a warrior about the kill. I know of the skills to end life in both man and beast."

Although his grey eyes touched hers only briefly she saw the disbelief in them. He examined the sword in his hands, admiring the delicate workmanship on the gleaming blade inscribed with the magical runes of Tiw to ensure its owner victory in battle.

"This sword was your father's?"

"Yes."

"It is a noble weapon. What is it called?"

"It is Elatha." There was pride in Averil's voice.

"I will take Elatha back to its rightful place. And see you do not lay hands on it again." He smiled. "I would not have you instil fear into my warriors."

Conflicting emotions beset Averil as she watched him leave, anger at his sarcasm and begrudging gratitude that he had killed the dog quickly and cleanly, thus sparing it further suffering. She wondered what kind of man this half-brother of Girdar was.

Chapter Five

Heavy summer rain beat down on the wooden storage hut which was also Averil's prison. She had been working in the kitchens preparing food all of the day and was exhausted, her hair was still damp from running back and forth to the hall in the pouring rain but now she lay with her cloak wrapped tightly around her against the firewood, listening to the rain banging relentlessly against the walls as the storm raged on unabated. Averil shuddered involuntarily. She had harboured a fear of such weather since she had seen one of her father's retainers, a strong warrior, veteran of many battles, struck down by lightning. The image of the horrible death had never left her – would that the Gods would take her vengeance on Girdar with the aid of the forked tongue of death! Girdar. In truth she was in turmoil, she wanted justice for her family. But always the truth that there was a new king, a new order in the land, and her demands would not be heeded. Her mind was going around in circles again as she fell into a fitful sleep.

* * *

The laughter and talking in the hall was subsiding as men threw pallets onto the floor and began to sleep off the effects of too much food and drink. Girdar sat back on his chair, knocking the girl he had been idly fondling off his knee as he looked around for Ranulph. Ah, there was his half brother enjoying the company of a wholesome girl on the straw by the roaring fire.

"Get me more mead." Girdar growled at his spurned companion who has just got up from the floor, The girl hastily hurried away to do the Lord's bidding, glad to be free of this man well favoured in looks but with a heart as dark as a demon.

* * *

The hot sun beat down as Averil and Edgyth walked hand in hand through the blanket of blue flowers which covered the woods with fragrant beauty. As Averil looked around, the scene began to change, the green trees became gaunt and lifeless, ugly giants standing amidst withered and dying plants, chill winds gusted all around as the sun dissolved, the cold reached through the dream........the door of the hut burst open, banging against the firewood piles with a dull thud, waking Averil abruptly to meet her nightmare. Girdar. Framed in the doorway. Averil stumbled to her feet, still disorientated, her heart hammering.

"It is long past time to claim my rights over my captive."

Fear gripped for only a moment and then a dark anger overwhelmed her, she reached into the hidden pocket of the cloak beside her and found much to reassure her – the dagger was in her hands..........

"Rest assured that what you claim would never be offered freely to a murdering bastard such as you!"

For a second Girdar was incredulous, then he burst into derisive laughter. "So you wish to fight me?"

"Come on then daughter of Aethelstan." He pulled his own dagger from his belt. "Kill me!"

"It will be my pleasure!"

He lunged at Averil, but to his astonishment she parried the thrust, once, twice and a third time wrong footing him so he fell back. His guard dropped for a precious second and she stabbed at his exposed body but his arm came up protectively, she slashed at it, cutting deep, cursing at missing the mark. Blood spurted from the wound, soaking his shirt, he glanced disbelievingly at the cut. She took advantage and went for the kill, but he was too quick and she was too close, he caught her wrist with his bloodied left hand and wrenched the knife viciously from her grasp. She'd lost it – been too eager – not kept her head..... he pulled her close, ripping agony through her as he squeezed his arm against her spine, his face swam in front of her as consciousness threatened to slip away.

"Hurts doesn't it?" his voice a disjointed hiss against her ear as he relaxed his hold just enough to take away the edge of the excruciating pain.

"You are lucky that I still choose to take my pleasure. For it gives you just a little while longer to live." Averil struggled violently, despite the pain, his blue eyes burned lust and death as he forced her to the ground, he was pressing down on top of her, she could smell the honey sweet aroma of mead on his breath, her nails sought his face but he anticipated the move, catching her wrists in one hand and pinning her arms above her head while his other hand ripped at her tunic.

"It will be a shame to kill you, for you are indeed beautiful – everywhere" horror gripped as he touched her. From the corner of her eye she saw the dagger glinting on the floor, he had relaxed his grip on her wrists as her reached down between her thighs......disgust, revulsion, desperation.... if she could just get out of his hold.... could reach the knife..........

Suddenly the burden of his relentlessly pressing body was no longer on top of her own, it was falling away, hitting the wall with a heavy thump. Averil staggered to her feet.

"Get out." it was Ranulph, he had half turned to her, she saw Girdar get up, a warning cry froze on her lips as he smashed his fist into Ranulph's face, sending him sprawling. Averil ran for the knife, but the snarling Girdar, his mouth oozing blood, pushed her out of the way, making a vicious stab kick at Ranulph's body, but Ranulph was not as dazed as Girdar supposed, he grabbed his brother's foot and flung him backwards against the firewood. Averil was looking for the knife, knowing it must be beneath the firewood Girdar had fallen on.

"I said get out! Go to your bower!" Ranulph shouted.

The Gods! She would never get the dagger back now! She ran out, hardly noticing the lashing rain soaking her to the skin as she made her way to the hut which had been her bower.

* * *

Lightning cracked in the sky, lighting up the hut, Averil had washed herself with a pitcher of water, rubbing at her body almost frantically, anxious to wash away the filth of Girdar's touch. She now sat on her bed with a fur lined cloak from her belongings wrapped tightly around her to help stop the shivering, as the delayed shock of the ordeal took a grip on her. Her mind still witness to what had happened, reliving every minute, every feeling, had she not been hampered by the chain and not allowed her emotions to take hold she might have killed him instead of just uselessly slashing his arm! She closed her eyes and saw Girdar's eyes burning with lust and death – he had meant to kill her afterwards....had not Ranulph stopped him. Ranulph. Why had he done that? The trail of thought came to an abrupt end as the door banged open and shut and a dark figure emerged into the light of the flickering candles. It was Ranulph, his face was badly bruised and there was dried blood on his lips. His eyes swept over Averil, if he hadn't heard if from the semi-conscious Girdar himself, cursing her, and seen the wound and the weapon with his own eyes, he would have thought it beyond belief that she had actually challenged his brother to a knife fight and then sliced his left arm with deliberate, expert precision. He had to admit that the thought of Girdar's mortification at being wounded by a girl – and one such as this – was very gratifying. But he, Ranulph, had underestimated her, they both had, she was in chains by the Gods! And where had she got a dagger from? Now here she sat, the supposed helpless victim who had turned on her attacker, her red gold hair wild, her freshly scrubbed face of haunting beauty deathly pale and still marred by the bruise Girdar had inflicted in the hall. He noticed the hands which knew how to handle a weapon were trembling slightly as they clutched at her cloak.

"You are unharmed?"

Averil nodded, her nerves stretched taut, not knowing what to expect from an enemy who had come to her aid.

"This is yours I believe?" he held up the dagger, still stained with Girdar's blood.

"Yes."

"I shall keep this." he pushed the dagger into his belt, a sardonic smile on his lips "for my brother's protection."

"He threatened me with death." The words tumbled out as though spoken by someone else, a release from her overburdened heart.

"I am not surprised given that you sliced his arm. In truth, a slave who attacks her master's kin for whatever the reason would be seen by many as a very poor bargain."

The words seared through Averil...pulling her back to her senses....what a fool she had been! For just a moment she had actually thought that he had been protecting her! She was HIS property! Of course he had saved her. From the same fate at his own hands! She glared at him, a potent mixture of anger and humiliation bringing heat to her face.

"Once more I expect honour from you and once more you twist my words to suit your own purpose!"

Ranulph slowly wiped the blood from his mouth with the back of his hand as he considered her. "You are without doubt an ungrateful bitch. Perhaps I should have let Girdar have you."

"And loose the chance to break me in like a new prize mare yourself? Like the filthy pig that you are!"

The silence in the room was deafening as Ranulph coolly contemplated her.

"Two things you should know. The first is that I am not my half-brother. The second is that those who Ranulph, first son of Ealdorman Leofric, bestows the very great honour of choosing to bed do so willingly." He walked over to the door and then turned back to face her "Oh yes, there is a third. You are a slave. And as such are so far beneath me that you will have to work harder than most to get there."

He took his leave. Averil leapt to her feet, picked up a goblet and flung it at the closed door with all the force she could muster.

* * *

The day dawned with a sharp brightness as the men prepared the horses and supplies for the journey to Oswin's hall. Ebba went quietly about her work in her lady's bower, not wishing to disturb the fitful sleep of her mistress. As she was folding clothes into a small oak chest Averil awoke with a dreadful cry, sitting bolt upright in the bed. Ebba dropped the garment she was holding and ran over to her, calming words on her lips..... for a second Averil looked at her as though she were a stranger.

"Lady. It was only a dream." Averil flinched as Ebba squeezed her shoulder, the girl noticing an ugly purple bruise fanning out from it onto her Lady's bare arm.

"Yes. Only a dream" she threw back the covers and got unsteadily to her feet, refusing Ebba's helping hand.

"There is water for you to wash with ."

"A wash?" disquiet rippled through Ebba at Averil's unexpected, mirthless laughter. "I need immersion in boiling fat to take away the filth which has touched me!"

"Lady...you..you...were..." Ebba's voice trailed off as she struggled for the appropriate, shocking words.

Averil's voice was vicious as she spoke almost to herself. " I almost had him Ebba – I injured his arm but I was too eager to end it, my father always chided me for letting my heart rule my head when fighting, now I know that he was right."

" I do not understand!"

"Girdar tried to rape me last night – I stabbed him in the arm and his noble brother came to my rescue" the heavy sarcasm was not lost on Ebba.

"Christ in Heaven! You should have escaped when you had the chance!"

"No. That was not the way then and it is not the way now Ebba. I am still Aethelstan's daughter – and no-one can change that. I will have justice for my kin. I do not know how, but I will." Her voice was suddenly brisk. "Now. Pass me the water for I am in sore need of it."

Ebba did as she was told. "I was bidden to ready you for a journey this morning."

"A journey?"

"To King Oswin's hall."

"Am I allowed to take my possessions?"

"I was ordered to pack what you would need."

" It's alright Ebba, do as you were bid, I shall wash myself."

"Do you wish this to be taken?" Averil saw Ebba was holding her finest garment. The kirtle was pure white linen and the overdress was sea green silk, lovingly embroidered around the hem with intricate flower patterns by her mother's own hand. The silver girdle to clinch in the waist was there too. Memories of the last time she had worn the lovely clothes came flooding back, it had been at the feast to Ecre, mother of the Earth. There had been much merriment and she had danced with all her brothers, spinning delightedly about the hall.

"Lady?" Ebba was speaking again, dragging her back to the present.

"Pack everything Ebba. I want nothing left for Girdar's whores!" the words were barely spoken when there was a heavy banging on the door, making them both jump.

"Enter." Averil's tone possessed all the old authority she had once commanded. The door was dutifully opened by the blacksmith Leif.

"Lord Ranulph has ordered you free of your chains for the journey." Leif's honest features spoke their pleasure, she recalled his anguish at having to chain her in the first place, and found a genuine smile for the craftsman of her father. "You must come with me to the workshop."

Averil followed him out, so, she was not to be taken to the new King's hall in rags and chains. Did perhaps Ranulph believe such things would make him appear different from Girdar? If so, he was mistaken.

* * *

"What is this Girdar?" Ranulph's voice was a demand as he walked into the courtyard, surveying his brother's men side-by-side in preparation with his own retainers getting ready to move out.

"It is what you see Ranulph. We are preparing for the journey to Oswin's Hall." Girdar turned to his brother, his top lip ripped and swollen from their fight of the night before, his arm was bound beneath his shirt. Averil's stab wound had been cleaned and sewn up, it would leave a scar for Girdar to remember her by.

"So you do not trust your dear brother to look after your interests." Ranulph regarded Girdar's smashed mouth with satisfaction.

"You will be interested to know that I leave Ulric and Grimwald here with a few of my men to look after that which will undoubtedly be named mine."

"I am impressed at your good sense Girdar, it's a pity your other dealings have not been so favoured."

"Nor yours Ranulph. Your attack on me last night has not been forgotten."

"The girl is mine. Though I am unsure that you would have got your way – given that she was in chains and in possession of a dagger." Ranulph allowed himself a smile at Girdar's discomfiture at his taunt, as he cut short the conversation by turning away to organise his own men. The part Averil had played in wounding Girdar had not been mentioned to any of the warriors for obvious reasons, it was taken Ranulph had been responsible when they had a drunken brawl. Ranulph recalled how good it had felt to smash his fists into Girdar, fighting without weapons had a special kind of exhilaration, primitive compared to the skill of the sword but effective and deeply satisfying, especially when your opponent was someone as despised as your own half brother, who now claimed this place as his own by right of conquest. The thought brought Aethelstan's sword to Ranulph's mind. Elatha. He recalled Averil's pride as she repeated the name. It was a beautiful, noble weapon. Unworthy of his half brother. He, Ranulph, would take it.

"Lord." The gravel voice of his most trusted retainer and finest warrior Edred brought his thoughts to a halt. He turned to see the bear like, bearded Edred dressed in skins as always, despite the late summer weather, striding towards him, dragging rather than leading a spirited dappled grey mare.

"Lord, this mare is giving me trouble, it has thrown two of my best warriors already. I am told it belongs to Aethlestan's daughter." Edred's weathered face broke into a smile as he tugged at the leather bit to control the frisky animal. "I venture to say that I am hardly surprised."

"It would be a pity to leave behind such a valuable horse. Let her former mistress ride her to Oswin's hall."

Edred bowed briefly and turned to leave.

"And Edred."

He turned. "Yes Lord?"

"Keep close but discreet guard on the girl."

Edred's eyebrow shot up for an instant before he placed his fist on his heart in salute and took his leave.

* * *

Averil was wrapping up her comb and mirror in a piece of soft rawhide when Edred entered the bower, his eyes alighting with momentary interest on the black-haired slave, then dismissing her as far too young and skinny, before turning to her proud mistress, the cause of much enmity between his Lord and Girdar, although there never had been any love between them. It was plain to see why Girdar should feel so aggrieved by Ranulph's ownership, for the daughter of Aethelstan's loveliness was without question and certainly without equal.

"Your horse is waiting to be made ready for the journey." Edred's voice was gruff, befitting his wide, muscular bulk.

"My horse!" for a moment Averil thought she had not heard this warrior correctly. "Do you mean Egwina?"

Edred burst into laughter at the name, by the Gods! Ranulph would find this great sport, it was the same name as Girdar's Lady mother – how fitting! For in truth the spiteful woman had the face of a horse!

"I cannot see what you find so funny" even as Averil reacted to being the subject of such amusement, a bitter-sweet recollection came back to her of how the name had also provoked much merriment from her brothers, how they had teased her!

"It is a strange name for a beast." Edred's tone was without apology.

"The name is beautiful and fitting for such a noble creature." They were the same words she had used to the grinning Edric, even as she cuffed him playfully about the ear for his cheekiness. The happiness she had felt at the news she was to be reunited with Egwina vanished. Edred was still laughing to himself as he took his leave.

Chapter Six

The last of the sunlight was beginning to fade in the cool green wood as the entourage came to a halt. The women were sore from the constant jarring of the oxen-drawn carts they were travelling in and were glad to be on firm ground again, even though their work of preparing food from the copious supplies was just beginning. Averil reined in Egwina and gently stroked the mare's soft neck. They were both weary, for the pace set by Ranulph and Girdar had been a fast one and they had covered much ground, each hoof beat taking Averil away from everything she had ever known. In one night when her family had been killed, it were as though she had shed what was left of her girlhood and grown into a woman – now she was moving on into an uncertain future. Yet, if she closed her eyes she could imagine it was as it had been and she was riding Egwina through the forest as she often did during the long summer evenings, without a care in the world. Averil dismounted, reckoning from the direction of the setting sun they were driving deeper into the west. Heart heavy, she pulled the leather saddle from Egwina's back, leaving it on the mossy ground before leading the horse to the bubbling clear stream where some of the men had taken their mounts to drink. She recognised one of them as the weasel faced Egforth who had treated her so cruelly the first night of her captivity. As she approached he gave her a yellow toothed grin accompanied by a mock bow. Averil ignored him and settled Egwina to drink before crouching down and cupping water to sip.

"Surely a girl of noble blood such as this one should be drinking from a golden goblet eh lads?" it was Egforth's voice. Averil turned to see a group of grinning men closing in around her, she sprang to her feet, their salacious expressions sharply reminding her of Girdar's attack and that this time she didn't have a weapon for protection.

"Get you gone from here."

"Why? We like your company don't we?" the men roared their approval at Egforth's words. "Besides you interest us." Egforth licked his lips. "We're curious to see what our masters find so much to their liking." Egforth's face broke into an obscene smirk as he approached.

In the blink of an eye Averil had jumped onto Egwina's bare back, the horse reared, knocking Egforth and sending him sprawling into the water.

"So Egforth, at last you take a bath to wash away your filth!"

Averil's laughter was without mirth as she watched the dripping Egforth struggle to get to his feet.

"What in the name of the Gods is going on here?" the voice boomed as a couple of men were knocked to one side by the warrior Averil recognised as giving her the message about her horse.

"She knocked me into the water!" Egforth splashed out of the stream. "I swear I will make her pay!" he lunged towards the horse. Edred pulled the smaller man away, lifting him with ease from the ground by the scruff of his neck.

"Easy Egforth. After all she's just a girl. Not worth risking losing your gizzard for."

Uneasy murmuring broke out among the men as Egforth's wet face paled.

"It was just sport Edred. A joke."

" It is forgotten. This time." Edred dropped him to the ground, his bearded face splitting into a grin as the men dispersed back to the camp. Averil dismounted, watching Edred closely as he addressed her.

"It seems that my intervention was not entirely necessary."

"Nevertheless I thank you for it."

"Well, you are after all a valuable piece of my Lord's property."

"Ah yes. Property! The Gods! Why not put me with the livestock and have done with it!"

Edred found himself amused. "Nay Lady, even I, humble warrior that I am, can tell the difference between your noble self and a goat!"

Edred's laughter was good natured, infectious, incredibly Averil found herself laughing with him, feeling all the tension dissolving as they shared the joke.

* * *

The delicious aroma of the roasting pig reached into the corners of the dark night, kept alive by the dancing flames of the fires whose uses extended to deterring wolves and bears.

Averil sat on the grass by one of the carts, eyes closed as she drank in the night air tinged with whisps of wood smoke, knowing her favourite time of year would soon be here when Ecre, mother of the Earth, would transform the forest into a gleaming palace of burnished copper and gold.

"Lady." It was Ebba's voice "The men are ready to eat."

Averil's eyes snapped open, back to the stark reality of her new life. She had so far avoided much contact with the warriors by taking on the heaviest task of carrying water from the stream. Now she must serve these swine. She stood up and smoothed her thick, woollen grey tunic clenched at the waist with a black leather rope belt.

"Come Ebba. We will serve the mead and ale."

The two girls lifted one of the heavy barrels from the back of the cart and started to pour its contents into wooden pitchers Ebba already had with her.

"I will have some of the mead too Ebba." It was Eglif, her pretty face clean and her yellow hair unbraided and flowing down her back. "And I alone shall serve Lord Ranulph." The statement was a challenge as she looked at Averil.

Averil stared in disbelief at the serving girl – it seemed this pathetic creature regarded her as some sort of rival for Ranulph! Ha!

"Do not think Eglif that I should ever wish to take such a pleasure from you."

Eglif liked the words but not the manner in which they were addressed, it didn't seem quite right somehow. She flounced off, telling herself she wasn't afraid of the former Lady Averil, after all, she, Eglif was a servant, of higher status than a mere slave!

"Come on Ebba. Let's get this over with!" the girls walked over to the camp fires. Averil caught a glimpse of Ranulph laughing and talking with Edred, perfectly at ease, for an instant it were as though she was seeing him as a man for the first time, seeing him as Eglif did, the raven hair and colouring such as Ebba possessed, the dull red sword scar slashed diagonally across one cheek.

"Hey girl, bring the mead!" the shout broke through her thoughts and Averil walked over to the dice playing warriors.

"A great honour it is to be served by such a fine Lady!" the sarcastic remark prompted riotous laughter as Averil poured the drinks, determined to ignore them.

"She's a bit skinny eh Aldred?"

The bearded man called Aldred reached out to roughly squeeze Averil's buttocks.

"Hmm. Nice rump though!"

Averil knocked his hand away.

"At least it will give my Lord Ranulph something to get hold of!" the men erupted into fresh laughter – that was it!

"You can either have this mead in your goblets or over your heads, now which is it to be you miserable pigs!"

The jug fell as one of the laughing men dragged her onto his knee, Averil sank her teeth deep into the hand which imprisoned her and found herself dumped onto the floor as her former captor roared in pain, must to the general amusement of everyone around. She picked up the empty jug and marched off, tasting her tormentor's blood in her mouth and wishing it belonged to Girdar or Ranulph.

"Hey! Bring us ale here!" Averil turned to meet Edred's gruff call – to be seared by Ranulph's gaze. She felt herself squirm under his look as she went back to the cart to refill the jug. On her way back she saw that Eglif was tending to Ranulph and Edred, so, the stupid girl had her uses! Sparing her at least for now the indignity of pouring mead for he who regarded himself as her master, Averil's heart was almost light.

"My master wishes ale." Egforth's whine voice brought her around. Girdar. Averil followed Egforth, she had not seen Girdar because he was a little away from the main fire, lounging on his side on the grass, resting on one elbow, he was deep in a conversation with a retainer - while his free hand was thrust inside the tunic of a tearful black haired girl whose breasts he was busy groping. Ebba! Blind fury rose in Averil, taking over her senses.

"Get out of my way!" she almost knocked over Egforth as she half ran over to Girdar, pushing her way past the men, ignoring their calls to be served.

"You wish for ale?" the tone was quiet, bringing an amazed look from Ebba. Girdar carried on talking without turning, merely lifting his goblet. Averil leant over then made as if to trip over his foot, flinging the contents of the jug over him. Girdar leapt to his feet, knocking Ebba away as if she were a dog, his blue eyes blazing with murderous anger.

"You bitch!"

"It was an accident. I tripped over your foot." It was a blatant lie and he knew it, he caught a flash of a glimpse from Averil to the fallen girl. So. He saw the slave was backing away from him and reached down and grabbed her by the hair, bringing her to his knees at his feet.

"Your clumsiness is noted. From now on this slave alone will meet my needs day – and night" a travesty of a smile twisted his smashed lips as he wrenched Ebba's tangled hair, extracting a sob of pain which cut into Averil's heart.

"She is a young girl!"

"Think you I care?" His laughter was cruel.

"You bastard! You are lower than an animal!" incandescent with rage, Averil screamed all her hatred at him.

"It is enough!" Ranulph's command sliced through the air as he took hold of Averil's arm, pulling her out of Girdar's reach.

"Your property has an unfortunate tongue Ranulph, you should have it removed." Girdar's expression was savage.

"What? And spoil that lovely face?" Ranulph smiled. "I think not."

He dragged Averil away from the camp, forcing her to almost run to keep up with his stride and ignoring her demands to be released as he took her into the silent darkness of the forest. Averil's heart was thumping wildly, her emotions in total disarray as he pushed her against the bark of a tree, a pale grey moon glinted above, but she could see his face only in shadow.

"If as you say Girdar has threatened to kill you, you are making his case for doing so very strong."

"I spoke only the truth!"

"Have you not yet learned it is not always wise to do so?"

Averil saw the wisdom of his words, by acting with her heart she had probably made the situation worse. Guilt, distress, anger at her sheer helplessness to do anything to save Ebba bombarded her.

"He said he was going to rape Ebba! She is just a girl!"

"What? "

" Ebba. My British slave. She is an innocent!" Averil's voice was savage as she focussed all her fury on Ranulph " Far too young to suffer the vile attentions of Girdar! Are all men filthy dogs such as you and your brother? Coupling without thought or feeling!"

Without warning he caught her in his arms, his mouth came down hard on hers, forcing it open to meet his own. The kiss brought every nerve inside Averil tingling into life, even as she struggled against him, her emotions reeled at the never before experienced gush of raw feeling. He released her lips, still holding her in an iron grip, his grey eyes unfathomable.

"A dog would take you now, kicking and screaming. Wouldn't he?"

Averil couldn't bring herself to speak as his breathtaking closeness battered her with a fresh storm of emotion.

"Although you refuse to say it you know the answer." He released her. "Now you understand me."

He left her alone. She leant against the tree, sliding down it to the ground, her whole body shaking, acknowledging that which her mind didn't want to recognise, Ranulph's compelling impact on her senses as he gave her the first kiss she had ever had. A wolf howl tore through the air, it's cry almost mournful. Averil stood up quickly and ran back to the safety of the campfires, away from the threat of one wolf and back to the threat of he who bore the creature's name.

* * *

Ranulph emerged grim faced from the night and walked over to Girdar who was sitting laughing and joking with his retainers and being served wine by the terrified Ebba.

"I would speak with you brother." their eyes met for a moment." "In privacy." Girdar waved his men away.

"You girl" Ranulph's command almost caused Ebba to jump from her skin."Get you gone! "

Girdar got to his feet. "So. What is it Ranulph?

Ranulph moved close, his voice low, so there was no chance of being overheard.

"I will tell you what it is Girdar and it is simple enough. I am fast reaching the point where I have had more than I can stomach of your ignoble behaviour and I do not wish the violation of a young girl added to your already overlong list."

"You do not tell me what to do Ranulph."

"Think you I am merely telling you what to do?" Ranulph leant in closer, his voice a hiss in Girdar's ear. "Let me spell this out for you in a manner you will understand. I will personally see to it that you will not gain the noble title you so seek if you heap anymore dishonour on our father's house."

Without another word Ranulph took his leave, walking over to his own campfire and retainers.

Chapter Seven

The days past, clustering together for Averil into drudgery and travel with no respite. Summer was fading, the forest gradually assuming a flaming mantle of red gold finery as they moved on their way. Since that first night Ranulph had not spoken to Averil and she had kept out of both his and Girdar's way. Much to Averil's relief Ebba went about her duties unmolested and although she kept pushing the thought away, she could not help wondering if it was because Ranulph had somehow intervened. Ebba had told her how Ranulph had ordered her to leave and then had close conversation with Girdar that night.

It was late afternoon when they came upon the wide, grey road of flint and broken stones. Averil offered a word of thanks to the Gods for the people who had built it – for it made the journey less troublesome and they would be able to camp comfortably on the soft grass by its side. Egwina trotted along with fresh heart at the solid road beneath her hooves and the pace was quickened considerably. In the distance Averil could see the ruins of what must have once been a magnificent villa, it's crumbling stone walls humbled, yet still a poignant reminder of a way of life which was now dead. They reached it as the red, setting sun cast a bloody swathe across the sky, casting a fire glow on the beautiful, cracked mosaics of gods and fantastic creatures which adorned the floor of the courtyard in which they came to a halt. Averil dismounted, taking in the surroundings, imagining what they must have once been like. There was a stone fountain at the heart of the courtyard, the stone cherub atop it which had spewed water through his mouth was missing a chubby arm, his body weather-beaten. Weeds had sprung up in drunken disarray through cracks in the surrounding walls at the middle of which was a wide, pillared doorway.

"Well, this is as fine a camp as ever I've seen!" Averil heard Edred speak as she pulled off Egwina's saddle.

"It is the work of giants – perhaps of the Gods themselves. I do not like staying here in the darkness of night!" Egforth's reply was fear filled.

"You speak like an old woman! Whoever or whatever built this place are long gone from it – do you know any God who would reside in such a ruin!" Edred laughed dismissively as other disparaging comments were made about Egforth's fears..... yet as Averil set about helping the women prepare for the evening meal, she felt there were those who shared Egforth's fright.

* * *

Night was beginning to fall, Averil was sitting on one of the courtyard steps filling a jug of mead when she saw Ebba struggling with a heavy bucket of water dragged from the stream which ran beyond the villa. Averil went to her aid immediately.

"Ebba, here let me help you."

Ebba flashed Averil a grateful smile,.

"Thank you but I think it should not be wise. For I take this straight to Girdar's retinue."

Averil's heart dived. "He still hasn't touched you?"

"No Lady."

"I thank the Gods and your own for it. Soon we will be at our journey's end and you will just be one of many slaves and servants."

"I overheard Girdar say this land is part of King Oswin's estates and we will be at his hall on the morrow."

"Hey girl! Quickly with the water!" the man's command broke off their conversation. Ebba moving as swiftly as she could to obey. Averil returned to the step, sitting down heavily, heart reaching out to the girl who had once been her slave and was now a firm a friend as she would ever have.

The central fire lit up the night, casting eerie shadows on the crumbling courtyard walls. Tonight, as in all other nights, Averil helped the others serve the men and was free of the task of waiting upon Ranulph, whose every need was anticipated and met by Eglif, her pretty face dimpling with accommodating smiles. She saw Eglif fluttering around Ranulph, squeaking delightedly as he sat her on his knee and began to laughingly kiss her neck. His action reminded Averil for a split second of the devastating effect of his lips on her own – the gush of raw feeling...... she hastily pushed the recollection aside, as she had done many times before, denying and then accepting and excusing. It had been the first time anyone had kissed her, it must be that was always the effect such a new experience produced....she had been overwrought with emotion after what had happened with Girdar and Ebba.....her eyes had lingered on Ranulph for longer than she realised and, in a heart-stopping instant, as he lifted his mouth from Eglif's neck he almost caught her gaze. Averil looked away quickly, going about her business of pouring the ale, what was wrong with her? To stare as she had, and if he had actually caught her doing so! The jug was emptying quickly, now would be a good time to refill it, Averil made her escape to the carts where the glow of the fire only partially penetrated the night, she wished she could curl up in a corner somewhere and stay wrapped in the inky blackness of the dark until the morning..... a thought hit her - the ruins would offer her that and the chances of her being followed were slim as the men were fearful of it. Quickly, she took out a thick beeswax candle from the supplies and climbed onto one of the mead barrels by the courtyard wall to light it from a torch burning in a rusty sconce. Now, she would be able to find some much needed solitude. Taking her cloak from the back of the cart she made her way through the large doorway. A full moon shone pale light through the window of a large, spacious room, but Averil was still glad of the wavering candle flame, for it allowed her to take a closer look at the wall, decorated with a running scroll design featuring bizarre bird like creatures whose colourful feathers fantailed at their backs. Such work of artistry, perhaps it was as Egforth had stated on their arrival, the work of the Gods! The connecting room was smaller, under her feet the floor was decorated with a riot of colourful mosaic, black, orange, yellow and red all intermingled into square and chain patterns. Shining the candle on the walls Averil saw to her shock they were adorned with the naked bodies of men and women. She stepped closer, curiosity gripping her as she studied the entwinements of the couples involved in all manner of aspects of love making, their expressions ecstatic......remembering what Eglif had said of Ranulph's body...fearsome strong..... rather like these naked men on the walls.....and the women's bodies soft and yielding as her own..... she ran her fingers along the outlines of the beautiful paintings......the sensations Ranulph had brought to the surface with just one kiss came flooding back....what would it be like if they were so joined?

"You should not wander around on your own." Edred's voice filled the room and made Averil jump, she whirled to face him, almost dropping the candle.

"Edred! You frightened me!"

"Better me than someone worse." he remarked dryly. "My Lord Ranulph wishes you to serve him."

Averil felt her heart dive as she looked upon the bearded face of the man who, of a fashion, had become a kind of friend.

"Surely you should be conveying your message to Eglif?"

"My words are for you and no other."

"Very well."

Averil wondered why now she had been brought to Ranulph's attention, she was certain he had not seen her shamelessly watching him sport with Eglif. What in the name of the Goddess had she been thinking doing that anyway! And not only that, her thoughts as she had been looking at the paintings! She must be beset by some sort of madness! She followed Edred out of the villa with a sense of dread, filling a jug of mead by the cart and then following Edred over to Ranulph, already being fed roast meat by Eglif as he played dice. Averil bent over to fill his empty goblet on the grass next to him, she had just straightened up when Eglif flung the jug from her hand, her face a mask of fighting fury. It all happened so quickly Averil could hardly take it in.

"Get you gone unless you want your fine eyes torn out!" Eglif screamed "Only I serve this Lord!" the affirmation was accompanied by peals of laughter from the warriors, Averil saw Girdar was highly delighted, relishing a situation she knew she HAD to get out of calmly – and very quickly. She would not be forced into demeaning herself by exchanging words in this way, especially when those words were over Ranulph!

"Indeed you are more than welcome to do so Eglif as I have told you once before. I was only acting on his orders."

Hands on hips, Eglif regarded the girl whom she had grown to hate with a passion only akin to the burning love she felt for Ranulph. She wasn't a fool, she'd seen the way he watched Averil, knew he lusted after her. Yet, he had not laid claim, and that bothered Eglif more than sharing him with her, it was as though this girl, with the air of superiority she no longer had any right to, was different from any other. Well, it was not so, and now she, Eglif, would prove it.

"You are a liar!" Eglif pounced with the swiftness of a cat, throwing her surprised victim to the ground and landing heavily on top of her, Averil automatically acting to protect herself from the nails which came at her face, moving her head away as they rolled in the dirt as the men cheered encouragement. Averil could vaguely hear them and the foul names Eglif was screeching as she tugged hard on her hair...sweet Nerthus! She must put a stop to this! A good punch in the jaw should do it. Averil rolled over with Eglif, trying to get on top of her attacker, but before she could do anything the girl was pulled away from her by Edred, who held her easily while she kicked and screamed her protest, for a moment Averil lay on the ground, relief flooding through her, then she got unsteadily to her feet. The humiliation! She thought her heart would burst with it, the shame of being dragged down to the indignity of scrapping like an animal with another woman! Over a man! With as much dignity as she could command she stalked away from the laughing warriors back to the courtyard.

* * *

Averil sat leaning back against the cart, her head pounding where Eglif had torn at her hair. By the Gods ! The vicious bitch would have taken clumps out if Edred hadn't stopped her! She closed her eyes, breathing deeply, slowly but surely getting back command of herself and rational thought, realising that Eglif must be crazed with love for Ranulph to have done such a thing and feeling sorry for her - for that love had nowhere to go – Ranulph would not pledge himself to a serving girl. It was beyond reason why Eglif should be jealous of her, Averil, who as a slave was lower than she was, added to which she had done nothing to inspire such jealousy. Well, nothing Eglif knew of, unless she had mystical powers and had read Averil's mind when she was looking at the naked paintings in the villa! Despite everything, Averil saw the grim humour in it all and found herself laughing out loud at the thought, her staring at him earlier kissing Eglif's neck was as nothing compared to those highly charged imaginings which would make the fertility goddess Hretha herself blush! In truth, she was a little crazed herself!

"I see you are restored."

The laughter died on Averil's lips as she opened her eyes to see the subject of her wanton thoughts standing in the flesh before her. She felt her face flame and the heart she had brought back under her command momentarily skipped a beat.

"Yes." She scrambled to her feet, using the time to avoid Ranulph's gaze while she gathered her wits.

"Good. For you have not finished serving me."

"Say you?" Averil could only stare at him. "I have just been attacked for so doing! I hope that you have explained all to Eglif, as I place value on not being set upon!"

Ranulph held her in a steady gaze.

"Although in truth it would be difficult for those who did not know to believe it, you are, in fact, my slave, and your sole purpose is to serve me. On the morrow we will be at King Oswin's hall and it is long past time you took up your duties. So. You will bring me wine."

He left her and then called back through the night.

" Oh, and the serving girl has already been dismissed."

Averil watched his retreating back, Eglif had certainly had her uses, for up until now she had spared her close proximity to Ranulph and the demeaning task of actually serving him.

Chapter Eight

The barefooted slave girl deftly unwound the strips of linen from the honey-blonde tresses of her mistress Ingilda, who sat on a low chair, admiring herself in the polished bronze mirror she held. Ingilda's hair was usually straight but this ingenious method gave waves which were much more becoming to her round face. She brushed her hand across the skin of her pale cheek, thankful it was smooth to the touch, her blue eyes, though small, were not without their attractiveness and would be enhanced by the cornflower blue silk gown she planned to wear. Yes. She would do very well for this special day which would bring the sons of Ealdorman Leofric to the presence of their new king, her father......a momentary pain as the slave tugged too hard on the last of the cloth pieces – she delivered a stinging blow onto the girl's painfully thin arm with the heavy mirror.

"You clumsy oaf Brigid! Cannot I trust you to do the simplest task!"

The slave Brigid paled visibly but did not utter a sound.

"Come on – comb it out now!" Ingilda barked the order, her words almost drowning the sound of the knock on the bower door.

"Enter." Ingilda's voice had changed in an instant to a kinder tone.

A tall, long-nosed woman entered. She was dressed in a grey linen gown, her hair covered with a fine blue silk head-dress fastened around the forehead with a thin silver rope band. Ingilda waved Brigid away, struck by the unexpected appearance of she who was at once mother and stepmother to the men she had just been thinking of – perhaps it was an omen.

"I am come from your mother the queen who wishes you to attend her as soon as possible."

"My thanks." Ingilda bowed her head politely to the much older woman whose blue eyes were smudged underneath with thin, hard lines.

"Your hair is most becoming" the compliment slipped easily from Egwina's tongue, she knew the vanity of the only daughter of King Oswin as well as her weaknesses.

"It is a new art which my mother thought of for those of us whom the Gods have chosen to favour with gifts other than the curling of hair."

"I am sure it will bring you much admiration." Egwina's tone was maternal, her smile indulgent. "Shall I comb it for you?"

"You would do me a great service, for this slave is worse than useless!"

Brigid backed away immediately, knowing from long and bitter experience that such remarks were usually accompanied by a slap. Egwina picked up the comb and smoothed it through Ingilda's hair, soothing the girl, bringing to her mind Egwina's words about the style courting admiration – wondering if it would come from this Lady's son and stepson.

"Do you look forward to the arrival of your kin this day?" Ingilda asked.

"Ever since the messenger brought news I have been longing to look upon my dear sons." The words were seeped in motherly sincerity, only Brigid saw the hard smile which accompanied them and shivered at it.

"I have heard much of your sons. It is said they are both great warriors and in the hunt have no equal. That they....." Ingilda stemmed the flow of words, she had been about to mention their noted prowess as lovers, the Gods forbid she should forget herself enough to mention such a thing to their mother!

"You were about to say princess?"

"I was about to say that they have met me once but would probably not recall, for I was but a child."

"Ah yes, I remember, it was but a few short years ago when Ranulph and Girdar joined your father's great hunt to capture game for the goddess Ecre's feast."

"Ranulph tested his skill with the sword against many warriors to entertain our kin."

"And what of Girdar?" Egwina's question brought a picture into Ingilda's mind – the white blond Girdar, whose eyes were as blue as the sea, his face clean shaven as his brother, but possessing an unmarred handsomeness which set him well apart from the scarred Ranulph.

"He excelled himself at the hunt." Ingilda remembered how the setting sun had shone down on his bright hair as he had walked around the courtyard with her father, surveying the impressive cull of animals.

Egwina stopped combing and stepped in front of Ingilda to admire her work.

"Ah yes. Girdar has always taken pleasure in the chase. He has little interest in that which he can easily take."

Ingilda's heart leapt, was this perhaps, a mother's advice on how to ensure he who was sought after by every woman who encountered him? To the demons! She would take the chance, what was there to lose?

"And does that apply to princesses?"

Very bold! Egwina was delighted, her gamble had proved to be correct, for she had taken as true the careless gossip amongst the women about Ingilda's fancies for Girdar and Ranulph and skilfully steered this vain creature in the right direction – away from the despised Ranulph, whelp of the Briton whore, and towards her dear love.....he own son, Girdar. For he alone was worthy to be son-in-law to King Oswin.

"I think my Lady, that it especially applies to princesses" the two exchanged sudden, conspiratorial smiles.

* * *

Averil dismounted from her dappled grey mare in a large courtyard which was a hive of sweated activity. Workmen were busy constructing wooden outbuildings to the side of an impressively large hall which was more than twice the size of the place which had served her own family. Doors pierced four sides of the rectangular building elaborately buttressed by wooden props on the outside. Averil guessed it was possibly sectioned off inside to accommodate another room for the new King and Queen and noted wryly that had the late King Ethelbert seen the manner in which this Ealdorman lived, he would perhaps have been more sensitive to his kingly aspirations.

"Hey." the familiar voice of Edred brought Averil's train of thought to an end as she turned to see him walking towards her, leading his chestnut mount.

"You are to come with me to the stables, after which I shall show you to Lord Ranulph's quarters."

"Can I take my possessions from the cart first?"

"Possessions?" Edred shook his head slowly, his tone teasing. "I am not sure whether a slave should have any possessions Lady."

"And I am not sure whether a slave should be addressed in such a manner Master Edred."

They laughed together as they walked side by side, past the timber skeletons of the new buildings.

"The Hall of our new King Oswin is noble indeed Edred. Are the workers perhaps building quarters for his retainers?"

"Aye, that is so. Many have achieved new rank until King Oswin. It is believed my master will soon become an Ealdorman as is his father."

"And Girdar? do you think he too will be awarded this noble title?"

"I do not doubt it will be so. There will also be land to go with it, although Girdar shall receive more than my own Lord if his mother has anything to do with it."

"His mother?"

"The Lady Egwina"

"Ah! Now I see why the name of my horse so amused you Edred. I am curious to know what kind of woman is mother to Girdar."

"She is as you would expect her to be - for one who has given birth to such as he."

Averil turned startled eyes on Edred at the frank admission.

"Oh aye. Girdar's heart is known to myself and everyone in my Lord's service."

"Including your master?"

Edred laughed. "Do you think that he of all people would not know his half-brother's worth? It is why I was charged to protect you on the journey here."

Averil's heart dipped." What say you? Protect me! From Girdar?"

"Aye. I am my Lord's best warrior. It was a good choice."

Averil's mind was whirling......what twist was this!

They had reached the stables. Edred was speaking.......

"Tell me, daughter of Aethelstan, do you have a fine gown among your possessions?"

Averil was too distracted to be surprised by the sudden inquiry. "Yes. Why?"

"Perhaps you do not wish to know of my thoughts but I will give them nonetheless. The life of a slave is one of drudgery and abuse. The Gods have blessed you with a beauty which puts you above every woman at this hall" he lifted her chin with a gentleness which was surprising. "Use it!"

* * *

The room was a simple one, low timbered, furnished with benches at either side of a magnificent wooden chair inlaid on the arms and back with silver scroll work. A tall, handsome man entered, his fair hair, hanging loose around his moustached face was peppered with grey, denoting his age, not betrayed in the powerful frame clad in a belted knee length tunic of fine brown wool.

"Ranulph! Girdar! By the Gods it is good to see you both again!" the man went over to his sons who sat opposite each other, taking first the elder Ranulph in his arms for an embrace and then the younger. Girdar marked the greeting, it was as it had always been. Ranulph first. In everything.

"You have both served the king well and brought honour to our house." Ealdorman Leofric beamed his approval at the sons of whom he was immensely proud.

"And will our reward be in keeping with our deeds father?" this from Girdar, who had sat back down on the bench.

"Assuredly, for you defeated the two men who would have caused the most trouble to the new king."

"Does that mean we will be given all the property and titles of those we cut down in battle for our liege?" Girdar asked.

"So my youngest son wishes to assume the mantle of the mighty Aethelstan?" Leofric laughed. "I cannot see why you should not be given that which you so bravely took."

Ranulph looked hard at Girdar, the words leaving a bitter taste, how brave was it to slit a warrior's throat as he lay sleeping?

Girdar returned the gaze, knowing what was going on in his brother's head…..and knowing too he had the means of breaking him. The girl!

"Did you hear that Ranulph? Our father would have me take everything of Aethelstan's, which of course will mean the girl."

"The girl?" Leofric looked from one to the other of his sons.

"Girdar is speaking of Aethelstan's daughter."

Leofric grasped at a thread of recollection, once he had visited Aethelstan's hall with King Ethelbert. She was but a child then, red-gold hair, pale skinned face, eyes of green fire – Averil. Some said she had lived up to her early promise of great beauty and it seemed it must be the case, for there was bad blood between his sons over this. Girdar's plain to see but Ranulph's, as always, more hidden from view.

"Explain yourselves."

"Should I be awarded Aethlestan's lands then his daughter is mine according to our law."

"That would be so Girdar – had you not lost her to me on the turn of the dice." Ranulph looked to Leofric "Your youngest son's skill at the sport is not what it was."

Girdar leapt up, the atmosphere was tense enough to slice with a knife.

"What in the Gods is this? My sons bickering over a slave! Cannot you settle this amicably?"

"What is won in the battle and at the dice is one and the same. The girl is mine." Ranulph didn't take his eyes from Girdar.

"We shall see dear brother" Girdar's voice was tight, his antipathy smouldering. He turned his attention to his father.

"With your permission I shall take my leave to seek out my mother."

Leofric nodded his assent and Girdar strode from the room.

"Well Ranulph? Are you to carry on this quarrel? There is no woman yet born worth enmity between those bonded by blood!"

"In all justice father you can see that this is not of my making. Girdar, as you know, has never liked loosing anything."

Leofric sighed his reluctant agreement. "Aye Ranulph, you are right in this."

"We also know Girdar's fancies do not last. This will soon be forgotten and replaced by another grievance!"

"Perhaps you are right, though I do not like bad feeling between my sons. Come. Let us join my fellow Ealdormen in the hall. We have much to speak of."

Even as Leofric outwardly dismissed what had happened between his sons who he well knew did not warm to each other, his mind was busy. He knew Girdar only too well, this situation could deteriorate rapidly should Girdar be given Aethelstan's lands, for then his feeling of injustice at having lost the girl he had captured with them and considered part of his reward could easily fester and grow out of proportion. Perhaps it would be wise to speak to the king on this.

* * *

Edred thumped the wooden chest full of Averil's things down on the straw strewn floor of the large hut. It was sparsely furnished with a small table, a high backed chair and a large wooden bed with a straw stuffed mattress covered with linen and furs.

"Not much I own." Edred remarked. "It must have been used for storage at one time. Still, at least it will give privacy and it is large. You must get candles, a washing bowl, goblets and a pitcher or two of mead from the kitchens. I shall take my leave now. Remember my words!"

Edred closed the door behind him and at last Averil could try to get her thoughts into some kind of order. Ranulph must have believed her about Girdar even though he had treated her claim with such contempt, otherwise why had he charged Edred to protect her? She would never have guessed from his words or manner towards her that he would do such a thing. And what about Ebba? Had he protected her too? Her head began to ache from the swirl of thoughts ......she must distract herself....she turned her attention to her belongings, opening the chest Ebba had packed to reveal her finery. On top of the sea green gown were a bunch of dried flowers, their heady aroma brought back her past, Averil separated the colourful blooms and scattered them around the floor of the hut. The fragrance bringing a little of home to the spartan surroundings. She went back to the chest and took out her bronze hand mirror, studying her reflection with a detailed attention never before afforded, Edred's words still fresh. Yes. She was good looking, she had seen the way men looked at her, it was not impossible for her to find a husband here. Even though she was a slave she was still of noble blood and lust had a way of pushing other considerations aside. Yes Averil, she told herself contemptuously, why not sell yourself to the highest bidder on the marriage market! She slammed down the mirror in disgust. She put on her cloak to get the things Edred had mentioned, eyeing the bed, noting it was softer than anything she had laid her head on in a long while, perhaps later she could test it, for only the Goddess Nerthus knew how much she needed to clutch at the unthinking blackness of sleep.

* * *

Egwina embraced her son warmly before standing him a little away for a critical assessment of his appearance.

"You are as handsome as ever my son. You will be the finest Ealdorman at Oswin's hall!"she gave him an affectionate smile.

"But of course mother!" Girdar disengaged himself from his fond mother and sat down in the high backed oak chair which furnished her parent's bower.

"Now, tell me all the news. I wish to know who is the most favoured and therefore the most land rich of our new king's followers."

"The new king has many whom he favours, no-one has been given special attention – as yet."

"So there is room for an ambitious man to make his mark."

"In ways that perhaps that man has not yet considered."

"Oh?"

"Ingilda is now a princess and has happy memories of her last meeting with the handsome warrior sons of Leofric."

Girdar smiled, his sapphire hard eyes calculating.

"And does she perhaps remember Girdar better out of the two?"

"Could you doubt it?"

"There must be others who seek out the king's only daughter."

"But none have your obvious advantage."

"Which is having you for a mother?"

Egwina laughed shortly, ignoring the observation.

"Ingilda is much taken with you. She needs only gentle handling....."

"And the riches and power her father would bestow are mine."

Girdar finished his mother's sentence with a flourish as they traded a look of perfect understanding.

Chapter Nine

Night had fallen when Ranulph entered his hut to ready himself for the feast with his new King. Six tall candles burned brightly in their iron holders and the heady scent of dried flowers filled the air. There was a large pitcher of mead and a goblet on a crudely fashioned wooden table next to a small oak chest. Averil lay on top of the bed in a deep sleep, her mass of red gold hair spread on the cover around her. Ranulph took off his cloak and poured himself some mead, raising an eyebrow as he saw a silver comb and bronze mirror laid by the pitcher. He sat on the high backed chair and put his legs on the table, contemplating the sleeping girl as he sipped the smooth, sweet drink. The Gods! But she was beautiful - and more so in slumber without her cutting tongue. Ah yes. The cutting tongue. How had she so far described him? Filthy swine and filthy dog. She certainly knew how to get around a man with honeyed words! Here was a female who cared nothing for womanly wiles! Now here she was, sleeping peacefully on his bed, in a hut she had scented with her possessions laid out around her as though this place were her very own bower...... .as it very well might have been had she been more accommodating to her lawful master.

"Hey " his shout echoed in the hut "Wake up!"he banged the goblet loudly on the table.

Averil stirred, opening her eyes sleepily, for a moment not awake enough for full realisation as to where she actually was – she saw Ranulph sitting watching her and was immediately back to cold reality.

"It is time to go to work. "he said "I need water for me to wash and some fresh wine."

She got up without a word and grabbed her cloak before taking her leave, just eager to be away from his presence. As she ran to the kitchen a chill wind whipped her, it did nothing to cool the heat of her temper as she smarted under the directness of his orders.

* * *

The flickering candlelight threw Ranulph's muscular semi-naked body into sharp relief as he splashed the warmed water across his torso. He wore only knee length grey linen breeches and his long black hair hung loose of its usual pigtail. Averil averted her eyes as she held the bowl of water, not being able to help remembering how she had thought of his body whilst looking at the paintings in the villa, and trying to blot out the thoughts and feelings she had experienced then.

"Pass me the cloth" she did as bidden, to say she disliked serving him thus was an understatement, but at the same time she reasoned, at least it showed her how out of keeping such thoughts and feelings were. He went over to the bed where he had left his dark brown leather tunic of mail. Averil had placed a clean white long sleeved undershirt next to it, along with his black leather shoes with cross garters and a black cloak.

"Tonight is a special occasion for our house. My father Leofric will see both his sons rewarded for their loyalty to their new king." Ranulph put on his shirt, the whiteness bringing his bronzed skin into sharp relief.

"And will your brother receive Aethelstan's land?"

"I do not know how it will go. The only thing I am sure of is that he will not receive Aethelstan's daughter."

Averil's breath caught. Girdar came tumbling into her mind, she knew the meaning of real hatred when she thought of him, and, like it or not, Ranulph stood between herself and the man who had murdered her kin in cold blood.

"You shall serve me at the feast." Ranulph's order cut through her thoughts. "Dress yourself."

Averil went over to the chest and took out her best gown. With her back to Ranulph she took off her tunic, under which she was dressed in a kirtle, and slipped on the exquisite green silk dress, fastening it about the waist with the delicate silver girdle given as a gift by Aethelstan. As she ran her comb through the cascade of thick, wavy red gold hair which reached to her knees, Ranulph poured himself another drink and lay back on the bed to watch her. Averil faced him, confident in the knowledge that she had never looked so lovely.

"Do not you think you are a little overdressed? Change into something more fitting."

Averil felt the blood drain from her face, at that moment realising that she had wanted him to admire her! What was she thinking! Angry with herself, she went over to the chest, hands shaking with emotion as she retrieved the plain grey tunic she had worn on the journey and replaced the beautiful gown with it, tying it with a plain leather belt before turning to him.

Ranulph looked her up and down." You must remove that too." he pointed to the pendant of sacred rock crystal on which she had placed the gold ring she had found in the sword.

The crystal had been given to her by her dear father to mark the day of her birth!

"You treat me no better than an animal! Perhaps you wish me to follow you into the presence of the king on all fours!"

"That will not be necessary. Your attire now fits your status." His tone was calm and mstter-of-fact, as though Averil had said nothing untoward. He got up and fastened his sword about him.

Averil's gaze was drawn to the elaborately worked silver hit of the weapon within the scabbard. Her heart leapt. Elatha!

"You have the sword of my father!"

Ranulph put on the cloak, clasping it with the cruciform garnet brooches, gleaming blood red in the candlelight.

"Another thing of Aethelstan's Girdar shall not have."

"You have no right!"

"Whose hands would you prefer Elatha in? Mine or Girdar's?" he picked up her cloak and threw it at her. "Ah! Silent at last."

He left the hut, Averil following him out, her emotions in turmoil.

* * *

Ingilda looked radiant in a blue gown which emphasized the colour of her eyes. Her flaxen hair hung in smooth waves and she wore a thin silver circlet around her head. She was aware of admiring glances as she served her father and those who sat at the high table with him, as was her bounden duty as princess. Leofric was there without his sons who had yet to be presented to their new king. She knew they were to wait in the room at the end of the hall until they were bid to enter by her father, who would greet them formerly and speak of their new status.

Sweet red wine had been flowing freely for some time when Girdar was finally summoned. Ingilda stood behind her yellow haired father, blood quickening as she watched the younger son of Leofric walk confidently down the length of the hall, magnificent in a light grey leather tunic of chain mail and a pale grey cloak fastened with silver cruciform brooches. The white blond hair was tied in a pigtail, pulled back from his square-jawed, handsome face. Ingilda knew hers would not be the only heart to skip a beat at his presence. He stopped in front of King Oswin and bowed, his deep blue eyes resting for a brief moment on Ingilda, sending a thrill of pleasure through her.

"Girdar." Oswin's voice boomed around the now silent hall. "I am pleased to greet you as the newest of my loyal Ealdormen."

"My sword and my life are pledged to you my king."

"Let it be known that you will be granted lands which once belonged to Halliwell."

Girdar stiffened momentarily – not Aethelstan's! He bowed – was Ranulph to get what was his!

"I am deeply honoured King Oswin"

The retainers banged their goblets on the tables in slow applause as Oswin beckoned Girdar to his side.

"Come Ealdorman Girdar, and join us in a goblet of wine."

Girdar did as he was bidden, keeping his bitter outrage on a tight rein. Ingilda brought over a pitcher of wine, offering him a drink with demurely lowered eyes, such maidenly modesty, he had seen it so many times and knew it counted for nothing. Yes. He would take Oswin's precious daughter for himself, then let him see the king deny his son-in-law!

"I count myself twice honoured tonight" his voice was soft, the words only for Ingilda "Not only am I made an Ealdorman but served by a princess."

Ingilda hardly dare look upon Girdar, so excited was she by the words, yet, she remembered what the Lady Egwina had advised, she must not be too amenable, she was, after all, a princess.

"You are fortunate indeed" she treated him to a cool, don't touch look, denying the hot message of her eager body.

So. She would give him a good game then, before she succumbed as they all did in the end....King Oswin turned to Girdar with an amiable smile.

"I am told your brother has arrived and will now be called to my presence."

Ingilda noticed Girdar's profile harden for an instant as Ranulph came through the main doors. Someone entered a little behind him and stood to one side, Ingilda saw it was a girl, but could make nothing of her, for she was wearing a grey cloak with the hood up.

"You are welcome to my royal hall Ranulph." King Oswin's voice rang out as the dark haired Lord bowed to his liege.

"I have called you here to bestow on you the title of Ealdorman."

"I am deeply honoured."

"As Ealdorman Ranulph you will be granted the lands of Aethelstan."

"I thank my king and offer him my allegiance"

Girdar's fury boiled as he watched Ranulph took his place with the other Ealdormen at one of the long tables at the side of the hall. Aethelstan's lands were HIS by right of conquest. His swine of a father must have had a hand in this! Ranulph. The favoured older son, who always got what he wanted! Now he had Aethelstan's land and that beautiful, deadly bitch Averil, who could be used against him at any time! He wanted her badly, and not just to kill. He picked out the cloaked figure who had entered with Ranulph and melted into the shadows as though to be out of the way – but not away from me my fine Lady ..... never away from me.....

"Ah. You are here at last" Ranulph took a short respite from sharing conversation with two other men to speak to Averil. "Take off that cloak and bring me some wine"

As Averil did his bidding, silently cursing him, she found herself the subject of surprise and then bold scrutiny from Ranulph's companions. Of the women, Egwina noticed her fist, as she sat listening with much politeness and little interest to the boring conversation of the haughty Queen Ethelburga on the women's benches. Who was this waiting on her scar-faced stepson? Whoever she was she was undeniably lovely. Her skin was pale and unblemished, the hands which held the wine pitcher long and slender – and that hair! A deluge of thick burnished copper. A sixth sense caused Egwina to glance over at Girdar, who was watching the girl with a ferocious intensity. What in the Gods was going on here? She didn't like to be presented with new situations without warning. Who was this girl? Egwina must know. She begged the Queen's forgiveness to be excused, siting her Lord husband's apparent drunkenness as the cause. She found Leofric in a corner playing dice with a group of men and enjoying himself immensely.

" My Lord. I would have words with you." Egwina broke into the game as Leofric threw a bad set of numbers.

"Well Lady, what is it?"

"Do you know of the girl who is serving our son Ranulph?"

"Ranulph?" Leofric craned his neck and caught sight of Averil. The Gods! she had turned out better than he could have ever imagined! Now he understood why his sons were at each other's throats.

"The girl is Averil, daughter of Aethelstan."

"Aethelstan!" Egwina's quick mind homed in on this new development. "Why is it she serves Ranulph and not Girdar? Surely she is his captive. He took the hall!"

"It appears Ranulph won her on the turn of the dice, his luck was obviously better than mine!" he laughed shortly as one of the company made a winning throw.

Egwina looked once more upon her white blond haired son, seeing the situation and it's dangers, as Girdar's slave the girl was no problem, but for Ranulph to take this unmatched beauty away from him........curse that whelp of the British whore! He could ruin everything!

Ingilda filled her father's ornate amber glass goblet, acutely aware of Girdar's presence, believing his gaze upon her, dare she turn and smile? Why shouldn't she? The smile froze on her lips as she saw Girdar looking, not at her, but in another direction, even as he laughed and talked with the man at his side. Ingilda looked away quickly, seeing where Girdar's eyes had been directed......the tall, slender girl who served Lord Ranulph. The girl was beautiful, her red gold hair flowed in envious waves down her back, gleaming in the glowing torchlight. A swift stab of jealousy prodded Ingilda, for such beauty made her all too aware of her smaller stature. So what if Girdar admired the serving girl? Why not, he was a man as any other, once she and the other noblewomen had retired as was customary to leave the men to their entertainment would he take this girl? What if he did! She was being ridiculous, this girl was just a servant, a quick tumble in the straw for Girdar.

"Princess. Your mother feels it is time for us to retire." Lady Egwina was beside her. Ingilda followed the older woman to the women's benches from where Queen Ethelburga bowed to the king, as did the rest of her retinue, before making a stately exit.

Averil stood beside Ranulph and watched them go, as she and her mother along with her women had gone from her father's hall in the past, before the feast degenerated into coarser realms.

"Go back to my quarters." Ranulph didn't bother to look at Averil as he gave his order. Averil did not need telling twice, she slipped away, muffled in her cloak, wondering at the command and despite herself, begrudgingly feeling grateful for it.

Chapter Ten

Averil awoke, the straw had not been too uncomfortable and she had covered herself with her cloak to keep warm. She had waited tensely for a long time for Ranulph to return and eventually given up her vigil in the early hours. Ranulph! She rolled over and saw him lying on the bed beneath his cloak and some fur skins, his chest was bare and one arm was wrapped around a half covered naked woman, whose ample bosom pressed against his flesh even as they both slept.

Averil scrambled to her feet as though kicked into action as understanding hit. She knew the woman. It was Eglif. They had coupled here while she lay asleep on the floor at their feet! Abhorrence flooded through her, and she had felt a kind of gratitude to a pig such as this for letting her leave the Hall early! Ranulph stirred, as if mesmerized Averil watched him stroke one of Eglif's fulsome breasts, her own pulse quickened as she imagined herself enclosed in the warmth of his arms, his hand rubbing against her bare skin.....sweet Nerthus! She must get out of there before he woke up and took Eglif again, ignoring her presence as he had hours before. Hands shaking for reasons she did not now care to even think of, Averil picked up her cloak and tiptoed to the door, it creaked slightly as she opened it a little, just enough to slip through.

"Make sure the bread you bring to break my fast is warm and the water fresh" Ranulph's command froze Averil for just a second as she hurried out, thankfully breathing in the misty morning air.

* * *

Ebba kneaded the bread dough on the large wooden table which dominated the kitchen as she eyed another black haired girl who stood next to her, tearing lean pieces of meat from a cooked chicken. Ebba was certain the girl was a Briton, perhaps from her own land of Elmet.

"What is your name?" Ebba asked in her native tongue.

There had been a time when Brigid had often spoken the language of her forefathers. She had been born a slave at this hall but her long dead mother had never forgotten her origins.

"Brigid. And yours?" the words were faltering, but to speak them in her own tongue meant much.

"I am Ebba"

"Whom do you serve?"

"No-one now. She who I once served is now such as we." Ebba stopped work for a moment, startling Brigid by her manner, it were as though she felt sorrow for her former mistress.

"Who is it?"

"Averil. Daughter of Aethelstan."

"Was not Aethelstan's land's taken by one of Ealdorman Leofric's sons?"

"Girdar." Ebba's heart beat faster with a fear she still experienced whenever she thought of him.

"There are many so called fine women at this hall who would have gladly swapped places with she who was captured by him!" Brigid's sarcastic laughter died on her lips as she saw the effect such light hearted banter had on Ebba, who now glowered at her.

"If you knew this man as myself and my Lady did you would not find anything about him to make sport of!"

Impulsively Brigid reached out to the girl who was of her own race and took her hand.

"I am sorry Ebba. I did not consider my words."

"No." Ebba shook her head. "It is I who should be sorry, how could you know of the black heart of he who is as handsome as one of his pagan God's? I thank Christ my sweet Lady is the property of his brother Ranulph!"

Ebba's loyalty to this Averil was unmistakable, Brigid decided she must be rare indeed to inspire it, for she herself would cheerfully throw her own mistress, the vain and cruel Princess Ingilda, to a pack of hungry wolves.

"Forgive me Ebba if I anger you once more. But I cannot understand how you could have such great concern for one who you once served as a slave."

"My Lady could have escaped when Girdar's warriors mistook me for her and sought to abuse me, but instead she gave herself up and protected me from harm."

Brigid believed at first she had misheard, it had been so long since she had conversed in her native tongue.

"Gave herself up and protected you?" Brigid was incredulous.

"So now you see why she is worthy of love, more so from her former slave."

"My mistress the Princess Ingilda inspires only hatred in me, for I have endured her cruelties for many a long year."

"Ebba! It does my heart good to see you!" the greeting startled both girls. Brigid found herself looking at someone of her own age with red gold hair clumsily pulled back in an unruly braid from a pale face of haunting beauty.

"And you too Lady!" Ebba motioned to her new found friend. "This is Brigid. She is of my race and serves the Princess Ingilda."

Averil noted the tall girl was much alike in her dark colouring to Ebba. "You have my greetings Brigid. I am glad Ebba has one of her own people as companion."

Brigid saw the words from one who had as much noble blood as her own mistress were without guile and truly meant.

Averil turned to Ebba. "Are you to work in these kitchens then? Girdar has not been near you?" Brigid glimpsed a flash of green fire in Averil's lovely eyes as Ebba nodded in reply.

"Then I shall thank my Gods and your own!"

They touched hands in a gesture of fellow feeling. Brigid did not fully comprehend the way of things, though she was certain Averil despised Lord Girdar and guessed he must desire she who hated him.

"What are you doing here Lady?" Ebba swiftly turned the tide of their talk, the question shadowing Averil's face for an instant.

"To fetch food." She couldn't bring herself to divulge more, especially in front of Brigid.

"There is hot bread by the fire and fresh water in that barrel in the corner. I'll get it for you." Ebba readily volunteered, wiping her floury hands on the cloth wrapped around her tunic.

"No Ebba. I do not want you to risk any displeasure. I can do it myself! I am glad to have seen you well."

The two Britons returned to their work in silence, glancing at Averil as she went about her tasks with an in-built dignity which told all who cared to see that here was the daughter of the chieftain Aethelstan, Ealdorman to the late King Ethelbert.

* * *

Egwina stepped into the bower of the King and Queen from the sharp cold of the autumn morning, welcoming the warmth wafting in waves from the crackling fire burning brightly in the hearth. Her mistress, Queen Ethelburga, wearing a woollen night garment and a soft brown fur cloak draped around her shoulders, sat in front of the blaze, eating slices of roast chicken.

"Good morning Egwina. You looked chilled to the bone! Come, warm yourself." The queen's invitation to take advantage of the fire was gratefully accepted. As she did as she was bid Egwina felt herself under close scrutiny.

"The king is to hunt today with your sons."

"The king does my house much honour."

"Would that my own sons were old enough to share their pleasure – it is a pastime they will much enjoy with their royal father." Ethelburga spoke with pride of her strong boys – Oswin, after his father, and Cuthbert. Both still only children, young heirs to their now royal house, prey to the vulnerability of their youth. If only they were of the same age as Ingilda....ah, yes.... Ingilda.

"My daughter is much taken with your youngest son" the queen's stare was probing, had her shallow-hearted daughter been encouraged by this woman in the great attraction she had been unable to keep to herself?

"Once more my house is honoured." Egwina replied.

"Ingilda is now a woman grown and must make her choices where she sees fit. But, she is also a princess and I would have her choose wisely."

"Girdar, unlike his half brother Ranulph, is of the pure stock of our race my Lady. His skill and bravery as a warrior are beyond question – it was he who took the hall of Ethelbert's greatest warrior Aethelstan."

Ethelburga considered, of course, Ranulph was the son of Leofric and the British princess he had captured, Girdar was Egwina's true son, and, as such, she would be ambitious for him – enough to further his case with her daughter. And what of Girdar? Was he as ambitious and as cunning as his mother? To be son-in-law to a King was indeed a prize.

"And do you think Girdar would be a good match for my daughter?"

Egwina's heart leapt even as she counselled herself to tread carefully.

"What mother would deny such a question?"

Queen Ethelburga smiled faintly.

"I doubt if there is any woman alive with sons of her own who would. But daughters too, are loved, and I would have mine well matched to he who would care for her."

The Queen's expression marked a clear warning, without giving Egwina time to speak once more she clapped her hands to summon a slave, the action terminating the conversation.

"Now. I am to dress. I wish to give the King good luck before he rides on the hunt."

Egwina was glad of the dismissal. For the Queen, in her own understated way, was an astute woman and she didn't like to be the subject of her close inspection for too long.

* * *

Averil returned with the food, mentally prepared to encounter Ranulph and Eglif together in bed. But Eglif wasn't there, only Ranulph, who was dressing himself as she arrived back.

"At last. Come, bring over the food. I am hunting with the King this morning and wish to do it on a full stomach."

Averil placed the tray on the small table. There was bread, chicken and a pitcher of fresh water alongside two goblets.

"What's this?" Ranulph lifted up the spare goblet. "Did you think to break bread with your master?

"When I left you were not alone. I thought that as you and Eglif had shared much through the night you should want to share your morning meal."

"With a serving girl?"

"Why not? She was good enough to share your bed."

"Why is it my slave should take the side of a girl who once tried to tear out her eyes?"

"Let us say I do not like the way your treat women."

"And no doubt that includes yourself." Ranulph poured some water, mixing it with a little red wine from a small flagon already on the table. "And how have I treated you since you became my property? Let me consider. I have allowed my brother to attack you and forced you into my bed against your will." He sipped the drink, his grey eyes not leaving Averil's face.

"There are other ways to ill treat, and you, Lord Ranulph, know them all."

Their eyes locked, the bang on the door broke the spell, yet even as Ranulph bid whoever was outside to enter, he still watched Averil.

"Lord." It was Edred, his gaze touching Averil for a few seconds before he bowed to Ranulph. "Your mount has been prepared for the hunt."

"Just so Edred." He drained the goblet. "Bring my cloak." This order to Averil as he stalked out, compelling her to follow into the courtyard, where a large group of men with their horses, breath smoking in the morning air, had gathered for the sport. As she almost ran to keep up with Ranulph, Averil noticed a yellow haired girl in a rich cloak standing in the doorway of the hall, the slave Averil recognised as Brigid by her side. This then must be the princess, she saw Ingilda's rapt attention was fixed on the white blond Girdar, standing talking with another man, both of whom Ranulph was heading towards.

"Ah Ranulph!" Girdar greeted his brother with a brittle smile. "Let us hope we have good sport, for then our Liege will be able to judge which of his new Ealdormen possesses the best skill at the hunt."

"The hunt is not to compete but to enjoy." Ranulph half turned to Averil, snapping his fingers for his cloak which she handed over immediately, hoping for leave to go. There was a flicker of surprise in Girdar's blue eyes before they riveted her, she met him head on with a look of pure detestation.

"Your slave's swift obedience is like that of a good hunting beast Ranulph" in a move too unexpected to avoid he caught hold of Averil's wrist, wrenching it with savage pleasure, Averil stifled a cry of pain as she struggled to be free. "It's a pity your bitch cannot run with the pack." He flung her at Ranulph, and she would have fallen had he not caught and steadied her with a rough gentleness which shocked her and then moved to stand between herself and Girdar.

"Your remark surprises me Girdar. For you more than anyone should know that this particular slave is far too high bred to mix with dogs."

For a split second Averil thought she had misheard, there was no mistaking the whitening of ill suppressed fury on Girdar's face at the words. Both men's leather gloved hands reached for their swords. There was a gasp from those around at the swift action and the men around them stood back.

"And perhaps those too weak to take what they want Ranulph. I trust the serving girl Eglif enjoyed herself in your bed last night?"

Averil's heart thumped, the slur on Ranulph's manhood brought conflict closer, if they were to fight! Would Ranulph win as he had when he rescued her from Girdar's rape attempt?

"Lord Ranulph" his name was almost a sigh, the voice speaking it was sensuous as silk. "Remember you promised never to speak of that woman again to anyone after this morning." She stroked his arm, the bewitching, knowing smile of a lover on her lovely face was irresistible as she pressed against him, her intervention snapping the crippling tension. There were nudges and salacious smiles from those who watched, envying Ranulph his luck.

For an instant, there was shock in Ranulph's grey eyes, then it was gone as he slid his sword back into its scabbard and took Averil's slender hand in his own.

"It will be as you desire."

Girdar felt the blood pounding in his head, Averil had gone to Ranulph willingly, something she would not do for him! So now his hated brother had both Aethelstan's land and his daughter – both his by right!

"I wish you well with your new whore" his blue eyes tore into Averil.

"It does me good to hear such brotherly consideration for my happiness." Ranulph led Averil away as Girdar mounted his horse, his eyes boring into Averil's retreating back. Ingilda turned on her heel, grasping Brigid's arm painfully and dragging her inside the hall. She had witnessed the scene with growing anger, jealousy and disbelief, who was this slave that she should cause Leofric's sons to almost cross swords over her?

Averil was telling herself she had been forced to do what she did, if they had fought and Ranulph had been defeated.... the idea was barely tenable, for she would once again be in Girdar's clutches. Like it or not, Ranulph stood between them. But so convincing a display! It had been as though she were outside herself, watching someone else in disbelief. They walked towards Ranulph's grey stallion, who was champing at the bit to be gone, Averil felt the warmth of Ranulph's hand in her own and sought to free herself.

"Do not tell me you no longer wish to hold my hand after the pleasures we have shared?"

"Would that you were so touched with fortune for it to be so."

Edred stifled laughter, by Tiw but she had pluck! She had given a sweet victory to his master over his brother without need to resort to the sword, though Ranulph could have taken Girdar easily. Now, she put this Lord firmly back in his place. And she was supposed to be the slave! Ha. Never underestimate the power of a woman, and certainly not one such as this one, who must have been kissed by the Gods themselves to be blessed with such beauty and wit.

"I much prefer the behaviour you displayed in front of my brother. Though I swear I am becoming used to your insolence."

Ranulph freed her reluctant hand and mounted the excitable horse, stroking the mane to instill calm.

"Come Edred, We have a good day's sport ahead."

Dismissed without words, Averil took her leave with much relief, feeling her emotions in a stranglehold and seeking to sort them in some sort of order.

* * *

The furious princess swept through the empty hall, Brigid running at her heels to keep up, gratified at the damning effect the scene between Averil and Leofric's sons had had on her mistress. Ingilda stormed into her bower and flung off her cloak before rounding on Brigid.

"Do you know who the red haired slave of Lord Ranulph's is?"

"Averil mistress. I understand she is the daughter of the warrior Lord Aethelstan." Brigid experienced deep satisfaction at imparting the knowledge, knowing how much more uncomfortable it would make Ingilda, for this was no mere woman of the land but someone with blood as noble as her own.

"Aethelstan." The name was said almost to herself. Girdar had captured Aethelstan's hall, had this Averil creature been his before she was Ranulph's then? The way he had looked at her! Her heart lurched with jealousy.

"She is the daughter of a traitor!" Ingilda's pale blue eyes were alive with indignation, Brigid took a protective step backwards in anticipation of the blows which usually accompanied such outbursts.

"What else do you know of this slave?"

Brigid maintained a dumb, deliberate silence, feeling a little light headed as she registered that for the very first time the tables were turned. Ingilda could inflict a beating but she, Brigid, now had the power to do greater harm - to the vain heart, lost to Girdar.

"Do not risk your hide Brigid! Now tell me what else you know."

"She is spoken of as courageous and noble. Thought to have been doubly blessed by the goddess Nerthus herself with kindness as well as unrivalled beauty." Brigid watched Ingilda blanch as she digested the information.

"And what other kitchen gossip have you heard?" Ingilda's disbelieving tone didn't fool her slave for an instant. By Christ! Why should she not twist the knife, just a little, scant repayment for her years of ill treatment.

"Well? I asked you a question Brigid!"

"Sweet mistress....I....." Brigid's voice was cleverly feigned humility, laced with extreme distress.

"Answer me!"

"That both the sons of Leofric desire her more than life itself princess!" there was an awesome silence in the room – broken by the cracking blow across Brigid's cheek.....yet even as her face throbbed with pain, Brigid felt content, knowing what she had just done to Ingilda was far more damaging than any physical punishment could ever be.

Chapter Eleven

Girdar splashed the warmed water across his bare arms and chest, the hunt had been successful and now he needed to wash away the stink of sweat and blood, after all, he did not yet want to upset the sensibilities of the princess, there was time for that after she and the power she brought with her were his.... providing of course Ranulph and his whore did not seek to discredit him. The idea, planted at Aethelstan's hall, had long been growing in the back of his mind. When she was the frigid, untouchable virgin Ranulph had threatened him to defend her slave Briton. Now she warmed his bed how much more potent would be her influence to sway him to her side against his half brother, for despite the hostility between them, to divulge what had happened would bring with it a slur on their house and cause his father, whom Ranulph honoured, much grief. But the Averil he had seen that morning was a different matter, could she persuade Ranulph to champion her cause and tell of what had really happened at Aethelstan's hall? The disconcerting reflection ended at the entrance of a cloaked figure.

"Mother! To what do I owe so unexpected a visit?" Girdar snapped his fingers for a cloth to wipe himself. Egforth jumped to obey, cringing under Egwina's stare.

"Your servant may leave us Girdar." Egforth immediately scurried to the door, closing it behind him with soft deference.

"Well?" Girdar addressed Egwina as he slipped on a white linen shirt.

"I understand you and your brother almost fought over the daughter of Aethlestan this morning."

"You know Ranulph and I do not need much to flare our ill-feeling – just as it has always been."

"Do not trifle with me Girdar! I am not the only one who has seen the way you look at this slave. Your lust could cost you the princess!"

"You mistake my intention." Girdar considered Egwina carefully, she was perhaps the only person he could really trust with this, his mother would never betray him.

"How so?"

Girdar moved to the door, opening it quickly to make sure that anyone crouched against it listening would fall at his feet. Satisfied they were not overheard he returned to his mother.

"My lust for the daughter of Aethelstan is not for pleasure, only the urge to still the tongue of someone who is dangerous to us all."

"Dangerous? A slave? Explain yourself!"

"The slave has a grievance."

"Which is?"

"She mistakenly believes her father and brothers did not die in battle but were killed beforehand and has demanded blood feud."

Egwina digested the information, the real meaning only too clear and confirming what she had always suspected – that Girdar had defeated one such as Aethelstan had always caused her disquiet, she had not wanted him, but Ranulph, to be given the task, knowing how dangerous an opponent Aethelstan could prove to be. But this was not the time to think on what had passed.

"She did everything according to law?"

"Within the day of their death and in front of witnesses, including your stepson Ranulph."

Egwina's breath caught "Ranulph knows?"

"He took the girl as gift of his silence."

Egwina sat down on the only chair in the room, her mind working. Surely Ranulph would not betray his house, yet the animosity between himself and Girdar was strong, and could easily be fuelled when Girdar became more land rich and powerful as husband to the princess....then of course, there were the persuasive powers of one such as Averil, which could be formidable....

"Who else knows?"

"Two others."

"They are here?"

"No. I left them at Aethelstan's hall. But I have sent word for them to go my new hall which was once Halliwell's."

"Can they be trusted?"

"They are my own men. Sworn to serve me before our Gods unto death!"

"Although if needs be it would be easy to take care of them. As we must the girl."

"I have longed for that particular pleasure."

"It must be done without suspicion! Your brother will bring us all down if he finds out what we have done!"

Girdar leant over his mother, pinning her with hard blue eyes. "Why stop only at the girl?"

Egwina followed his train of thought, to rid herself of that thorn in her side, the arrogant, swaggering Ranulph, favourite of her husband, constant reminder to Leofric of she who he had always believed was his only love! The slave princess. And now, danger to her son. It would take some planning, but it could be done.

She stood up, pulling her cloak around her.

"Spend your time winning the princess back to your side and avoiding a clash with your brother. We will talk again." Her lips were corpse cold as she kissed him on the cheek before taking her leave.

* * *

The brown bear snarled ferociously as he tried to free himself from the chain around his furry neck which held him fast to the wooden post in the centre of the deep pit. Averil's sympathy reached out to the imprisoned beast as she stood amidst the crowd of spectators who had gathered around excitedly in anticipation of the fun of the bear bait. King Oswin was already there, discussing with Lord Leofric the merits of the dogs which were to bait the bear. The moon faced Ingilda was at her father's side, laughing out loud at the poor beast's attempt to escape his bloody fate.

The crowd parted as a burly man wearing a dark leather tunic came through with four snapping hunting dogs straining on their leashes leading the way. The audience murmured at the sight of the animals, which would mean the baiting would soon begin – as would the betting on how many dogs the bear would kill before it finally succumbed. To her dismay, Ranulph led her to the front of the onlookers, she didn't want so good a view of the horror which was to come, the mere thought of such brutal treatment to an animal repulsed and sickened her. It was a sport her menfolk had always enjoyed and one which she had viewed only once – she well remembered it – half way through, to her lasting mortification, she had almost fainted and had been teased for a long time afterwards by her brothers for her weakness – a quality not normally associated with their feisty sister. A dreadful thought hit her, suppose she were to react the same way here?

"Now we have better sight of what is to come." Ranulph looked down at Averil.

"I do not wish any sight. I wish only to leave."

"Why?"

"I despise this sport, it is savage cruelty."

"The bear is a noble beast who will die as the Gods intend men to die – fighting – there is nothing wrong with that."

"Except the time is not of the beast's choosing."

"Your sympathies continue to surprise me, extending as they do to a slave, a serving girl, and now a bear!"

"I say again that I wish to leave."

"But not enough to ask me."

"I am asking you!"

"No. You are telling me. Although should you wish to persuade me otherwise with the sweet voice of this morning I may grant your request."

Averil stared at him, to give him what he wanted would demean her. Sweet Nerthus! could not she manage to get through one bait? She was being ridiculous! Averil kept a grim silence. Ranulph focused his attention to the pit.

"Very well. You will stay here until the end."

Would that she could kick him into the pit and unleash the bear on him, how then would she enjoy the sport! Yet it was not what she had thought hours ago, then she had afraid of losing him, no, not him, she told herself firmly, his protection.

"Do you think the four dogs are strong enough to tear at this large beast?" the inquiry from someone behind drew Averil's eyes to the bear, now frothing at the mouth with anger and frustration, she felt her heart would break for it.

There was a sudden silence as Oswin gave leave for the entertainment to begin with a wave of his hand. The dogs were thrown into the pit, growling and snapping, they circled the enormous bear, whose paw flayed one across the stomach, leaving a bloody imprint. Averil closed her eyes as the wounded dog yelped with pain and fury and then leapt at the chained attacker, but although she cut out the gruesome sight of what followed she couldn't blot out the terrible sounds of a violent struggle to the death between the tormented animals. There was much shouting for the dogs to kill the bear, as each failed and met it's gory end, there was a mighty roar from the crowd. And then it was over, the wretched bear, cut and bleeding, in agonizing pain, but alive, with the broken dogs around him.

"Bring more dogs!" Oswin's command sent the dog handler running to obey. The crowd were shouting, gloating on the wounded bear's suffering as it howled it's defiance. She saw Girdar was now standing with the Princess Ingilda, who was taunting the bear with her companion's laughing approval. The new dogs were flung into the pit, their presence extracting a roar from the spectators as they hit the dirt floor, and, with bared teeth, went straight for their prey. Averil was full to bursting with anguish and pity as the dogs brought the noble creature down. The terrible ripping sounds as he was torn apart washed a tide of nausea over her, she closed her eyes, her head spinning from the sheer horror of it all and unwittingly leant against Ranulph, darkness threatened, she pushed it back as her mind screamed in protest, desperate for control of her rebellious body....but....Ranulph caught her before she slid to the ground in a faint and lifted her in his arms. So. This was why she had been so eager to leave! Here was a woman of many contradictions. She could face an attacker with a dagger but not stomach a bear bait! He watched the bear meet a brave end before carrying her through the crowd.

* * *

Princess Ingilda had watched Averil pass out at first with incredulity and then with deep satisfaction, even more so as she saw Ranulph make not much of it, lifting her in his arms and watching the bait until the end. And had not Brigid said he and Girdar desired this so called courageous creature? So much for courage! This one didn't have the nerve of a babe when it came to even watching a bear bait! It was all lies, she had been duped by that harlot Brigid, or was she merely duping herself, had she not seen the evidence of her own eyes? That very morning, she had watched Ranulph and Girdar almost cross swords, this Averil seemingly the cause of their dispute.

"Your brother is having trouble with his slave Lord Girdar." Her nonchalant tone was not in keeping with the intensity of her gaze. "If you care to look over there you will see the stupid creature has fainted."

Girdar glanced over at Ranulph and Averil before returning his attention to the pit. "My brother has bad taste in women. He prefers them weak as milk."

Ingilda noticed that as he spoke he rubbed at his left arm.

"But possessing some beauty" she pressed "You cannot deny the slave is beautiful." The words tasted sour, their truth an affront to her vanity, but she must know.....

Girdar shrugged. "She is beautiful like the brooch you wear."

Ingilda's heart dipped, then turned as he took her hand.

"She is a possession and nothing more. To be used and discarded at will."

Ingilda could have laughed out loud, and she had thought this slave was somehow a rival! Believing the words of a Briton! She lowered her eyes as Girdar congratulated himself on his performance. She was his. His whenever he chose, as was the power which would be her dowry.

* * *

Ranulph kicked the hut door open and placed Averil on the bed, the action jogging her back to consciousness.

Averil's initial confusion as she came around giving way to acute embarrassment as she remembered what had happened.

"I'm not sure which was the best sport " he said "the bear meeting a brave end or the bold daughter of Aethelstan fainting at the sight of blood." He handed her a goblet of wine. "Here, drink this."

Averil took a deep draught of the wine, all too painfully aware she was under Ranulph's scrutiny.

"I gave you the chance to leave but you chose not to take it."

"I had no wish to make the request as you suggested."

"Yet you chose to give me soft words in front of Girdar. Why did you do that?" the snap question caught her off guard, she was expecting more taunts about what had happened.

"Well? I find it hard to believe that you, who are never lost for words, have none to say to me."

Averil recalled her bewildering emotions that morning which she had, until that moment, skilfully pushed back from her mind, the gentleness of his touch when Ranulph had caught her, his standing protectively in front of her, the rush of warmth when he had come to her defence , threatening to cross swords with Girdar.....and then the spark of real fear that he might be harmed, and not only because that would leave her at Girdar's mercy.....

"Why did you defend me against him?" she asked.

"Why should I not? You are my property and only I have the right to speak to you in such a way."

Of course, it all came back to the same thing, Averil thought bitterly, she was Ranulph's possession, like one of his horses.

"I am still waiting for the answer to my question."

"It suited me to lie."

"I do not understand why you did not seek to watch he whom you hate taught a lesson. "

Averil could not find an answer, refusing to meet his gaze.

"Of course." He went on "in the unlikely event of the fight turning to Girdar's advantage and my falling under his sword you would have lost my protection from him. Or is it that my slave feared only for her master's safety and nothing else?"

Their eyes caught, Averil looked away quickly, for he had spoken the truth.

"Believe what you like" she leapt up and made to leave, he blocked her path.

"I choose only to know." He moved toward her, she took a step back from him, her betraying heart pounding at the thought he could discover that which she had only just admitted to herself.

"There are other ways to find an answer" in a swift movement he took her in his arms and his mouth came down on her own. Averil was battered by the same sensations which had crashed through her consciousness with such fury only once before - when he had kissed her in the forest, but this time was different, then she had battled to be free, now she found herself not wanting to resist.

He lifted his mouth, still staying suffocatingly close.

"Did I not once tell you that those I choose to take always come to me willingly?" his voice was seductively soft, but the effect of his words on Averil was devastating. Despite all reason and sense her betraying heart and body had been on the very brink of melting, giving in to a depth of feeling she never knew existed, matching what she had finally thought was true passion from him. But it was not so. Ranulph felt only conquest. A true victory over his brother!

"Yes, you did," her voice was playful, she smiled while slipping from his arms.....the stinging slap she delivered left an angry red hand mark across the scar on his cheek.

"Do not EVER deceive yourself that I am your whore!"

With a curse Ranulph moved to grab her, but she evaded him, sprinting to the door and almost making it before he imprisoned her waist from behind, lifting her from the ground. She kicked out against him and pushed down against his hold as he carried her back into the room.

" Let me go you swine! Were I a man I would kill you!" Averil spat the words while struggling against him.

Without losing his vice-like grip, he brought her around to face him, holding her close."Were you a man you would already be dead"

Averil was breathing heavily from the exertion of the struggle. He was reminded of the first time he had seen her, chained in Aethelstan's hall, remembering how he had been struck by her beauty and the same courage she displayed now. She had actually dared to slap his face by the Gods! In truth he had never met a woman like her –she was without equal .....she was magnificent......what sons she would have! He released his hold so abruptly Averil almost fell on the floor .... she was stunned for a moment at his action ...what in the name of Nerthus!......he had dropped her as though he held fire......she could only stare uncomprehendingly at him as he strode over to the door.

"I do not need you to attend me at table tonight. Make sure food and wine are ready to break my fast on the morrow" the order was given without a backward glance as he slammed the door behind him. Sweet Nerthus! How could she have allowed these feelings for Ranulph to develop! She must be mad! It was a nightmare which there was no waking from. She was in love with him.

Chapter Twelve

Bitter winds swirled autumn leaves in a dizzying dance around Averil's feet as she may her way across the courtyard. Dawn had broken a few hours before, bringing with it the cool promise of a hard winter. Averil slipped into the heat of the kitchen, noticing her entrance had for some reason attracted the close attention of the women, some of whom paused at their work. A touch on her arm brought her around to be met by Ebba holding a goblet of piping hot mead.

"It is cold outside Lady. I thought this would warm you."

Averil accepted the drink, revitalised more by the warmth of Ebba's friendship than the fire trail of liquid down her throat.

"I hope Lord Ranulph is kind?"

The whispered inquiry startled Averil, before she could question it, the black haired girl Brigid had joined them.

"Would you have some more to drink?" Brigid offered mead from the jug she carried, Averil noting with alarm disfiguring bruises on her pallid cheeks.

"Thank you Brigid." Averil held out her goblet to be filled once more. "What happened to your face?"

Brigid looked at Ebba, Averil sensing unspoken words which brought with them a feeling of discomfort.

"My mistress's anger does not end swiftly, her punishment for words of truth is a prolonged one."

"Will you explain your meaning?"

Ebba replied hurriedly, before Brigid could. "Princess Ingilda saw Lord Ranulph and Lord Girdar almost clash swords over you in the courtyard before the first hunt after their arrival."

Cold now clenched Averil's stomach, dispelling the heat of the drink.

Brigid carried on. "She was mad with jealousy and I, as always, was to take the brunt of it. Only this time I made it worthwhile. I told her how much Lord Girdar burns for you, how he and Ealdorman Ranulph desire you more than life itself!"

"What!" Averil cut her short with her angry exclamation.

"It is small satisfaction for what she has done to me! Though it has made my position much worse, as my mistress continues to beat me for it."

Brigid hung her head miserably, Averil was immediately sorry for her outburst, she touched Brigid's arm.

"I am sad to see you so badly treated Brigid."

Averil had hardly finished speaking when a voice piped up. "Lord Girdar courts the bitch princess already in heat for him while he and his brother fight over their turn to rut their accommodating whore!"

Ebba gasped, Averil glared at the laughing women, the deeply offensive remark sparking a blaze of fury in her - how dare these low sows so speak of her – she would give them something to think about!

"Shut your filthy mouths and get about your business!" there was a shocked silence at the imperious command. "Or this whore shall see to it that the queen hears how every last one of you has so called her daughter!"

The women stood stunned as Averil's words sank in, she had admitted she was a whore! If it were so then the other rumours that she served two Ealdormen who battled for her affection would indeed make her powerful and her threats far from idle.

Averil snatched up a loaf of bread and a pitcher of water from the table.

"Come Ebba. We will leave the chickens to lay their eggs."

Averil swept from the kitchen and slammed the door behind her. Ebba had to run to keep up with her as she stormed across the courtyard and finally came to a halt by the great hall, leaning against the rough wooden wall.

"Despite what I said in there I am not Ranulph's or anyone else's whore."

"I knew that it was so Lady."

Averil smiled, her temper dissolved. "I am glad of it. Although I see this rumour has made me another enemy as well as Girdar."

"The Princess Ingilda."

"I would ask you to keep your eyes and ears open for me Ebba. It may be that she who desires Girdar could be just as dangerous to me as he is himself."

They clasped hands, the action expressing more than words could ever have done.

* * *

Leofric wiped white flecks of ale from his beard with the back of his hand as he turned to Ranulph, who sat next to him at the long table.

"And when do you plan to return to your land my son?"

"Soon father, before winter takes too strong a hold."

"It looks as though your brother will not follow your example."

Ranulph followed his father's gaze which rested on Girdar, sitting at the high table, engrossed in conversation with the Princess Ingilda.

"A match made by the Gods – or my stepmother?"

"It is not yet a match Ranulph, though Girdar has been working towards it being so." Leofric's steady scrutiny switched to his oldest son. "Whomsoever wins Ingilda will also win power."

Ranulph turned his full attention on Ingilda, attractive by virtue of youth, generously proportioned with large breasts, pale skin, flaxen hair, she would provide warmth in Girdar's bed and their sons would be royal. He had thought of sons before..... Averil's. Her face came into his mind's eye. Averil. Compared to Ingilda she was a burning torch to a flickering candle.

"Power, father, is never sure – despite whom you take to wife."

Ranulph spoke casually as he poured himself some ale.

"And would you be so wise had the princess been the daughter of Aethlestan?"

"You can rest assured the Gods have not as yet created the woman who will affect my judgement."

"And do you not call it ill-judged to begin your stay at Oswin's hall by almost crossing swords with your brother over a slave in his courtyard?"

"That was between Girdar and myself."

Leofric surveyed his oldest son, seeing Ranulph's mother in the raven hair, the stubborn set of the jaw which spoke of the same unbending nature she had possessed.

"I once thought as you my son. Yet even as I believed it, I burned inside to possess that which my rank should have denied me – your mother."

Ranulph was taken aback, his father had never spoken of his relationship with his mother, who had died when he was just a babe in arms.

"Aye, even when your mother was a slave none could mistake her for any other that what she was – a Princess." Leofric's eyes shone as the sweet memories came flooding back. "It was I who had to prove myself to HER by the Gods!"

Leofric took a swig of ale then caught and held Ranulph's gaze. "It is easier to slay warriors in battle than to capture the heart of such a woman – for it cannot ever be taken, it must be freely given. To do so you needs must lay down your sword. You will only win when you accept defeat."

Leofric smiled as he grasped Ranulph's shoulder. "Think well on my words Ranulph. For such a victory is sweeter than you can ever imagine."

He got up without another word, leaving to join a group of men playing dice by the roaring fire. Ranulph watched him for a long time, lost in thought.

* * *

The evening was nearing its close when Egwina approached her stepson, sitting broodingly alone.

"Would you care for wine Ranulph?" Egwina stood over him.

"Why not?" Ranulph swigged the last dregs of ale and banged his goblet down for Egwina to fill up with the rich red liquid until it almost overflowed, leaving the jug empty.

"Your hand is unsteady tonight stepmother." Ranulph grinned wickedly. "Could it be your mind is elsewhere, on the mating of our dear Girdar perhaps?"

"I hardly feel such a lewd question to your stepmother deserves a reply Ranulph. Now, I must take my leave of you, the jug is in need of refilling, your father has a great taste for this brew."

Ranulph watched Egwina's stiff back retreat, his glance alighting on the flaxen haired Eglif, laughingly shrugging off the wandering hands of one of the noblemen she was serving ale to.

"Hey! Serving girl! Over here!"

Eglif treated him to an unmistakably salacious look before slapping away her troublesome Lord and moving over to him, hips swaying invitingly.

"Ah Eglif, it has been a long time since I have seen you." He pulled her onto his knee and began to explore the familiar territory of her body, the action inciting squeals of delicious delight.

"And do you want some ale then?"

"You know what I want Eglif." He stroked the fulsome breasts through the low cut tunic, feeling Eglif shiver with excitement as his fingers toyed with the now erect nipples straining through the material.

"You are too forward" Eglif's protest was without any conviction as she savoured the thrill of his touch, he bit her neck as his hand travelled inside her tunic and up her bare legs. Eglif leant against him as he explored her thigh.

"Let us leave." His voice was thick with desire as he withdrew his hand and she got up, almost knocking over the goblet of wine which Ranulph retrieved with a lightening reflex.

"Do you want this? It's fire will keep you hot."

"You know that I need nothing to keep myself burning for you." Her blue eyes sparked their message of willing acceptance as she drained the goblet.

Ranulph led her outside and pressed her against a rough wooden wall, seeing little of her in the inky darkness, she could have been anyone – she could have been Averil. "We can have comfort later. I want you now." His voice was low as he tugged at her dress to reveal soft naked thighs and promptly lifted her up. Eglif groaned with pleasure as she entered her and they each gratified the other, her legs entwined around him in a sure grip as they took their fill.

* * *

Averil lay on the floor wrapped in furs, sleep was elusive but she had to grasp it in case Ranulph returned, something he did not always do. The door burst open, her eyes closed, she must pretend to be asleep.

"For shame that we should disturb your mistress!" Averil held her breath as she identified the voice.

"My mistress?" Ranulph threw off his cloak, looking over at the slumbering form in the corner of the room. "Ah yes, do not worry. She is sleeping." Eglif giggled drunkenly.

"Remember you promised me comfort this time."

"And I thought you enjoyed being taken against a wall."

The words conjured up a stark image for Averil which brought with it an unexpected jab of jealousy which she hastily put down.

"And so I do. Though I much like the feel of your naked flesh against my own." Eglif pressed her mouth hungrily against Ranulph's as he eased her onto the bed. Averil could imagine everything that was going on, Ranulph's hands stripping Eglif before he took off his own clothes, the torchlight dancing across their naked bodies, his mouth probing the yielding flesh. She tried to blot out the pictures, putting her hands to her ears under the furs to cut out the sounds of their energetic lovemaking, she could hardly endure the thoughts which bombarded her, for she was at least honest with herself to know that she wanted to be the one in Ranulph's arms, and that was the worst thing of all to come to terms with.

The room was silent, but Averil could still hear what had passed. Had he known she was not asleep? Had he done this to insult her? How could she feel the way she did about such a man! The questions she had no answer to whirled inside her brain, catching her in a dizzying vortex which eventually span her into a troubled slumber.

* * *

The heavy, laboured breathing woke Ranulph with a start. The light from the torch still burned brightly above the pallet, casting a dim glow on the girl who lay half covered by bear skins, her face unnaturally white and her yellow hair matted with perspiration.

"Eglif!" Ranulph shook the naked shoulder, it was cold as ice even as it slithered with sweat. "Eglif! Wake up!" the breathing was noisy now, rattling in her throat. She was undoubtedly sick. This was women's' work.

Ranulph jumped up, dressing himself in his loin cloth and then pulling on his leather tunic as he went over to Averil and shook her awake..

"I want you to look at Eglif, there is something wrong with her."

"What do you mean wrong? Is she sick?" Averil rubbed her eyes as she woke from a deep, troubled sleep.

"She has a sweat and her breathing is strange."

Averil looked over at the still form, whose every rattling breath laboured as though each would be the last, she had heard this dread sound only once before, long ago in one of the farmer's huts before her horrified mother had found her there and taken her away – from the presence of death. A creeping fright took a tenuous hold on Averil's senses, she wished the rock crystal was about her neck to ward off what could even now be upon herself and Ranulph.

"Has she vomited?"

Ranulph shook his head.

"You are sure?"

"Yes. I am sure."

Averil felt easier, she had limited knowledge but was certain there was always vomiting before the onset of the sweat which heralded the scourge which she greatly feared had taken hold of Eglif – the plague. Yet she still went over reluctantly to the sick girl, surveying her face, noticing a barely discernable discolouration about the mouth which was rapidly fading. What was this? Her heart twisting, Averil hastily examined Eglif's hands, noticing the same on the fingertips, with growing alarm, she lifted the furs and saw the same fading blue-black tinge on Eglif's toes. Nerthus protect them! For she recognised this thing which held Eglif in its grasp, that which could be taken for the plague, wrought from the ghastly fruit of the midnight blue flowers which grew in secret places in the deepest parts of the forest. Poison! The horrifying revelation crawled along Averil's flesh.

"Well? Can you tell what is the matter with her?"

Averil whirled on Ranulph. "Did you sup together?"

"No. She was serving in the hall."

"You are sure she took nothing to eat or drink which was yours?"

An image of the wanton expression on Eglif's face as she accepted his wine and drained the goblet came to Ranulph's mind.

"She drank my wine. Are you...."

"You didn't have any?"

"No. I gave it all to her. " Ranulph looked deep into Averil's eyes and read what he had already begun to suspect. "Poison?"

Averil nodded.

"You are certain?"

"I have seen this before in our village. The faint discolouration appears for a very short time as the poison begins its work and then disappears without a trace, giving the impression death has come from the plague."

"Can nothing be done to help her?"

"I am not skilled in the art of potions but I know there is no antidote for that which has been used here – the death juice of the blue flower." Averil leant over and stroked the matted hair from Eglif's face, tears stung her eyes, her heart full of pity at so terrible an end to a young woman not much older than herself.

Ranulph's face was grim as he looked down at Eglif's comatose form.

"This poor girl received that which was no doubt intended for me. Sweet gift indeed from she who has always held me dear – my loving stepmother Egwina!"

Only Eglif's ragged breathing pierced the still silence of the room, echoing the shocking pronouncement.

"It cannot be! She is your mother in the eyes of the Gods!"

Ranulph's mirthless laughter was frightening. "And my stepmother intended me to meet them, by poisoning the last of the wine she carried and giving it to me, I do not doubt that you would join me later."

Averil's heart missed a beat.

"You have told me yourself Girdar wants you dead. While you live there is still a chance you could disgrace him with your allegation of murder."

"Which is the truth from his own lips."

"Whatever the case, you are a danger to Girdar and consequently to his ever faithful mother Egwina."

"But I cannot see why you too should be victim."

"I am a more powerful enemy than yourself, Girdar must believe you are my loving mistress. If I found out you had been murdered it might incite my wrath which could also lead to his downfall."

Averil's blood ran cold as she saw he could well be speaking the truth, it were as though she could actually see Lady Egwina and Girdar voicing their fears and reaching a solution which neither dare utter but only confirm with a glance which spoke a thousand words.

"Your Briton. Can she be trusted?" Ranulph's question sliced through her thoughts.

"Yes."

"Then go and get her from the slave quarters and bring her back here, make sure you are not seen. I shall get Edred."

"What do you intend to do?"

"Just bring her here."

Averil picked up her heavy cloak and was gone, out into the night, hardly daring to think as she ran to fetch Ebba.

* * *

Dawn was near to breaking when the four gathered in the room at the foot of the bed where Eglif now tossed fitfully, obviously in pain.

"Edred. You and the Briton will take the girl. You know what to do."

Ebba clutched her throat, confusion and fear had taken hold of her since being woken up by Averil's urgent whispers. As they rushed through the night to Ranulph's quarters, she had learned her Lady's life was in danger and she must be charged with a grim but necessary duty if she were to help her….and then to find Eglif in so terrible a condition.

"Do not worry Ebba." Averil had taken her hand. "You are in no danger from Eglif, she has sickness which was inflicted upon her by my enemies."

The meaning was not lost – poison! No doubt meant from Averil, could it be the work of the jealous Princess Ingilda?

"Can you ride girl?" Edred addressed Ebba with his accustomed gruffness, relieved with the nod she gave by way of reply.

"Good. Then let us make haste before the sun rises."

"Remember what I told you to say at the gate Edred" Ranulph grasped his retainer's arm. "Sit Eglif in front of you, you can pretend she is asleep or drunk. They must not guess her condition."

Edred bowed to his master before wrapping Eglif in furs and picking her up.

Averil ran to her oak chest, retrieving a rich blue cloak lined with black fur which she handed to Ebba.

"Take this dear Ebba." She wrapped the magnificent garment around Ebba's old woollen cloak. "Trust me and do not fear Edred. He is a good man and will make sure no harm befalls you." They embraced tightly, loathe to leave each other.

"Come on. We must move." Edred barked his command impatiently, as with one backward glance Ebba, almost lost in the gorgeous cloak, followed him from the room, closing the door with her accustomed gentleness, the action searing Averil's overstretched emotions. Her one dear friend now gone from her, poor Eglif to die a horrible death, a fate which might have been Ranulph's and then her own….pent up grief and horror welled up and threatened to overwhelm her…… Ranulph looked over at her, she looked ashen, pain and sorrow easy to read on her face.

"This night has taken its toll on you " his voice had a soft edge which Averil had never heard before, it was enough to touch her overburdened heart, she wanted more than anything for him to just hold her in his arms and comfort her, when he took her hand and sat her down on the bed she did not resist. "Rest yourself."

"Thank you" she smiled up at him and for one sweet moment their eyes met without conflict.

" I cannot have my betrothed looking as though she has spent the night with death."

The shocking words impacted on Averil's overwrought senses as if someone had thrown ice cold water over her. What in the name of Nerthus!. The words just tumbled out, she could not stop them.

"Betrothed! To you! Are your wits addled!"

For just a split second Ranulph's face darkened before regaining composure. "No. I am perfectly in charge of my wits. I had no idea the thought of the honour of becoming my wife would fill you with such horror."

Averil could only stare at him, she was so upset that she had reacted without thought, he had twisted her words, like he always did, that was not really what she had meant!

"There is much to do. I would have you sleep."

He left her alone. She fell onto the bed, physically and emotionally spent.

Chapter Thirteen

Melodic humming seeped through the darkness of Averil's sleep. She sat up to see a plump, apple-cheeked woman deftly sorting out the clothes in the oak chest.

"Who are you and what are you doing here?" Averil's demand was tense.

"My name is Breda Lady. I am here to meet your needs." The tone possessed a deference Averil had not experienced in a long time.

"By whose authority?"

"By Ealdorman Ranulph. He has charged me to be your servant while you reside at this hall."

What in the name of Nerthus! He had been serious about the betrothal! It must be so. For here she was returned to her former status– Breda was speaking once more.

"I have sorted out your garments and shall make sure all your clothes are kept fresh and clean. There is warmed water to wash and I am clever enough with the comb to dress you hair."

As the woman fussed about her, Averil responded as though she had never experienced anything else but the attention of others. For although in name a slave, she had always been the noble daughter of Aethelstan in heart and mind.

* * *

Leofric was rubbing his hands together for warmth when Ranulph entered the anteroom.

"Ah Ranulph. What is it you wish to talk of that is so important to drag me from my bed?"

Ranulph loosened his damp cloak as he faced his father. "I have decided to marry Aethelstan's daughter."

Leofric treated his eldest son to a searching look. "An interesting decision – and a swift one."

"Not as swift as you imagine father, your words to me last night were well thought on. Do you think the king would accept it?"

Leofric stroked his chin thoughtfully.

"I and my house are held in high favour and I have King Oswin's ear in many things. Aethelstan and his male kin are dead and his house is now extinguished. This girl is no threat but is of noble blood. Why should she not marry and give her loyalty to new kin?"

"I thank you father, your words are wise. Now there is something else I must ask. I shall need your witness at my giving Averil freedom before we marry."

"You will take her to the place where the great roads cross?"

"It is right it should be done there – henceforth she can choose her own path."

"We shall do it this very morn, before the meeting of Oswin's council."

"I should wish our marriage conducted at the beginning of the ceremonial feast to mark the autumn sacrifice of the surplus cattle."

"You are in much haste Ranulph, though I do not dispute such a good choice of time, the high priest can incorporate both the celebrations."

Leofric went over to his son, planting both hands firmly on Ranulph's shoulders.

"I congratulate you on so wise a path. She will give our house fine, strong sons to be proud of."

The two men embraced, Leofric failing to notice the fixed expression of his oldest son.

* * *

The wind howled around the partially denuded trees, swaying them eerily, a mass bow of respect to the tall cloaked figure of the girl who stood in the middle of the point where two cracked stone roads crossed. Two men on horseback stood on either side of her, their horses champing at the bit, restless from the onslaught of the elements.

"I ask you Leofric, Ealdorman of King Oswin, to witness the freeing of Averil, daughter of Aethelstan from her bondage of slavery to me, Ranulph, Ealdorman of King Oswin and oldest son of Leofric's house."

"I Leofric, bear witness to what has passed. Henceforth the Lady Averil shall be a free woman."

Averil looked beyond Leofric's solemn countenance to Ranulph, searching for some trace of emotion, but his face was unreadable. She glanced away, accepting Leofric's hand to lead her to Ranulph, who helped her onto his black horse.

"I shall speak with the king as soon as we return Ranulph." Leofric mounted and the three galloped off without another word, moving swiftly through the bleak, inhospitable landscape.

* * *

"I saw Ranulph in the courtyard barely ten minutes ago looking very much alive" Girdar confronted his mother, seated in a high backed chair in her bower "I thought you gave him a dose strong enough to knock down a pack of wolves!"

"I did." Egwina's eyes were sharp as she regarded her son, fury at her failure biting. "It means that the son of the British whore cannot have drunk it."

"If he didn't then who did?"

"No-one. The potion leaves no trace and makes it look as though the victim has the plague, there would have been report by now if anyone had drank it. It must have been thrown out with the slops."

Girdar paced the room. "There is something else here. Nothing involving Ranulph is ever simple. If there is any chance at all that he knows...... "

"How could he?" Egwina's tone poured scorn on the conjecture.

"Are you sure you did not see anyone else drink the wine?"

Girdar's question prompted a recreation of the scene of the night before in Egwina's mind. After she had given him the drink she had meant to keep close watch on Ranulph but the queen had unexpectedly demanded she and her ladies leave the hall early.

" I have told you. If anyone had drank it they would be dead or dying by now and everyone would think we were infected with the plague. "

Girdar took in her words, she was right of course. "I bow to your opinion mother."

"Next time I will watch him drink it!" she got to her feet, the subject closed.

"Now, we will go to the hall. Your father wishes to speak to us before we break bread with the king."

"Do you know why?"

"If I did I would tell you. Perhaps he wants to know when his youngest son will become Oswin's son-in-law."

"You will be the first to hear of it when it happens."

Egwina accepted his hand, squeezing it gently with maternal pride as they left the room.

* * *

Breda clucked around Averil as she helped her into the gorgeous green gown which Ranulph had regarded so contemptuously on the first night at Oswin's hall. The servant's podgy fingers were surprisingly nimble as she dressed her lady in no time, finishing off by tightening the silver girdle around Averil's waist.

"Now your hair Lady."

Averil submitted herself to Breda's attentions, not paying much heed to what was happening, taking the time to concentrate on working out what Ranulph may be planning.

"Do you wish it bound or loose?"

"Loose." Ranulph answered the question as he entered the bower.

"It is well as it is Breda." Averil confirmed the order, for it would not do to cross he whom she was betrothed to.

"Are you ready Lady?"

Averil turned to him, noting he was dressed entirely in black, the only relief from the sombre colour the silver rings of chainmail sewn to his leather tunic. She wished Breda out of the room, for there were a number of questions crying out to be asked.

"I have brought you this to replace the one you left behind." He placed a green cloak he carried about her shoulders.

"Thank you." Averil smiled graciously, aware of Breda's interested gaze.

"I am to present you to the King and then the high priest who will perform our ceremony of marriage."

"And when do you plan to complete my happiness?"

"Just before the feast to mark the autumn sacrifice."

Shock seared through Averil, the feast day of the slaughtered cattle..

"But that is in two days time!" the thoughts had formed words before she could prevent them.

"Believe me. It is not soon enough." He lifted her hand, turned it and kissed the palm, his eyes signalling a warning.

"Your happy news has overwhelmed me!"

"As I knew it would" he took her arm and led her outside, past the half finished building in the courtyard.

"I had no idea your plan would be so swift!" Averil lowered her voice, not trusting the apparent emptiness of the surroundings. "Two days is but little time to act."

Ranulph stopped with surprising suddenness, his expression unreadable in the glow of the flickering flames from the torches in the courtyard sconces.

"My plan will take a little time after our wedding."

" You mean you intend to make me your wife!"

"Is that not what betrothal naturally leads to?"

"Do not make jest of this!"

Ranulph pulled her close.

" This is not a game. Eglif will soon be dead and I would have been in her place with you soon to follow."

"Do you think I do not know that!"

"You act as though you do not. Girdar's actions against me have brought revenge for your kin within your grasp. No-one must suspect this union is anything other than true."

"And no one will! I will be everything and more to you in the company of others be they noble or slave. But know you this – even though our servants will find us each morning sharing the same bed – that is all we shall share."

The sound of voices as two cloaked men entered the courtyard.....

"For shame!" her laughter was light and teasing "Cannot you control yourself – let me go at once my Lord!"

Ranulph's eyes darted beyond her to the men who now came into full view, causing him to release his hold and wordlessly take her to the hall.

* * *

Egwina looked for Leofric in the throng of men and women who awaited Oswin's arrival for the evening meal. Seeing him she called out his name, his warm smile in response catching her unawares, for she was unused to warmth from her husband, deference and respect but never, ever, warmth. Egwina had gone into the marriage with high hopes – believing herself in love with the man who saw the union as a means of consolidating the power of two houses. But, she had soon discovered his inner self was forever reserved for she who had long been ashes. The Briton. Ranulph's mother. The birth of Girdar had filled the void in Egwina's life, at last she could give all the love Leofric would never accept....Girdar meant more than life itself to her. These thoughts washed over Egwina as she made her way to Leofric, seeing Girdar with the princess from the corner of her eye. It would be the son of Egwina who would triumph – not the son of the she demon slave who embraced Leofric even in her death sleep!

"You are well tonight Lady?"

"As well as ever and curious to learn why myself and Girdar should be summoned to you."

"I see Girdar is too interested in the company of Ingilda than that of his father, though I cannot blame him."

"I shall tell him what you wish to say."

"Your eldest son is to wed."

Egwina looked merely politely interested, barely flickering her profound shock at the news – for she knew who it was Ranulph planned to take to wife, even as she inquired it of Leofric.

"And who is to be a daughter of our house?"

"The daughter of Aethelstan. Ranulph has already given her freedom with myself as witness."

"And what has the King said to this?"

"I have spoken to him and he does not object."

"Should you not have consulted me on this matter?"

"As you consulted me on your plans for Girdar?" Leofric's face was impassive, not betraying how he felt – did his wife think he was a complete fool? That he did not know of her subtle manipulation on behalf of Girdar, whom she loved better than herself?

"I work for the strength of our house."

"Then you will see how good a choice is Ranulph's. The girl is of noble blood, her stock will enrich our family."

Egwina said nothing, flaming at a turn of events which could easily have been avoided had Girdar told her the truth sooner. A slave poured a goblet full of wine for Leofric, she watched the blood red liquid, contemplating on the poisoned cup served to Ranulph.

"See Lady. Our son has arrived."

Egwina's eyes followed Leofric's and many others as Ranulph entered with Averil on his arm. She had removed her cloak and wore a sumptuous green gown. Her red gold hair cascaded in shimmering waves to her knees, its only adornment a slim silver circlet around her head. There was no need for jewellery, for nothing was needed to enhance the loveliness the Gods had granted.

Girdar's words to Ingilda were stemmed in mid-flow as he caught sight of Averil, head held high, acknowledging with an assured smile the unspoken tributes to her beauty. She was a bright, fierce star who made all other women pale into insignificance in comparison.

"What does your brother think he is doing bringing his slave here like this!" Ingilda's voice was high as she saw on whom Girdar's attention had been diverted.

"I cannot guess what must be on his mind." Girdar gave Ingilda a laconic smile, marking her jealousy.

"I shall find out why he has brought her here." He made to leave, anticipating the catch on his sleeve.

"I wish you to stay here with me Lord Girdar." Ingilda could not disguise her petulance.

How simple it was to play her, thanks to Averil, yet he was rapidly tiring of the game, knowing how it would end.....

"Do you want me to stay by your side while we both live?" he raised a questioning eyebrow as the meaning sent tremors of delight through Ingilda, he had moved breathtakingly close and it was though no-one else was in the hall but the two of them, she nodded her consent, unable to trust herself to speak.

"I shall speak to the king as soon as I can."

Ingilda ached to be alone to him, to feel the touch of his mouth on her own, she shivered with anticipation of the much longed for moment.....the commotion caused by the king entering the hall stemmed Ingilda's unmaidenly imaginings as everyone made way for King Oswin, resplendent in a cloak of midnight blue cloth woven with gold and silver thread. Queen Ethelburga was at his side, wearing a gown of the same hue but without the glittering addition displayed by her royal husband. Oswin surveyed his followers, his looks lingering, as always, on the women, but this time with a purpose, to seek out the would-be bride of Ranulph, who even as a slave in a simple dress had not escaped his notice. Ah yes, he had her now, dressed as befitting her true rank, not just lovely but magnificent – blessed indeed by the Goddess Nerthus, and a prize for any man. He stopped in front of her, his steel blue eyes taking in every inch of Averil's body, missing nothing.

"I welcome you to my hall Lady."

Averil bowed her head in respect.

"I wish both you and Ranulph joy in your union."

Girdar stiffened slightly as Oswin's congratulations rang out, igniting an eruption of fury and fire within – that son of a slave whore was to take she who rightly belonged to him, to wife! No wonder she had allowed Ranulph to bed her with the thought of wedlock in the offing! The crafty, sly bitch........

"Did you know of this?" Ingilda demanded an answer from Girdar, the question barely sinking through the black virulence which assailed him.

A flutter of emotion she did not then recognise as fear brushed Ingilda's heart for an instant as she looked up at Girdar's granite hard profile. She touched his arm, a gentle tug on Girdar's senses reminding him of her presence – did Ranulph know somehow of the poison and plot to bring him down by supporting his wife's accusations of murder? Although, as son-in-law to the King his position would be better to deal with any accusations of even the wife of an Ealdorman.

"It is as much a surprise to me as to you. But I can do nothing but wish him the blessing of the Gods – as he will give to us." An appreciative smile played on Girdar's lips as he took her hand and lingeringly kissed it – dazzled by so obvious a display of affection, Ingilda failed to see it did not even begin to penetrate the frigid ice in his blues eyes as Girdar's mind worked, for he must be well prepared for anything Ranulph may throw at him.

Chapter Fourteen

Hundreds of squat candles cast their vivid luminescence over the temple full of people, whose voices mingled in a melodic chant. Wisps of spiced incense spiralled into the atmosphere, it's heady, eye-stinging aroma permeating every corner of the richly furnished place of worship, adorned with hangings depicting all manner of wild and wonderful creatures woven in glinting gold and silver thread. Ranulph and Averil made their way to the stone altar under the fierce gaze of the black-bearded, red-robed High Priest. Ranulph wore black, relieved only by the two blood red garnet studded cruciform brooches pinned to his cloak. The richness of Averil's green gown was underlined by the circlet of fresh evergreen leaves pinned around her head. In her mind Averil offered fervent prayers to the Goddess Nerthus, who must surely understand and plead her case before the deities of wedlock who presided here, explain why she, Averil, must go through a sacrilegious act, forced to enter the sacred bond of union with a man who she had love for but which she needs must deny because he had no love for her. As they reached the stone slab altar, the chanting reached a crescendo, only to be stilled in an instant by a wave of the priestly hand.

"Most mighty Gods of union, look you now upon these two creatures of the Earth Goddess Ecre" the High Priest's resounding voice boomed in awesome majesty, then he gazed at Ranulph, waiting for him to speak.

"I Ranulph, first born son of the house of Leofric, wish to take to wife the woman Averil."

Two silver bowls were before them, Ranulph dug into one to retrieve a handful of dark soil, Averil watched transfixed as the fruit of the earth goddess trickled through his strong fingers into the empty bowl in front of her. "Here is symbol we shall share our toils." He bowed briefly to Averil then stooped to pick up a shield leant against the altar, it was of leather and handsomely set with gilt bronze oval mounts.

"And here is symbol that we share our perils." He placed the weapon of war onto the slab before Averil. Shivers ran through her, despite the warmth of the temple, she could feel the eyes of those assembled on her back. It was her turn to make her affirmation and she must do it well.

"I, Averil, only daughter of the house of Aethlestan, wish to pledge myself to the man Ranulph." Elatha lay on the altar, glinting in the candlelight. She picked up the mighty sword of her father with two hands and gave it to him.

"Thus I give a gift of arms, symbol of my pledge to share all with my husband – in peace or war." Her voice stood firm, even as she uttered the sacred oath she wished with all her heart what had passed had been real – that Ranulph, son of the house of Leofric, had truly meant his vows, spoken not through necessity but through love.......he replaced the sword on the altar and then kissed her forehead, marking the end of the formality of the ceremony and starting the celebrations. He caught Averil around the waist, almost lifting her off her feet as he led her to the King and Queen, who sat at the forefront of the temple. Ethelburga draped a garland of red berries around Averil's neck.

"I wish you well in your bond. May it prove as fruitful and as lasting as that which now encircles you."

The king led the way out of the temple into the great hall. Averil felt herself swamped by merriment and goodwill which served to magnify an already painful situation as she was swept along with the tide of the feast marking both the slaughter of the autumn cattle and their marriage.

* * *

There was much laughter as the company who had eaten and drank their fill mingled with each other at the feast. In honour of their marriage, Averil and Ranulph had been seated at the King's table, with the advantage to them that all their food and wine had been tasted beforehand. Averil had no appetite and had eaten very little, but the wine gave her a kind of solace, for she could divorce herself from the truth of the situation, it was much easier to pretend under it's benign influence. She stood a little apart from those making merry, sipping her wine.

"My sister." Girdar's unexpected intrusion made her start.

"I wish to welcome you to my family with a token of the high esteem I hold you in." The small silver dagger he handed over to her was finely wrought, the handle worked into the repellent body of a serpent. "I more than any know how much you value this weapon for your protection."

Averil looked at the hideous weapon while hastily contemplating his words – was there hidden meaning in them and the gift? An implication she needed to protect herself because Ranulph was not her true husband? No. Her act had been too good, tempered as it was, she though bitterly, with too much truth from herself.....she was just jumping at shadows.....

"I thank you for your gift Lord brother and I shall give this noble weapon to my husband for safe keeping." She placed the dagger in her silver belt.

Girdar regarded her with hooded, suspicious eyes. "I see the great honour of becoming my bond sister has improved your manners." His hand brushed hers as he leaned close. "Though I hope the time will come when I shall teach you some more."

"And what is it that you wish to teach your new sister?" Ranulph's cordial inquiry as he appeared and placed his arm protectively around his new wife's shoulder brought Girdar up short, his face clouding a fraction of a second at the unexpected intervention, before breaking into an amicable grin.

"What else Ranulph, but the art, perfected by she who will soon be my wife, of staying conscious during a bear bait!"

"An interesting offer Girdar. We shall drink on it." Their goblets clashed together in a toast before they drained them and Girdar took his leave.

Ranulph kept his arm around Averil as he looked down at her "What did he say to you?"

"Nothing of any import. He gave me this." She handed Ranulph the dagger from her belt "No doubt in memory of the last time we were alone." For the briefest of moments they exchanged true smiles.

"And what is this?"It was Leofric, his laughter robust. "Cannot you wait until the feast is over to be alone together?"

"It seems not father, though you cannot blame me my impatience!"

"Custom must be met Ranulph." Leofric winked. "Though I think we can hasten it along eh? Go daughter, you may begin your preparations in your bower to greet your new husband."

* * *

Egwina watched her new daughter carefully as they entered the hut. Evergreen leaves were festooned around the walls and scattered on the furs of the bed. Breda stood to attention as her mistress appeared, puffed up with pride at the beautifully displayed decorations which she and a handful of others had worked long and hard on.

"Welcome Lady. Everything has been prepared."

The sweet smell of scented dried flowers lightly touched the air. Averil saw they had been strewn on the clean straw which covered the floor.

"It is very well Breda. I thank you."

Egwina regarded Breda with distaste as she bristled with disapproval at her new daughter's familiarity with one so low.

"Leave us!" Egwina's haughty command sent Breda straight to the door and fired Averil.

"Breda." Averil stopped the servant in her tracks. "You will stay until I command otherwise." Averil met Egwina's withering look head on, she would not have her new authority usurped.

"Do you care for wine?" she asked her new mother-in-law.

Egwina masked her outrage – the low bitch! - who was no better than this snivelling servant herself!

"I thank you. But I shall leave you to ready yourself for your husband."

"As you wish" the two women exchanged glassy smiles before Egwina departed. Averil breathed a mental sign of relief, she had no wish to be in that woman's company, no more than she would wish to be with a slithering serpent with venom tipped fangs.

"Should I undress you Lady?" the inquiry brought Averil back to the reality of the bitter present. Her wedding night with Ranulph, who set even the very blood in her veins alight, and who thought of her only as a possession – a man as cold to her as the snow and ice the winter brought. The wine seemed very attractive, something to give courage to face the night ahead – it had already stood her in good stead at the wedding feast.

"Where did you get the wine from Breda?"

"The communal vat in the kitchen Lady."

"When?"

"Only minutes before you came here. Do you not wish it?"

"No. It is perfectly good." Satisfied it could not be poisoned, Averil poured herself some of the heady red liquid and drank most of it in one swig.

"Perfectly good Breda. Now. You may undress me."

* * *

The wine was having a very pleasant effect. Averil had drank enough to feel a little carefree and mused how pretty the decorative leaves looked as she sat up on the bed, understanding now why her father had favoured this brew before all others.

Bursts of rowdy laughter – her heart turned, she realised she had not had nearly enough wine to deaden her feelings..... now here was her dear husband! Her sweet, kind, Ranulph, whose honeyed endearments never failed to enchant, who loved her beyond reason.......ah, how she ached for it to be so! And how he must never know her true feelings. The door burst open and Ranulph and a group of men, all blissfully drunk, almost fell inside, she recognised one of them as none other than Ealdorman Leofric, who now addressed her with a heavy slur in his voice.

"My dear daughter. We have delivered your husband to you and mighty sorry we are to have kept you waiting!"

"You have all done your duty and may leave me to my pleasure." Ranulph ushered the company from the bower, Averil smiled as all, to the last man, bowed drunkenly to her on their way out, for had they not, she thought with dark irony, brought her loving husband to her?

"I thank you all." She smiled and raised her goblet of wine to them in salute as they left.

Ranulph, who had feigned drunkenness for his companions, cast a disbelieving glance at Averil's flushed face.

"Do not you think you have had enough wine?"

"No. Have you? Or did I imagine you just arriving with a group of companions so drunk they could hardly stand up? "

"For one who does not wish to be a wife in truth you sound like one. " He unbuckled his belt. "Well? Take off your clothes."

Averil's heart leapt as she felt the blood drain from her face. "I told you I would be your wife in name only!"

"And I told you I take nothing that is not freely given. "

Their eyes met for a moment, Averil looked away, hardly daring to feel.

"We do not wish the slaves to find you fully clothed after our wedding night." He threw the dagger which was Girdar's gift over to her. "Here, feel free to kill me if I touch you."

Averil was thunderstruck, in truth she wished she had drunk herself senseless. This was a new twist, she looked at the dagger then at Ranulph,....he was actually undressing..... Nerthus preserve her! She picked up the dagger and looked away, he was taking ALL his clothes off, she felt her face burn red and then her body.

"Do you wish me to undress you?"

"No!" she covered herself with the fur and took off her shift, throwing it to the floor, moving as far to one side of the bed as possible, hardly believing what was happening as he got into bed naked beside her.

"I wish you good sleep." He turned his back on her and went to sleep, as though it were the most natural thing in the world.

* * *

Averil had been awake for what seemed like a very long time, listening to Ranulph sleeping. Her lying naked beside him obviously not hindering his slumbers whatsoever whereas for her, him naked beside her was a completely different matter. They were as far apart as possible but it were as though the heat of his body was infusing into her own, melding into it, which was madness! But try as she might, Averil could not stop the wild desire within her for him to just turn and take her in his arms, could not stop the memory of the feeling his kisses had aroused, .imagining him kissing her the same way now while they were naked together.....his hard, muscular body pressed against her own.......sweet Nerthus! She HAD to put her shift back on and get out of the bed, she would stay awake all the night and join him when dawn broke. Stealthily she moved to get up, he turned on his stomach and placed his arm across her body, pinning her down, his arm was warm against her, it felt as if the flesh were joining her own ....her body was so hot... hardly daring to breathe she lifted his arm gently and slid from the bed, quietly pulling on the linen nightdress and moving softly over to the table, taking long moments to catch her breath and calm down. She poured herself wine, planning to drink herself into as near to oblivion as she could.... the hand which stayed her action of lifting up the goblet made her jump. She whirled around to see Ranulph, his body covered only with a loin cloth .

"Is lying beside me so abhorrent to you that you must drink yourself senseless to do it? " his voice was soft.

"No! " fright constricted her throat, caught completely off guard, she had blurted out the truth. "Yes!"

"I would that it were no" their eyes met in the flickering candlelight, he moved towards her, she took a step back. "Is it?"

A perfect storm of emotion assailed Averil all at once, the predominant one anger, for she was sick unto death of feeling this way about him and fighting her own heart. She wanted so much to surrender. She ached to surrender..... to lie in bed naked next to him had been torture! She wanted to be his, but she wanted what he could not give her and she would not be his loveless whore!

"It makes no difference! I cannot give myself to a man who does not love me!"

There. The truth. It was enough. She had endured enough. Now he could leave her be.

"Think you that I do not love you?"

Averil's heart turned at the statement, hardly taking in what she had just heard.

"You are wrong Lady." She did not stop him as he reached out and gently stroked her face. "You are no longer my slave, but I have long been yours."

In a breathtaking moment he took her in his arms and his mouth came down on her own. Averil did not resist as his words reverberated in her heart, and at long last she gave in to all the pent up emotions that her entire being had so yearned to release. She wrapped her arms around his neck as his kisses became deeper, his tongue exploring her mouth as she answered it hungrily with her own. She was dizzy with desire when he finally lifted his lips.

"I wish to make you my true wife."

"I wish that too." They kissed as he pulled her down onto the straw strewn floor, kneading her breasts through the thin linen, making Averil desperate to feel his touch on her naked skin.

"Shall I take it off?" Ranulph's voice was a hoarse whisper.

"Yes" her answer was barely a sigh as he ripped the flimsy material away.

"You are more beautiful that I imagined"

The thrill of his touch as he at last stroked her bare breasts and kissed them, sent exquisite tremors along Averil's tingling skin. His fingers moved down her body and reached inside as he ran his tongue around her nipples. Averil felt as though she was one long exposed nerve ending as she gave herself up to the sensations of his expert touch and hot mouth. He licked her skin, trailing fire along the length of her body, his fingers finished their fine tuned work and he replaced them with his tongue, sending shock waves of raw pleasure crashing over her..........she called out his name over and over again as if from a long way away as her entire being shuddered in a pulsating, shattering climax. His face swam before her as she slowly came back to reality and was looking into his dark grey eyes as he brushed back her hair.

"I cannot find words for...what you just did" she smiled as she held his face in her hands. "All I know is that you can do that to me forever."

"Ah my love, the best is yet to come" he lifted her up and carried her to the bed.

Averil's blood was pounding through her veins with excitement, she longed to feel him inside her, he pressed his muscular body against her own and she received him with glorious abandonment as he entered her at last, piercing her virginity. Averil felt momentary pain and then she gave herself completely to their frenetic, passionate lovemaking, moving towards an explosive climax, and there was nothing but the heat and sweat of their demanding bodies pushing them to the very limits of pure pleasure.

Chapter Fifteen

Dawn smeared it's bloody hand across the rapidly lightening sky as the horsemen sped through the gaunt, frigid forest, ploughing up layers of snow. Steam rose from the sweating bodies of their beasts, snorting their exertion at the gruelling pace until at last they were pulled up to a shuddering halt before two riders waiting on the trail, a bearded man clad in tan and white furs and a slight girl, almost completely buried in the rich blue cloak which swathed her.

"Greetings Junward. You have made good time." The bearded man spoke to the flaxen haired leader.

"And will make better to test some swords for my Lord Ranulph, Edred." Junward grinned hugely.

"I am glad to see you so enthusiastic Junward! Come. We will soon be at Girdar's new hall."

The horses thundered on, leaving a mashed trail of muddied, spoiled snow, soon to be covered without trace by a fresh fall of thick flakes bursting from overburdened clouds scudding across the morning sky.

* * *

Averil's eyes opened on the present, focusing on the bulk which was Breda frantically folding and packing away her clothes.

Averil sensed, rather than saw she was alone in bed under the furs and the place where Ranulph had lain and held her close after their lovemaking had been long unoccupied. Ranulph. Erotic, shimmering images, naked bodies entwined, so much pleasure, undreamed of sensations, she had opened up and given everything. She felt herself burn and shiver, hot and cold, as a hungry longing gripped her – a longing for Ranulph who was not with her to greet the morn.

She sat up. "Breda, hand me my tunic."

The woman obliged immediately.

"Are we going on a journey?"

"Yes Lady. All those at the hall are leaving. Things are not well...." the woman's voice trailed off.

"Go on."

"Even words can bring us harm!" there was real fright in the near hysterical statement.

"Wait a moment Breda." Averil got up, wrapped a fur around her naked body, and went over to the wooden chest from which she took out a piece of soft hide. The woman gasped as her mistress opened it to reveal a glimmering piece of crystal, mystic symbol of the great goddess Nerthus, captured on a silver chain alongside a ring. Averil fastened the charm around her neck and fixed the servant in a steady, confident gaze.

"You may speak freely now Breda. Nothing will touch you under this protection."

"Grain is to be burnt." Breda said in hushed tones – the burning of grain was for the health of the living after death.

"Who has died?"

"One of the servants Lord Ranulph sent to prepare for your arrival at your new hall. There is talk.....talk....of...." the woman faltered, her eyes darting to the crystal. "the plague" the last word almost a whisper. Averil knew what she was going to say even before the words were uttered. She touched the pendant, and offered a wordless prayer to the goddess for Eglif.

* * *

A heavy pall of dark smoke hung over the hall from the still glowing pyre of blackened grain as Averil pushed through the tangle of people to the courtyard, unable to avoid snow sludge being thrown up by the wheels of wooden carts trundling away. The plague was an evil visitation and struck much fear into the hearts of all, for protective incantations and sacrifices had always failed to stop its devastating progress....although she knew this all to be a lie, part of a greater plan by Ranulph. How could driving the king away from his hall bring down those who sought their lives? The question swirled around inside her mind as she made for the stables, arriving splashed with dirt. Her faithful horse Egwina neighed with pleasure at the sight of her.

"There girl. It is good to see you too! We are going on a journey and I have come to prepare you." The mare snorted as though she understood.

"Lady." Two burly, bearded men she did not recognise came to a halt behind her.

"Your servant told us you would be here. We bring words form Ealdorman Ranulph."

"Well. Speak them."

"You husband has ridden ahead."

Averil's emotions reeled, to be left without a word after last night....the men were speaking once more. "You are to travel with the royal party. We shall be your protection."

"And where is it we are all to go to?."

The both stared at her in surprise. "Why to your own hall Lady."

"And we were told to give you this." One of the men handed her a folded piece of rawhide tied with strips of leather. Averil opened it to reveal the two garnet cruciform brooches Ranulph always wore.

"Lord Ranulph bade us tell you these belonged to his mother and are now the property of his beloved wife."

A surge of raw feeling coursed through Averil as she clutched the beautiful brooches to her. Feeling the men's scrutiny, she turned away to lead Egwina from the stall and the bustling stables with her two guards close behind, her mind full of Ranulph. They had reached the end of the long building, a cart piled high with belongings covered with furs rumbled past, blocking their path......daylight disappeared, filthy encased suffocating blackness, pain exploded in her head but only stunned. She wanted to scream, but could barely open her mouth, hardly able to breathe.....kicking, she was kicking, her legs were free, the precious brooches dropped from her grasp into the mud. Gripped sickeningly around her middle and dragged, feeling cold slush splatter on her legs, lifted, a violent thud as she hit living warm horseflesh, then another blow, this time sending her spinning into a bottomless pit of dark.

* * *

Averil came back to semi confused awareness, men's voices, laughter, she was on the ground. She blinked, ice diamond stars winked in the frigid night sky. She was on her back but warm underneath a thick fur, bound hand and foot with leather strips. Even as she struggled to be free of them she knew it was useless, her senses reeled........Who were those men? Why had they taken her? What had happened to those Ranulph had assigned to protect her?Figures, shadows in the darkness, men unburdening their horses, one lighting a fire. Voices once more but she was too far away to make out what they were saying – wolves keening in the distance. Her head was splitting, she closed her eyes and once more slipped into unconsciousness.

A large hand shook her into wakefulness, she opened her eyes and for a moment had no recollection of what had happened.....then it all came flooding back in painful detail as she faced one of her captors. He sported the same flaming red hair as herself, hanging in a single plait from a top knot, his moustache was long and he was unbearded. He wore brown leather, his sword in a sheath on his back.

"Hungry?" he held out a wedge of bread. "Here. Eat quickly. We go soon." The surly voice was strongly accented.

Averil knocked the bread from his hand.

"You can keep your food. I want to know who you are and where you are taking me?"

"Neither of these things you need to know."

"Do you know who I am? I am wife to Lord Ranulph, Ealdorman of King Oswin."

The man chose to ignore her as he pulled her to her feet.

"What happened to the men who were with me."

The man grinned. "They feast with their Gods Lady."

"Hurry it up Hamund!" a shout from one of the men sitting astride....

"You have my horse!"

The red haired man called Hamund laughed. "Beautiful, valuable and skittish Lady. Rather like yourself." He unsheathed a dagger from his belt and cut her bonds before dragging her to a chestnut stallion. "Come. Unless you wish me to stun you again. " He lifted her onto the horse and mounted it himself, she had no alternative but to clasp his chest as they set off, at a canter then a gallop, on through the silent morning which dawn had barely touched, through the cheerless forest to Averil knew not where.

* * *

The liquid dripped slowly into the open, snoring mouth of the noisily sleeping man, sprawled fully clothed on the long table of the hall, surrounded by the debris of a feast. He came to life angrily, his coughing and spluttering mingling with the genial laughter of he who had revived him.

"Well Ulric. No doubt the former master Halliwell would be more than pleased at what good care you have taken of this place." The sarcastic comment came from the hulking man who took a swig from a drinking horn he had poured over the now red faced Ulric who had sprung to his feet.

"I do not find your humour funny Edred." Ulric knocked the horn from Edred's hand, sending the contents splattering across the floor and bringing a frightened gasp from a cloaked girl standing in the corner shadows. Edred took his ease, sitting down and putting his feet on the table.

"What are you doing here anyway?"

"I have come to see you." Edred tore off a piece of meat from a half eaten chicken carcass and sank his teeth into it.

"You have a message from Lord Girdar?"

Edred wiped the grease from his lips. "Not Lord Girdar." the door banged open. "Junward, have you delivered our message to Grimwald?"

The flaxen haired warrior approached, the bloody jelly from the stiff, white severed hand he carried, oozed onto the straw.

"Grimwald did not like what we had to say. But I think we will soon get him to listen." Junward threw the hand onto the table as Ulric drew his short sword.

"You swines will lose more than your hands when I've finished with you!" Ulric dived for Junward who just missed the lethal edge of the sword, the move giving him just enough time to pull out his own. Tables and chairs tumbled as they clashed, two other men ran in, overpowering the warrior as he cursed them, snorting his rage. Edred strode over to him, his face grim.

"I am come from Ealdorman Ranulph Ulric. He knows what happened at Aethelstan's hall and seeks to put it right before the law. Only then can honour be restored to the house of Leofric."

"You too have taken the same pledge as I to your master – loyalty or death. You know I cannot break it."

" Don't be a fool Ulric! Your loyalty to the house of Leofric which you serve through Girdar comes before all others!"

Ulric continued to struggle. Edred turned away.

"Let's get him tied up and put on a horse."

As Ulric was dragged from the hall the girl came into full view. He remembered her, the black haired Briton, slave to Aethlestan's daughter. She of unmatched beauty protected by the wood sprites. Averil. Mortal daughter of the Earth Goddess.

* * *

Hamund set down the scorched meat and a skin of water onto Averil's lap, her hands were bound and she was tied by her neck to a tree. His expression was almost good natured.

"Eat Goddess. You never know where your next meal is coming from." His green eyes swept her appreciatively before he took his leave. He and the five other men wore their hair plaited and carried their heavy broadswords in the same manner on their backs. Mercenaries? Whoever they were, although they kept her tied up at night, they had not molested or attacked her, and had even given her furs to keep warm which showed that at least they did not wish her to freeze to death – surely this could not be part of Ranulph's plan – his own men, if Hamund was to be believed, had been killed.....there was another thought which she did not even want to contemplate but which kept coming back to haunt her again and again. The black clad, helmeted horseman appeared without warning from the gaping mouth of the night. Her heart stilled as she saw the men stand and greet the new arrival, one lifting the communal drinking horn in salute as he dismounted.

"Greetings men. You have done well." The horseman accepted a swig from the horn.

"Where is she?"

"Tied up with the horses." It was Hamund who spoke.

The man removed his helmet, firelight danced on the pigtailed, white blond hair.....the nightmare Averil had never really woken from was now back and this time she knew he would kill her. Eventually. She watched as he took another drink and then threw the horn over to Hamund who caught it expertly with one hand. She touched the crystal, making wordless incantations to the Goddess to get the fear which was rising within her under control. He wiped his mouth with the back of his hand, staring into the darkness which held her, then, crunching snow underfoot, he made his way over, his dark figure illuminated by the background fire glow. Averil's flesh crawled as he reached her and crouched down, he tugged at the neck strap, giving her no alternative but to face his cold blooded, triumphant smirk.

"So. You have come to the end of your path."

"You won't get away with killing me."

"Do you think that is what I am going to do?"

"My death is what you have long wanted."

"Not as much as the one that you will help me to achieve."

The silence was alive as the terrible truth dawned – Averil's eyes asked the question and were given the reply. Ranulph! And she. The bait.

"You are no match for your brother."

"You should know by now that I never risk myself in combat unless it is absolutely necessary. There are other, safer ways to be rid of Ranulph."

"You bastard!"

He twisted the leather, pulling her nearer, his voice the travesty of an intimate whisper. "Soon death will be all the daughter of Aethlestan will want. It will be denied. After I am done with you there will be good coin to be made from the slavers."

Averil spat in his face. His iceberg calm as he wiped the spittle away was more ominous than anger.

"Soon we shall be at my hall and I shall exact payment for this and other insults."

He slammed her back against the tree, a display at last, of emotion. Averil watched his retreating back, one word ringing through her head. Escape. She had to get away, there must be something workable....something........

* * *

The flame from a single candle spread a miserly glow on Ulric sitting cross legged on the straw in the small hut half heartedly throwing dice, a partially eaten wedge of bread and a pitcher of water by his side. His thoughts were grim company in this miserable prison at Aethelstan's hall. He didn't know what had happened to the mutilated Grimwald since their arrival and wondered if the severed hand had been joined by other limbs. He flung the dice down violently, feeling more and more like a rat in a trap, waiting for the sword to strike, while Edred's words repeated themselves, they were a way out of this. Did loyalty to the house of Leofric come before that of loyalty to Girdar? Girdar was his master, his Lord, provider of his horse and arms. Yet, another voice in his head, the voice of self preservation, reminded him that this was only through the bounty of his father, Ealdorman Leofric, since Girdar was not himself an Ealdorman until recently. The candlelight flickered as the door swung open and two men entered, one of them holding aloft a torch.

"Stand up in the presence of Ealdorman Ranulph." Ulric instantly obeyed Edred's order.

Ranulph leant against the piles of grain sacks, his arms folded as he fixed Ulric with an unswerving gaze.

"Well?"

"You ask me to break honour with my Lord and master."

"Your lord and master has broken the code of our people and brought dishonour on the house which you serve."

"But I am still bound by my pledge before the Gods."

"The Gods disowned my brother when he committed his foul deed – as they will any who stand by him."

Ulric stared at Ranulph as the words twisted and turned inside his simplistic mind, tuned only to fighting, eat and sporting, be it with women or dice.

"You may live in honour or die accomplice to murder. I shall leave you to think on it Ulric. But not for long. The King is on his way here and will soon know the truth."

Edred opened the door, the icy draught extinguishing the mean candle flame, leaving Ulric in complete darkness.

Chapter Sixteen

The bucket of warm water sat untouched in the corner of the bower at Girdar's hall which Averil was locked into. It was similar to the one she had once had at home, the same virginal narrow bed with the stuffed straw mattress and a table on which a mirror and combs must once have been kept. Averil sat hugging her knees on the bed, brooding in the gloomy darkness, her gaze fixed on a wooden bucket, brought by a pale reed of a girl barely an hour ago, along with a fresh tunic of pale grey wool and a linen undergarment. It was the sight of the girl which had given her the idea for an audacious, probably unworkable plan, but a chance nevertheless. To do nothing except sit and wait to be Girdar's victim was infinitely worse. So Averil had washed and put on the clean, but more importantly, warm clothes. A scraping noise alerted her that the piece of wood which bolted the door was being removed. She had another quick glimpse of a spear carrying guard who stood by the door as the girl came in once more, this time carrying a plate of meat and bread and a pitcher of mead.

"Put it on the table." Averil got her feet, her tone deliberately impervious. "You may take away the bucket."

The girl turned her back and went over to the corner,. In one swift, fluid movement, Averil picked up the pitcher, threw out its contents and slammed it against the servant's head with just the right amount of strength to do as little harm as possible when knocking her out. Averil prayed for them both and apologised in her mind for what she had done as she turned the senseless girl's body over and took off her cloak, fastening it around herself and putting the hood up.

"Wait girl!" she said loud enough for the guard outside to hear."Hand me some mead and be quick about it !"

She dragged the limp form into the corner - now she had to get past the guard. She shoved the hunk of bread into her belt and flung the tray at the door.

"Not get out you slut before I rip out your eyes" Tell your master to fry with the demons!"

Averil picked up the bucket and banged urgently on the door, a slave wishing to be free of the raving and ranting of a furious Lady. The guard was laughing as he opened it, just enough for her to slip out. It slammed shut behind her, a convincing sob caught in her throat at the ill treatment from the prisoner as she scurried away unchallenged into the cold freedom of the night.

* * *

Girdar smiled to himself as the guard opened the door for him to enter. Egforth was already well on his way with the message for Ranulph, who had Ulric and Grimwald. Ah, his clever brother. But not clever enough. The wheels had been set in motion, some terrible misfortune would fall on Ranulph and his new wife. Now for the daughter of Aethelstan. He had had the leather bindings removed so she could prepare herself, now he had brought them for later, or maybe sooner. She would soon be broken, humiliated. A single candle burned, the corner shadows enveloped the figure sitting there.

"Come here"

No movement, but he expected some soon, he wanted her to fight, to resist. Girdar strode over and dragged the unconscious slave to her feet, hardly believing it.

"Guard!" he threw the body to the ground and sped out, his voice a murderous roar. "You fool! The prisoner has escaped. Alert the men! Move yourself!"

* * *

The horses were restive, edgy at the unexpected disturbance. Egwina's white mane stood out amongst them. Gently, gently, beads of sweat on Averil's brow, nerves stretched taut, standing on tiptoe to get a couple of nose bags from the wall, filling them with fodder piled nearby in a corner, hauling them over to Egwina....men's loud, bad tempered voices.....

"What's amiss with those bloody horses? Can't a man play a game of dice!"

"Well go and see what's the matter with them then!"

"What's that?"

Averil heard it too. Shouting. She couldn't make out the words but knew their meaning. He knew! Clutching at the vital supplies she jumped onto Egwina's back, screaming as she lashed out at the already unsettled horses, their mouths frothed rage and panic as she urged them on and out to follow her in a stampede. Pandemonium broke out, men scattered to save their skins as the uncontrollable beasts ran riot through the compound, some didn't make it, falling in screeching agony beneath the bone-crunching hooves. Averil and Egwina moved as one, through yawning gates opened by the panic stricken guards to release the maddened horses, speeding into the forest as though pursued by the vengeful Tiw himself.

* * *

Averil's fingers were blue tinged as she broke the ice on the stream with a branch so she and Egwina could drink. It had been a long, hard night. Terror of the dark, wolf infested forest had been nothing compared to what would happen if Girdar recaptured her. But the Goddess had been smiling on them, for a break in the night sky revealed a glimmer of a full pearl moon, enough to light the way on their perilous journey. It would be impossible for them to come after her before sorting the utter chaos she had left in her wake, the horses would need to be captured and settled. The search party would leave by the light of the dawn, tracking her through the snow. At least she had some sort of start, walking Egwina to save her strength, ever listening for approaching pursuers, and then rest. They must be ready to flee the next day. Girdar had a very good chance of getting her before she reached Ranulph at her father's former hall where he must now be awaiting the royal party, expecting her to be with them. She sat on the hard stump of the tree in the silent forest, the only noise coming from the steady slurp of Egwina drinking. Her mind filled with her husband and what it would be like to lose him, to never again experience what had happened on the night they had bonded. Egwina moved over to her mistress, nuzzling her neck. Averil smoothed the silk soft mane.

"We will get to Ranulph. We MUST"

* * *

Girdar's expression was stone hard as he strode into the courtyard towards a small group of men, breath smoking in the freezing early morning air, holding their horses and watching their Lord uneasily. The flame haired Frankish mercenary Hamund walked with him to the sleek, black stallion patiently awaiting his master.

"This woman. She gives you much trouble." Hamund eyed Girdar's profile. "If she should reach her husband...." the question hung in the air.

"She won't."

Hamund shrugged. "I think only of our bargain. Myself and my companions expected very valuable merchandise as part of our payment."

"And you will get it. She's easier prey than a trapped wolf."

"Yesterday my friend, she was a prisoner in a hall guarded by trained fighting men, some of whom, thanks to her, are now talking with the Gods."

"You move as planned. Egforth has already left for my brother's hall. He will deliver the message and you will then do what I am paying you for."

"And the woman?"

"You can send one of your companions back here for her."

"We will expect compensation for what we have lost if it does not go well."

"You will get all that was agreed."

Girdar mounted his steed, snapping orders to the small pack of men behind him. Hamund watched him leave, stepping back to avoid the slush sprayed by the horses.

They moved swiftly at first, following a sure route. She was heading south east towards Aethelstan's hall, the initial tracks showing she had walked for some distance, gambling correctly on the assumption it would take them all night to capture the horses she had so successfully stampeded to aid her escape. As they rode on they discovered that fresh snow falls had made what appeared to have been an easy task more difficult. It slowed them down considerably, Girdar cursing himself for misjudging her as his trackers sought to find the path. Removing her bonds had been a mistake, a she-wolf backed into a corner would always bare her teeth and spring for the throat. A pulse throbbed in his temple as he contemplated the great trouble she had caused him, in particular his loss of face before the Franks who were in his pay.

"Lord Girdar" one of the trackers, way out in front, galloped back to his Lord, pulling in breathlessly "We have picked up the trail again."

"Good. It will not be long before we have her."

* * *

The merchant Aefrith trudged through the snow, the strips of cloth tied around his leather shod feet and wound around the thick legs of his knees were sodden. He tugged impatiently at the reins of the plodding oxen who pulled the cart containing his livelihood. He was just days away from the settlement which had once been ruled by the bluff chieftain Halliwell – gone now, it was said, to the Gods, along with all his kin. Aye, There had lately been much blood letting amongst the chieftains and now – a new King. It was all the same to ordinary folk such as Aefrith, times had always been turbulent. Those who ruled in these lands of wolves and woodland changed like the wind. Only the Gods and Trade, the two guiding forces in Aefrith's life, remained constant here. All men, be they rulers or slaves, needed what he had to sell to live. Salt. Collected from the salt-pans of the wild coast. Fiercely coveted by the flaxen haired men who boldly drove ships across the great sea, bringing all manner of precious things from distant lands. The Frisian. Led by their dread master. The oxen grunted their protest at so long without a break.

"Come on, you lazy beasts! Time to rest when the sun is setting." Aefrith carried on through the unwelcoming forest, looking forward to the time when he could strike camp and warm himself before a good blaze.

* * *

Averil pulled up to a halt as the sun set. Instinct screamed to carry on, but it was impossible to do so, their pace had been frantic, any further would burst Egwina's brave heart. The exhausted horse shuddered beneath her, flanks sweating and heaving. She dismounted, stroking and calming, tenderly whispering admiration and love, settling her quietly with one of the nosebags before sitting down on the jutting roots of a nearby tree. Averil looked up to the leaden sky, praying for snow to cover her tracks. She took the hunk of bread which the unfortunate serving girl had brought to her – biting into it hungrily, restraining herself from having more than two bites – just enough to sustain. Egwina munched contentedly, at least she'd managed to get some food for the horse, though she had to ration that too if they were to make it. She scooped up a handful of snow and assuaged her thirst from it's moisture. It was impossible in such damp conditions to light a fire without flint and tinder, and anyway, it was not worth the risk of being seen. She scrambled up a tree, trying to find at least a half comfortable position on a high, thick branch. Here would be the best defence against the wolves and other wild creatures. She must pray Egwina would be safe. If only there was someone who could help her! But she was utterly alone...her pursuers closing in, removing the small start she had given herself. Averil remembered one of the saga songs she had learnt about the Princess Triona. Had she not thought of it when she first saw Girdar? Triona had been brave, escaped the white haired demon within an inch of her life – only to be captured.

Dreams, fragments, a sacred grove, sun beating down on the gently swaying grass clasped inside it's circle – the black flowing hair of Triona, plaited with blue flowers, her beautiful rose bud smooth smiling then opening into a deafening scream..... Averil's eyes snapped open, disorientated, clutching at the branch, even as realisation hit she was sleeping in a tree. A sudden cramp knotted her legs, biting her lip to stop crying out, she frantically rubbed at her twisted calves. Egwina stirred, stamping her hooves, the noise shooting bolts of fright through her mistress. The horse disturbed. By man or beast? A sluggish half moon shone forlornly through the night mist, between the trees she saw a fire burning, a bulky figure hunched before the crackling flames, outlines of animals and a covered cart. Not Gidar. Maybe someone who could help! But for what? She had no coin, no gold, could the promise of reward secure aid? Could she risk asking a stranger, yet how could she afford not to? A split second decision sent Averil clambering from her hiding place, speaking gently to Egwina as she led her through the trees towards the fire glow until they reached the small clearing and the figure of a fur wrapped man.

"Greetings master."

The stranger was on his feet and facing her, hand on a small dagger in his leather belt. He was balding, grey bearded and of considerable bulk owing more to fat than muscle, his eyes looked beyond Averil, searching for possible accomplices, thieves came in many guises, she could be a ruse to distract his attention.

"What do you want?"

"Your help."

The simplicity and sincerity of the statement took Aefirth by surprise, he backed away nevertheless, his gaze still skimming beyond the intruder into the darkness. Satisfied there was no movement, he beckoned Averil towards the light of the fire so he could see her better. His breath catching for an instant as he admired how lovely she was, never had he seen anything to match those perfect looks, this was no coarse woman of the land but someone well bred and of good stock, she was worth more than a cartload of salt! His keen brain was busy working out exactly how much when his eyes alighted on the pendant around the slender neck, a mystic crystal hanging alongside....... No! It could not be! So she was a thief after all? Impossible! No-one would dare to touch such a sacred object, let alone wear it if it were not their own, for certain death would find them all and their kin, and it would be a long, agonizing torture......as Egfirth floundered in uncertainty, an all too familiar fear prickled his spine, the long healed lash marks across his back stung as if fresh, making up his mind for him, in seconds he was on his knees before the astonished Averil.

"Forgive me Lady. I did not know who you were!" his brown eyes rested on her neck. Averil was bewildered, what in the name of the Gods was going on? The man appeared to be terrified! Was he staring at the crystal of Nerthus? Surely......it was the ring! He was looking at the ring she had found in the pommel of her father's sword! Who did he think he was addressing? He scrambled to his feet.

"Please Lady. Come by the fire. I beg you to accept my hospitality such as it is." He ushered Averil to sit down on a cloak, close to the blaze, eager to please, handing over a wooden goblet of warmed mead he had obviously been drinking from, she noticed his hands were quaking – sweet Nerthus! What dread personage was she supposed to be!

"I am Aefrith. Seller of salt." A jittery smile accompanied the introduction.

Averil merely nodded her acknowledgement before drinking, buying time, whoever he thought her to be the stakes were too high to question him and risk revealing her true identity.

"In what way am I to help you Lady?"

Averil put down the goblet carefully, her voice deliberately lowered as she spoke.

"I do not wish to say anything which will endanger you...."

Aefrith shifted uncomfortably, sensing the web of politics and intrigue those in power were always crawling around, best avoided by such as he lest they were caught in the sticky strands and devoured. He spread his hands as if in supplication. "I am only an ignorant pedlar Lady with a head fit only to be filled with business. Tell me nothing. Just what you want of me."

"Very well. For now, I want to hide among your salt sacks while you take me south east."

"It is done."

Aefrith's nod was more of a bow, severing the conversation. She watched as he turned sullenly to the fire, trying to snatch the elusive recollection about the ring which had touched her when she had discovered it in the pommel of Elatha. Events had been such that she had had no time to think about the trinket around her neck. She closed her eyes – willing herself to remember......Aefrith poked the fire, cursing his ill luck, knowing the world had been a much safer place before she had appeared here. Yet what choice had he but to comply with her wishes? For she shared close blood bond with Finn. His Lord and Master. Mighty and dread pirate King of the Frisian.

Chapter Seventeen

The small band of men lead the weary, slush splattered, riderless mare through the trees. The faithful animal had tested herself to the edge of endurance for her mistress before finally forced to rest. Driving deeper into the heart of the forest, leading Girdar away from Averil, following the wrong trail.

"Where is she?" Girdar's demand rang out in the afternoon silence.

"The horse was without rider Lord." This from the leader of the group, who liked not to impart such bad tidings. That she could escape them once, and from a guarded compound was shaming enough, but twice to outwit them! She must have the blessing of demons!

Girdar regarded the snorting beast, once more he had underestimated Averil – and lost.

"Well! What are you waiting for! We go back and find where it was she left the horse!" he turned his mount, his men following his galloping lead, one riding at the rear with the mare in tow.

* * *

Night was falling when Averil and Aefrith came to a halt. The oxen had moved at a good, lumbering pace which was their fastest but still painfully slow, Averil had made what could be a fatal mistake by seriously misjudging how quickly they would travel. If only Aefrith had used horses to transport his salt! Each torturous mile covered reminded her of how slow they were going and how fast Girdar was able to move. She had released Egwina tearfully, hoping for a good lead, knowing in her heart the courageous beast would try to grant at least that, but at this rate time gained was being rapidly eroded. The weather had so far been her friend, fresh snowfalls serving to cover tracks, and she estimated they were a day, maybe two, away from Ranulph. Yet intuition told her that if she stayed with this cart Girdar would surely get her and Aefrith, the gut feeling made the decision for her. At first light she would take supplies and leave Aefrith to go on alone to his original destination, that way he would be safe and if Girdar had begun to follow the cart trial then this would be another false lead and give her the crucial time she needed to make it to the hall. Averil touched the crudely worked, heavy gold ring around her neck, fingering the garnet eyes of the boar – the ring had tipped the balance in her favour. Aefrith's help given because he thought her someone he was honour bound to serve, which could only mean close kinship to his master. However outlandish it seemed, the ring hidden in Elatha HAD to be symbol of blood bond. If only she would cast light on this! She had prayed to Nerthus to give her the full recollection of that which had only brushed her mind so fleetingly when she had found the ring, but to no avail. A half moon barely lit the sky as they sat by the flames, eating pickled fish from Aefrith's plentiful supplies.

"I shall leave you tomorrow Aefrith."

The pedlar raised a surprised eyebrow even as blessed relief at release from such a burden flooded through him.

"You will give me some supplies and carry on as though nothing has happened. If you are stopped you lost your way in the snow and have been alone. You understand?"

Aefrith nodded., "I know when to keep my mouth shut Lady."

"Aefrith" Averil hesitated, she wanted no-one's blood on her conscience. "If your story is not believed then you must tell the truth."

"Do not worry about me Lady. I know how best to save my skin, how do you think I have managed to live so long under the iron fist of my master?" to her surprise he smiled, perhaps she could now thaw some of the tension of his own making between them which had so far blocked every subtle attempt she had made to find out whom he served. She now tried once more.

"It is true there cannot be many who serve him who have the luxury of living to possess grey beards such as yourself!"

Aefrith was momentarily startled, the Lady's impish grin confirmed she had indeed been jesting with him at his master's expense.

"Aye. It is not for those who wish a long, quiet life, such as myself."

"You ply an honest trade Aefrith."

"But many would say a dull one Lady. You can be sure that cannot be said of those warriors who follow the king across land and sea. They would have their time on Ecre's soil no other way."

Averil hardly heard him, her senses reeling as she grasped the one important word of the entire speech. King. The boar's head ring was symbol of a royal house! Blood bond with a king! Aefrith was still talking, warming to the theme, she caught this king's name. Finn. The name echoed. It was of the sea. Of the

Frisian! A tribe who had been locked in conflict with the Anglii for generations. Such kinship would need to be kept secret!

"Your thoughts are far away Lady."

Averil looked to Aefirth but did not see him, probing into the impenetrable darkness of memory and once more dredging nothing.

"It....." the rest of Aefrith's sentence was severed, the oxen were disturbed, grunting their distress, the pedlar leapt to his feet, on the alert, Averil's instincts screamed as her heart dived – man or beast? Aefrith plunged a thick branch into the flames and brandishing the blazing torch went over to the animals, coaxing them into calm as he held the flame aloft to peer into the darkness.

"What is it?"

"Must be wolves Lady. I'll move the animals in closer and keep watch tonight."

Averil shivered, hemmed in by the night.

"You should sleep now Lady. Your journey on foot tomorrow will not be an easy one."

Without another word Averil climbed into the cart and lay down amongst the sacks, the firelight danced grotesquely on the canvas, a too poignant reminder of the terrible night when she had woken to find her world collapsing in flames all around. The past had been murdered by Girdar on that nightmare night and now the same man threatened to take away her future. Ranulph. She saw his scarred face once more, if only he were here with her now! She was doing everything possible to reach him, yet hardly dare think it were not enough, that she would be hunted down. The ring. If only she could remember.

* * *

Ebba stood motionless, watching the horsemen leave. Ranulph, Edred and four other men on their way to the hall which had once been Halliwell's and was now Girdar's to Christ knew what fate. The thought of her mistress being once more in Girdar's clutches filled Ebba with horror. Knowing well of his evil, his handsome face not betraying the ugliness of his soul. Lord Ranulph had held a murderous fury in tight check as he had learnt the two men he had left to guard Averil had failed and Girdar now held his wife and wished to see his half brother immediately. This delivered by the stooped weasel Egforth. Edred had told her that Egforth had been tortured into revealing Girdar had employed Frankish mercenaries to capture Averil, a fact which made Ranulph doubly uneasy, knowing as he did that Girdar always preferred others to carry out his murders for him. She clasped the fur-lined cloak more tightly about her, a lone, hooded figure at the gate, eyes fixed on the white featureless landscape long after the riders had disappeared from it.

* * *

Girdar's horsemen surrounded the cart which Aefrith, who had been ordered from his seat in the front, now stood by. The circle was broken to let in a white blond haired man astride a black stallion who Aefrith guessed must be the leader.

"You travel alone salt seller?" his men dismounted behind him as he spoke.

"Aye Lord. As always."

Two men came forward at a wave of Girdar's hand, they climbed into the cart and began flinging the sacks onto the ground, splitting some open and spilling the precious contents.

"What are you doing!" Aefrith shouted his protest as he stood helplessly by, watching his profits mingling irretrievably with the snow. "I told you I am alone!" he ran to the back of the cart. "Please stop this! It is my livelihood...." another man seized his arm in a bone crunching grip and dragged him over to Girdar.

"I must make sure you are not lying pedlar." Girdar's hard smile was without mirth.

"Why in the name of all the Gods should I lie? I travel alone as I told you."

Girdar leant forward on the saddle. "When did the girl leave you?"

"What girl? I don't....." his words cut short as the man who held him ran the cold steel tip of a dagger lightly across his throat, resting it at the base of his captive's ear.

"Do not play games with me pedlar! Now. I ask again. When did the girl leave you?"

"Two days ago." Aefrith's voice screamed panic.

"Relieve the pedlar of his ear."

"Yesterday morning!" Aefrith struggled as he shouted. "She left yesterday morning!"

Girdar's satisfied smile mirrored the grin of the retainer who held Aefrith at knife point. "Good. That is Good. Now what did she tell you?"

Aefrith shook his head vigorously. "I swear she told me nothing Lord. She said she would not endanger me by saying anything and that I must tell she had travelled with me if I was stopped."

Girdar leant back, seeing Averil only too clearly in the words, such consideration for this filthy low-life tradesman was typical of she who saved her hatred and contempt for the Ealdorman of the King!

"You will take us to where she left you." Aefrith's bulk was hauled up behind one of the other men as Girdar swung his stallion around, ready for the last stretch of the chase.

* * *

Averil's muscles ached as she carried on, her face grey with fatigue and pain, only taking short breaks when she could not put one foot in front of the other any longer, but even then leaning breathlessly against trees, fearful that if she should sit down, her body would refuse to get up again. She only had to get through this day and tomorrow she would be at the hall of her father....of Ranulph, the weariness was confusing her as she trudged on, taxing herself to the limit as she knew the brave Egwina must have done for her. If only she had the horse now, it could make the difference between capture and escape......Averil turned tired eyes towards the bright yellow orb piercing without warmth through the denuded trees, wishing it would set, for at least then she could hide inside the dark cloak of the night. She trudged towards the thick bark of a nearby tree and leant gratefully against it, taking a sip of water from the pigskin tied to her belt.

Girdar saw her first, a dark speck detaching itself from a camouflaging bark and moving slowly through the snow amidst the stark, lifeless trees. Averil. Exhausted. Hunted. The Prize.

"Stay here and give our friend his just reward!" he barked the order before breaking the stallion into a gallop.

A blood curdling scream pierced the air, Averil froze at the awful, agonizing sound – whirling around to see a lone, chain mailed horseman thundering towards her. Girdar. The scream was something to do with him, the thought jumped into her mind – Aefrith! She turned. Run! The useless voice – to where could she run where the spawn of a demon could not find her? And what perverted enjoyment he would get by chasing her like a hunted animal with no chance to escape! An ironhanded grip clasped her waist, picking her up and dumping her face down across the front of the leather saddle of the moving horse.

"I have you now you little bitch!" Girdar's words were a snarl as he brought his sweating horse around, one gloved hand holding the back of Averil's neck in a vice grip, pressing her face into the sweating horseflesh. "This is the last time you will ever escape me." Spurring hard, he thundered back to the cluster of retainers, throwing his captive onto the ground in front of him before dismounting.

"Well slave? Shall we see how your pedlar fares?"

Averil staggered to her feet, the men around breaking ranks to reveal Aefrith's portly figure slumped against a tree, blood seeping from the side of his balding head. No! He was dead because he had helped her! She was responsible for this! She ran to the mutilated pedlar, kneeling at his side and touching the ruddy cheek with gentle fingertips – warm, alive……relief engulfed her. His injury was the loss of an ear and the Gods has blessed him with unconsciousness which at least took away the pain for a time.

Girdar bent over the senseless Aefrith, examining the handiwork of his men with detached interest before turning to Averil. "It is lucky for you that I am a just man."

Sickened beyond belief or sense, Averil rounded on him.

"You call this just! This man knew nothing, all he did was help someone he thought was in trouble."

"You have just cost the pedlar his hand." Girdar's voice was flat, emotionless.

"No!" .

"You wish to make it both?" their eyes held, Averil looked away quickly, fearful the detestation she could not disguise would bring more horror for Aefrith.

Cold fury gripped Girdar even while he relished Averil's torment. This emotion! This care! For a fat, sweaty trader! He hauled her up, riveting her in a direct stare, their faces close enough to touch.

"Kill him."

"No! You cannot do this! He is an innocent man!"

"It is your choice whether it will be quick. Or slow." His eyes were chill as death. She could do nothing to change his decision, railing against it would make Aefirth suffer more. Girdar led his much sought captive to his horse, handing her over to one of his men while he mounted, then pulling her up in front of him and riding off without another word, leaving those who served him to carry out his command.

Chapter Eighteen

Ranulph and his men ate their cold supper with only a pale half disc moon to give them light. Edred, clad as always in the brown bearskins stretched across his massive frame, bit into the cold, salted meat with distaste – Tiw! But he detested the stuff, not the sort of decent food for any man.

Ranulph sat beside him, taking a long drink of mead from the communal horn before passing it on to his companion, he would have preferred it warmed but a fire would pinpoint them to any attackers.

"We'll stand guard in two groups of three tonight."

Edred raised a questioning eyebrow at the number of men on watch.

"I don't like the idea of Girdar employing mercenaries – we could be riding into a trap ready to be sprung by the Franks."

"As you say Lord." Edred spat out the half chewed meat in disgust.

"Not to your taste eh Edred?" Ranulph laughed at the abhorrence on his retainer's bearded face.

"Pah! It is tougher than the leather of my saddle!"

"It's a pity we do not have a fire to scorch that for you instead Edred." The good humoured remark form one of the others brought peals of gusty laughter from the company, Ranulph joined in, the amusement for a moment extinguishing the dark thoughts of Girdar with Averil which haunted him – the idea of his brother touching her tore at his insides – he should have taken her with him to Aethelstan's hall and to the demons with her slowing him down! His lack of judgement might well have cost Averil dear.....Girdar was already a dead man – if he had laid a finger on his Lady then Ranulph would make sure that his death would be a slow one.

Wolves keened mournfully, puncturing the freezing shroud of night silence as the shadow figures of Hamund and his men moved stealthily, the muddy earth which stained their faces melding them into the darkness. They had tracked their prey, Hamund judging Ranulph well – no fire and probably more than one sentry. Rustling movement, one of the men on guard, Hamund saw a dim outline of the body, a glimpse of a short bearded profile. The mercenary took out the length of thin leather from his tunic, wrapping each end around his hand – the guard hardly knew what had happened as the choking cord tightened murderously across his throat, cutting off any warning cry he might have made, expertly extinguishing his life in seconds. Hamund caught the corpse before it crumpled to the earth and propped it against a tree.

The horses whinnied, stirring Ranulph from a waking doze which was as near to sleep as he would allow, he sat up, senses on the alert. It was quiet. Too quiet. He picked out the three sentries on the edge of the campsite. All immobile. Ranulph drew Elatha from his scabbard and moved over to the snoring Edred, covering the big man's mouth to mask any sound he might make while being shaken into wakefulness.

Edred was barely on his feet when the six mercenaries emerged from the trees. With lightening like action the big man unsheathed his flat broad sword and dagger, there was a flash of metal as, with a roar, he sprang forward, the weapons alive in his hands as they sliced through the bodies of their attackers. Ranulph's other retainer had no time to stand up before Hamund pounced, skewering him where he lay, drawing the bloody blade from the body with expert ease before turning his attention to Ranulph, in time to see him plunge his sword into the chest of one of his men and starting to fight another one. Three of the Franks had taken on Edred, and one of them was already down, crimson spurting from a fatal chest wound. Three seasoned fighters against one should have been winning odds – but the giant's ferocious skill was fast narrowing them. Hamund came at Edred from behind, bringing a powerful arm across the big man's throat, clenching his teeth into a growl as he squeezed, the other two seized the moment, bringing him down with the brute force of their pushing bodies. Hamund rolled away and was up in seconds, seeing Ranulph was still fighting.....the violent unexpected blow at the side of his skull knocked Ranulph to the ground, the night was suddenly still, quiet as death.

* * *

Slurries of sleet had dogged the riders for most of the day, drenching them and the forest around, it was still falling when they dismounted onto snow slush, there wasn't even a dry twig with which to make a decent campfire. One attempt – a smouldering mass which didn't give heat or light – had been stamped out hurriedly, but not before it had gusted acrid, eye stinging smoke through the company, bringing loud complaints and curses from men shivering in sodden cloaks. A grudging half moon was the only illumination as they sat down on their saddles and ate cold rations, icy sleet still weeping from the black sky.

Averil sat at the edge of them, her back against a tree, her wrists were bound and she was tied to by her neck, nestled down into her cloak, emotions raw to the touch raged within, part of her had died along with the poor pedlar Aefrith, she had wept for him, and even as she prayed to Nerthus for him a nagging voice demanded by what right had she risked his life so she could save another. Ranulph. Girdar had planned his murder – this she knew deep in her heart – would he escape it? How miserable had been her failure to help him and prevent the death of the innocent Aefrith.....A wedge of preserved beef slapped onto her lap, she knocked it untouched onto the ground, looking up at the man who had flung it.

Slivers of moonlight shone through the dark trees, touching the face untainted by the cruelty which festered inside, she remembered that face reflected by another light – from a single candle flame, it had held the same triumphant expression when he had come to rape her..... in one swift movement which caught her off guard Girdar reached down and cut through her wrist bonds and the neck rope, then backed away from her as she leapt to her feet, wishing that this time, as at their last encounter, she had a knife.

"You wish protection from me?" it were as though he had read her thoughts, he threw the knife he had used to free her to the ground to the side of her. "Here."

Averil stood motionless, measuring the distance, knowing that if she tried to grab it he would be able to fell her to the ground.

Girdar rolled up his shirt sleeve to reveal the still angry red scar she had left with her dagger at her father's hall.

"See Averil. I already have your loving brand – do you not wish to add another – to the other arm? Or perhaps you would prefer to spit in my face once more?"

Girdar moved toward her, a grim smile on his lips, his white blonde hair was wet, matted to his scalp – she had nothing to lose, she dived for the knife – she felt the reassurance of the handle for a fleeting second before his foot came down on her hand, grinding it into the mud.

"How I have missed the sweet temper of Aethelstan's daughter." He hauled her up, imprisoning her arms behind her back with one hand and stroking her face with the other.

Averil recoiled in revulsion. "Your skin is smooth. Soft. Do I not touch you as a lover? As Ranulph?"

Averil blinked back the sleet which stung her eyes. "You disgust me!"

"Ah, and I have also missed your honeyed words." He pulled her close, turning her face to his.

"My Briton Ebba believes in only one God....."

"You give me instruction on your barbarian's religion!"

"She speaks of his goodness, of his struggle with the devil who spreads evil and dwells in the flame pits deep in Ecre's heart. Although I can never believe in her God, when I look at you, I believe in her devil!"

"I am your devil Averil – and you are mine" his hand reached inside her tunic, she fought violently to be free of him, they both fell to the ground, grappling in the muddy slush in now driving rain, Averil unable to fight off his pressing body....

"I have waited long enough to possess you." As Girdar forced her to submit cold reason fought through the numbing horror of the violation – he may take her body but that was all he would ever steal from the daughter of a noble house! She closed her eyes – blotting out what was happening – she was not part of all this......this was not her.....it was just her body.........

Girdar looked down at the woman who was now his alone.

"In time you will enjoy better the attentions of your master."

"Ranulph will kill you for this!"

"Alas Lady. The dead cannot take their revenge."

Dead. The terrible word pressed at her heart, crying out a denial. "You lie!" she searched Girdar's face to seek the truth and saw absolute confidence.

"You were too late. He was killed in an ambush on his way to you – just as I planned." Girdar's boastful, sure words suffocated Averil's hope....grief tore through her....

"I did have other plans for my brother's widow – but perhaps I shall keep you. For myself." He got to his feet and left her.....too much horror, too much to deal with.....Ranulph. Dead.

* * *

The mud stained warrior strode into the hall, glad of the warmth from the blazing fire which burned at it's heart, his stomach welcoming the rich aroma of roasting pig. He was weary from a strenuous journey with no rest, enough time had been wasted already, he was eager to finish his business.

"All is well Hamund?" Girdar's eyes fixed the mercenary.

Hamund drew the magnificent, silver-handled sword from beneath his cloak and threw it onto the ground before Girdar. Elatha. Girdar sat back in the chair, savouring the moment. Now he knew for sure that Ranulph, favoured son of the slave whore, was dead. Nothing stood in his way of power now. Taking the stupid, moon faced Ingilda to wife was just the beginning. Hamund picked up a goblet of foaming ale and downed it in one, noisy gulp before addressing Girdar.

"And all is well here? You have the woman?"

Girdar's glance slid over the Frankish killer who had struck a very good bargain, Averil would fetch a huge price in the slave market, only he who was the richest could possibly afford Ranulph's exquisite widow. Yet. The idea had begun to become less and less appealing. Now he had taken a small taste of Averil he wanted to devour her, put her away somewhere safe and secluded for his exclusive use – and why should he not? It would make union with Ingilda more bearable, and he would have the best of both worlds – power and the daughter of Aethelstan to do with what he wanted. But what about his bargain with the Franks? Was Hamund alone – his companions on their way back to their lands?

"Of course." He motioned for a slave to pour the mercenary more ale, watching as Hamund tore into a succulent leg of pork.

"And are your company on their way to the coast?" a casual inquiry.....Hamund threw the chewed leg of meat onto the floor, wiping the grease from the beardless chin with his sleeve before answering.

"Nay Lord Girdar. I came on ahead. They are only just behind me, awaiting a reward much richer than gold."

How true was this? Why not come together, so they could share the warmth of the hall. He must check it. Fast.

"More food for our guest!

Hamund lifted his hand in refusal. "My belly is well served Lord Girdar. The ride has been hard. I wish only now for a good sleep on a soft bed."

"And you shall have it my friend." Girdar summoned a slave with a snap of his fingers "Take our guest to my retainer's bower."

Hamund eased out his aching leg joints as he got up.

"I bid you sleep well Hamund." Girdar raised his goblet in salute as Hamund took his leave behind the boy slave who was overshadowed by the powerful, muscular body of the Frank.

* * *

Averil span in the black void of a dreamless sleep, the deep, resounding voice sending shock waves through the darkness, bringing back the aching sorrow of stark reality, the red moustached face before her familiar – it was one of the mercenaries who had kidnapped her, she opened her mouth to speak, only for it to be covered by a rough hand.

"Quiet! Do you want to get out of here?"

Heart pumping, Averil nodded vigorously, she didn't want to think why this man was doing this, all that was in her mind was escaping Girdar. Satisfied by her co-operation, Hamund released her.

"Follow me" he led her into the cold night, Averil jumped back as she saw a man leaning against the wall by her door, his glazed eyes staring into eternity. Hamund urged her on, they moved as flitting shadows, backs flat against the huts which stood between them and the outer wall. Averil squeezed Hamund's hand, nerves tying her stomach in knots as they moved nearer to freedom. They reached the wall. Hamund lifted her onto his shoulders and she scrambled over, getting as far down as possible once on the other side, before finally letting go and dropping to the spongy ground. He was beside her in seconds, half carrying her through the forest – running away as she had done once before, it seemed now so long ago, leaving behind the bloody carnage wrought by Girdar, but then she had been with Ebba, now she was with a warrior who was well prepared, as she ran, the question she had not even wanted to consider in her desperation to be free of Girdar now dogged every step – why had this man got her away? The reached a small clearing where a dark stallion was tethered to a tree, his back covered with warm furs. The Frank greeted his horse with words Averil did not understand, untied and mounted him.

"Come on" he extended a strong arm so Averil could scramble up behind him.

"Why have you done this?"

"I collect only what I am owed" he wheeled the horse around.

"You were owed me?"

"Payment for kidnapping you. I think Lord Girdar did not intend to let you go. Come. He may pursue us"

"At least tell me where we are going!" the request was almost lost as they moved on, gathering speed, Hamund weaving his mount through the mighty trees with skilful horsemanship.

"We go to the wild sea. To your new master. Finn."

Chapter Nineteen

Watery sunlight cast faint warmth onto the travellers standing on top of the sparsely grassed knoll, the dark forest, iced with sparkling frost, lapping at their backs. Before them a thick, ribbon river, pearl mist hanging gauze like over it's deep waters.

"We near the end of our journey." Hamund turned to Averil who merely nodded in reply, accepting his hand to help her climb up behind him onto the dark brown horse. They had spoken little during the long, tedious journey, each day of which had melted into the next. Soon, it would be the December feast of the Mothers, a celebration of life, but all those dear to Averil were now gone. Ranulph was dead and a part of her had joined him in the unending sleep. She thought of their lovemaking, his sweet words to her, his leaving the brooches of his mother for her. As she had only begun to realise the true depth of her love for Ranulph so she had lost him. Ranulph. Her family. All gone. But honour remained. And honour meant revenge. It burned within her, day and night, dominating her emotions..... she would dream of killing Girdar, running Elatha through him, experiencing the raw triumph of his death – a death which she WOULD make possible! For was not the great goddess Nerthus with her in this? Guiding her fate so she was now being delivered for sale to the one person who could take that revenge. The

Frisian king. Finn. Somehow she would find the secret of the ring about her neck – Nerthus would guide her....

Hamund kept his distance from Averil, he knew nothing of women, and did not want to know, yet he saw in this beautiful creature the dignity and courage of a warrior trapped in the vulnerable female body, were she a man he would be glad to fight by her side, and that, he had to respect and grudgingly admire.

"There is a settlement a few miles from here, we should reach it before nightfall." Hamund spurred the horse down the gentle slope, glad to be out of the wild forest and in open country where he could breathe again.

Averil looked over to the river, casting a prayer to its sprites for her success.

The sun was a burning red orb about to descend into the yawning throat of night when they reached the settlement, it's wooden buildings of various shapes and sizes to house people and livestock nestling snugly inside a circle of high fencing. They rode past strips of worked land, ploughed over for winter, reaching like swollen fingers into the surrounding landscape, a roadway from the gate led to the river on which bobbed small fishing boats of skins securely tied to a jetty. Plumes of smoke rose up from cooking fires, the rich, peaty smell mingling with the aroma of food, reminding Averil she had not eaten since the morning as they approached the gate, guarded by a cloaked sentry standing on a platform behind the wall. Hamund lifted his hand in salute.

"Greetings. We are here to ask shelter for the night of your master Margem."

"Your name and business?"

"I am the Frank, Hamund, friend of Margem. This is my woman."

The guard shouted out an order to someone below him as he watched them, trying to make out the woman's features, obscured by the hood of her cloak. It was not long before the gates opened to admit them, Averil feeling the sentry's eyes still probing her as they passed through the familiar sights and sounds of everyday life she had been so long out of touch with, cows lowing in their pens, playing children, some of the men up to their elbows in the communal vat of water, washing away the dirt and grime of the day before taking their ease over the evening meal. The main hall was a modest size. Smaller than her father's, Averil noted, as Hamund dismounted and lifted her down.

"I see I have been promoted from slave to bed partner."

"I do not want Margem to get any ideas." he tilted her chin to face him. "Just to make double sure. You are carrying my child."

"What!"

"Margem is my friend," he took her arm, leading her to the timbered hall. "He would see no reason why he couldn't share you – except when it may harm my unborn son."

He pushed open the door, sending a rush of cold night air into the warmth inside. Their host, who sat at the top table, called out Hamund's name, beckoning them in with a wave of the silver goblet he held. Hamund took Averil's hand in his as he approached the bulky, bearded figure of Margem whose long brown hair hung wild and unkempt, partially covering deep scars at the side of his face and a milky, sightless eye. A nasty disfigurement which Averil wondered how he had obtained.

"Greetings Margem. It has been too long since we last broke meat. "the two men embraced. Margem casting his good eye curiously towards the hooded, cloaked woman who stood by his friend's side.

"Yours eh?"

Hamund grinned, placing his hand on Averil's stomach. "Aye. Both of them."

It took only seconds for the meaning to sink in, prompting Margem to treat his friend to a congratulatory slap on the back.

"What celebration then for us. Come, let us drink to your son!" he waved them both to follow him to the top table, one of his retainers immediately gave his seat to Hamund while a serving girl motioned Averil behind the main table to a bench on which dishes were stacked. Averil sat down and accepted a goblet of warmed mead, finding the delicious honey liquid soothingly refreshing.

A girl was singing by the central fire, slim hands plucking at a harp, she couldn't make out the words but the tune was cosily familiar, as soothing as the drink.

"The religion of the Britons!" Margem's loud voice rang out. "Pathetic." He spat onto the straw to emphasize his distaste.

"I grant that their belief is strange." Hamund answered through a mouthful of meat.

"Is that what you call it! I call it an excuse not to fight. They have only the ONE God – and he preaches only love!"

"Aye" remarked Hamund "But it must take courage to stand and accept death without a fight in this God's name , as I have heard some of them have done."

Margem guffawed, shrugging off the comment. "Know you what the Britons call my liege Lord Finn?" Averil was instantly alert at the name. "Devil! The name of the demon who battles with their precious God!" his laughter was heartily derisory.

Hamund grinned. "It must cause the king amusement."

"And other rewards he makes the most of!" Margem took a swig of mead. "When he sweeps through the villages of Elmet to take their miserable hides the virgins are swooning with expectation at the thought of being despoiled by the devil!"

Averil watched the scarred Margem. So. Finn was a slaver who raided Elmet, the land of Ebba's people, who feared him enough to give him the name of the only demon of their faith – just as she had so called Girdar the night he had attacked her.... after he had ordered the murder of poor Aefrith. She pushed back the memories, but not before the image of the salt seller's face when he had first seen the ring around her neck came to her – he had been terror stricken! Margem was speaking once more of Finn, describing his adventures in the wildest, storm-tossed seas, bragging of the wealth he brought back from trips to mysterious lands. This Finn was the kind of man she needed to extract fitting revenge. She must delve the secret of the ring!

* * *

Forked lightening streaked across the night sky, casting a transient garish glow on the fortress courtyard in which the torrential rain had extinguished the torches, and picking out the drenched captives as they moved across the shiny wet cobbles.

"Come on, hurry it up!" the cloaked guard shouted impatiently, kicking a couple of the ragged men whose progress was hampered by the ropes which attached them together. He could see the wisdom in the order to get the new arrivals into proper shelter quickly. They were no use to anyone dead of exposure, though he wished he had not been unlucky enough to be chosen for the task, still, it could have been worse, he might have had to take them immediately to the slave compound in this vile weather. He opened the door to quarters he shared with half a dozen of his fellow guards and herded his troublesome charges inside, glad to bang the heavy door shut.

"Over there in the corner!" as he gave the command he caught the eye of one of them, a big bearded giant who supported an ashen faced man in one of his thick, powerful arms. His murderous hatred and contempt smouldered, striking a shard of fear into the guard despite the fact he could not possibly do any harm, roped as he was to the others.

"I said over there!" he shouted again as the group moved to do his bidding. As they all sat on the dry floor the guard discarded his cloak, wishing the time away when he would be replaced by those who were now eating their supper in the main hall and ruminating on the fact there were no women amongst the motley collection he was in charge of. The wholesome thought had barely escaped him when the door was pushed open and a burly man, his black hair plaited in the strange fashion of a top knot, entered.

"Greetings. I am the Frank Colwarn. I have come to view my two prisoners."

The guard recognised Colwarn, one of a band of mercenaries who sometimes provided his King with valuable merchandise. He led him over to the captives.

"What do you want now you Frankish bastard? To finish off what you started?" the giant growled, the guard saw the man he had been supporting had now slipped into unconsciousness.

"I never went along with Hamund's decision to keep you both alive for the extra coin your sale would bring. You should be thankful I brushed your master with the lash instead of cutting out his insolent tongue!"

"By the Gods Colwarn I shall live to tear your limbs from your body!"

"You shall live Edred to serve the Frisian King. Both of you."

Colwarn leant over the senseless Ranulph and touched his back, the guard's eyes widened as he saw the Frank's hand smeared with bright red blood.

"I see he is no fit state to be presented to Finn. No matter. There is time enough." He turned away without a second glance, striding to the door and stepping out into the deluge.

* * *

Averil sat on the edge of the bed, drinking fresh water and eating warm bread left by her side while she had been sleeping in the small bower for guests.

"I hope you have slept well?" the woman who addressed her was past youth, she was warmly wrapped in a rich, fur lined cloak, her blonde plaits streaked with grey. Yet her face still bore testimony to much beauty and her teeth were as clean as those of a girl.

"Yes. Thank you."

"I am Jarna, widowed sister of Margem. Your man sets much by you, now I see why."

Jarna looked the girl over and saw true, dazzling beauty, the likes of which she had never encountered even in her own bronzed mirror at the height of her youth – she placed a woollen bundle she had been holding onto the bed and rolled it out to reveal a lovely navy blue silk gown of unusual thickness.

"He has bought this for you to wear at the hall of Finn. There is also a new cloak, like the one I wear but of the same hue as the gown."

Averil fingered the rich material of which she had never seen the like.....which she would wear when she faced Finn.

"How far are we away from the main settlement?"

"Barely two days."

"And will the king be there now?"

"News is he has just returned from a journey and brought back much wealth."

"Your brother told us of it last night, he has high respect for the Frisian king."

Jarna sat down next to Averil. "My brother watched over Finn throughout his childhood. He served his father for many years, fighting by his side in all his campaigns. In his heart Margem still grieves for the loss of Casto."

Casto. The name smashed open the floodgate which had held so frustratingly tight shut in her mind – in a blinding flash she saw the tableaux which had so long eluded her – she had been so small on her father's knee, her two older brothers with solemn faces sitting at his feet. She had reached out a plump, child's hand to grab the pretty trinket Aethelstan was showing them, she saw again his indulgent smile as he prized it away from her, his mouth uttering the words kinship – kinship to Casto, in reward for....the image swam, blurred, evaporated.....

"Are you alright?" Jarna's concerned question, a hand on her shoulder, jarring Averil back – this king, Casto, was now dead, had he passed on the knowledge to his son?

"I have heard of your dead king. Tales of my people recall his meeting with the Anglii chieftain Aethelstan."

Jarna puzzled for a moment, then shook her head. "I know nothing of such a story."

"No matter" Averil half turned away from Jarna, quickly changing the subject. "Tell me of Finn's queen."

"There is no queen as yet. Though the King is much pressed to get himself one and produce a male Frisian heir – else who knows what crossbred bastard will one day claim his title."

"Crossbred?"

"By one of his whores. You have never seen the likes of those he brings back! One had skin burnt browner than a tree bark, caused it was said by the nature of the lands she was from, in which sunlight never sleeps."

"Had?"

"The last cold winter killed her – though Finn found her easy to replace."

The Gods he did! Averil looked at Jarna who was speaking once more. "You will learn much more of Finn when you reach his hall, which is where your man wishes to leave for as soon as possible." Jarna stood up, her tone brisk, bringing the conversation to an end. "Now. You will find both warmth and hot water enough in the kitchens to cleanse yourself."

"I thank you for your hospitality."

"I wish you safe journey."

"Will your brother give us his farewell?" a slipped in inquiry, perhaps Margem knew of the ring....

"He left to hunt as soon as dawn broke and will not be back until long after you have gone."

"Then I would be grateful if you could extend my thanks to him also."

"It will be done " the polite ritual over, Margem's sister took her leave, leaving Averil to thank Nerthus for showing her the truth and to pray that she help her remember why the kinship was given.

Chapter Twenty

The man sat in a high backed chair in front of a blazing fire which lit up the stone walls of his apartment, his nudity covered by a loin cloth and brown bear furs slung across his muscular shoulders. His yellow hair was pulled back from a high forehead and hung in a single, thick plait down his back, his face, the skin hardened and bronzed by years at sea, was clean shaven – a curious practice introduced to him by a skilful new whore who, for the present, amused him, an emotion which was far from his mind as he regarded with narrow green eyes the fidgety, thick set man who cowered visibly by his side.

"How many more problems do we have to overcome master craftsman before the ship promised me in the summer will be ready?" the soft tones conveyed threat more effectively than loud words could ever have done.

"There are problems my king, as I told you. The slaves lack understanding....."the man waved his pudgy arms, as if to reiterate his point "their work is..."

"Their work is your responsibility " the king picked up a glass goblet from the table next to him, taking a drink of the rich ruby wine it contained before turning back to his shivering minion. "By the winter's end I shall have my ship" a slight smile curled his mouth "or your head " he raised his glass, his face distorted through it's reflection. "The choice is yours."

The man bowed low, knowing he had been dismissed, eager to get out while he was still whole, he tugged at the heavy door with shaking hands to take leave of his master Finn, whose threats were never idle.

* * *

Averil tasted the tang of salt in the air as she rode behind Hamund towards the imposing grey stone fortress in the near distance. The impregnable building squatted atop a gentle rise watching over a harbour and settlement teaming with life. Her breath caught as she glimpsed the glittering sea which seemed to stretch into the distance forever – she had never before seen the huge expanse of water, only sang of it, and now, seeing it for the first time, she could not fail to be moved by such wild grandeur. Truly it was a home fit for only the highest Gods and Goddesses, and he who sailed ships upon it must surely risk their wrath unless granted their permission. They had reached the edge of the settlement when Hamund came to a halt, dismounting and lifting her down without a word, handing her a small silver phial from inside his chain mailed tunic.

"This will bring you a better future."

Averil turned the top, the contents filling her with confusion.

"What is this?"

"Your virginity Lady." Hamund fixed her with a steady gaze. "Blood which you shall spread to mark the taking of your maidenhood by Finn, the rest of the convincing is up to you."

"You would sell me as a virgin?" Averil found herself laughing, but there was no mirth in it "By the Gods Hamund, but your work will be well cut out in this – for I am the true wife of an Ealdorman and the rape victim of his brother!" she flung the phial at him, some of the blood splattering his face as he grabbed her arms and shook her.

"Listen to me!" his voice a roar "You are of no value to Finn if you have been despoiled, he will merely use then sell you. This way there is a good chance you will remain only his."

"And you shall receive more for the sale!"

"I survive as we all do. As you will have to learn to do." He released her, picking up the phial and replacing the top. "Take it. I said, take it!" he thrust it into her unwilling hand. "Let's move. I want to reach the fortress before night falls."

* * *

Averil leant against the dank walls of the narrow torch lit corridor, under the scrutiny of the two spear- carrying sentries who guarded the heavy wooden doors leading to the great hall. Hamund had entered alone, wishing to speak of his prize before it was presented. After what seemed like hours he appeared and led her into the hall, the like of which she had never before seen. A huge fire burned in part of a stone wall adorned with a variety of shields – some plain, others studded with semi-precious stones, there were also hangings of vivid colours featuring odd creatures, lit by torches burning in gleaming silver sconces. Before the main table a group of black haired dancing girls, their diaphanous gowns leaving nothing to the imagination, gyrated provocatively to the constant beat of a drum, suddenly, one of the onlookers roared and climbed over the table to grab and drag one of them off, whoops of encouragement accompanied the action as others swiftly followed suit. This. In the company of the womenfolk who sat supping on their separate benches! If she had ever doubted it, this clearly showed what scant respect this king showed for her own sex. Hamund led her to the top table and the man flanked by two guards wearing helmets bearing a boar's head crest. Finn did not acknowledge her arrival as he concentrated on words a man behind his chair was whispering in his ear. Averil saw that Finn was perhaps as old as Ranulph, and not black toothed or repulsive. His eyes were green, lined by the same sea weather which had hardened a strong face. He wore a black leather tunic and on his middle finger the image of the barbaric golden boar's head ring which hung around her neck.

"My Liege. Here is the merchandise we spoke of." Hamund's statement brought Finn's attention. He gestured to Hamund and sat back, one elbow on the arm of his chair, resting fingers under his chin as he watched the Frank remove the girl's muffling, hooded cloak with curious interest. No-one living could possibly measure up to the praise heaped upon her by so able and experienced a salesman as Hamund. Torchlight shimmered on a vision in blue silk, the knee length, waving mass of flame hair framed a face of exquisite, delicate beauty, the body was full breasted with a waist slender enough to span with one hand. As Finn took her measure he saw that her green eyes, which were the colour of the sea, were insolently taking his.

"Not bad Hamund. Though I think you ask too much. It is a price I would pay for a cartload of fair skinned virgin meat, not one portion."

There was a smattering of laughter from those around at the remark.

"My value, Lord King is more than you yet know." There was a shocked silence. The girl had spoken without permission. Finn's eyes sparked anger, fuelled as the girl before him matched it, unflinching.

"Your property offends me Hamund. Remove it before it is damaged."

"Not before I have spoken!"

There were gasps of disbelief as Averil's voice rang out. Finn gestured to his guards, who moved towards her.

"Hamund has not delivered a slave to be sold to a new master but a sister to her brother." She pulled out a neck chain lifting the ring which lay upon it. "This is our sacred bond. Given by your father King Casto to mine, the Anglii Chieftain Aethelstan."

The guards pushed Hamund to one side and grabbed Averil. "Take her away" Finn watched the girl being dragged from the hall, the silence around broken by a gentle ripple of murmuring from the thunderstruck audience.

* * *

Finn was pacing his apartment when a mud-splattered Margem entered, bowing low to his master, his good eye alighting on the two naked women who lay sleeping on the king's bed.

"Welcome Margem" the two men embraced. "You have made good time."

"I came as soon as I received your summons my liege."

Finn sat down by the fire, motioning for Margem to take his ease across from him.

"You knew my father better than any man alive Margem and were by his side in all his campaigns."

"The Gods blessed me with that honour."

Finn threw a golden object onto Margem's lap. "Look at this."

"It is your ring of kingship."

"No Margem." Finn lifted up the hand which sported his own ring. "THIS is my ring of kingship."

Margem looked once more at the ring, knowing before he examined it more closely it was identical to Finn's in every way, right down to the tiny scratched runes placed there by Casto's high priest to invoke the power and protection of the Sea God Pluna. He thought never, after all these years, to see it again.

"Where did you come by this Lord King?"

For a moment, the only sounds in the room were the crackling of logs and the shallow breathing of the sleeping whores as the two men faced each other.

"Why was I not told of its existence?"

"You were to have been, by the priesthood, when I, the last man to know of its history, was dead."

Finn leant back, waiting....

"Our people were at war with those who have always been our long standing enemy, the Anglii, the land was red with the blood of warriors. Your mother insisted on staying by her liege Lord's side, despite being big with child. You were born long before time in a tent on the edge of a battlefield and snatched from the dying queen by a band of mercenaries fighting for our enemies. They were deep in the forest before Casto discovered your loss and gave chase." Margem paused, remembering the desperate pursuit, the murderous anguish on Casto's face. We found the kidnappers dead and you safe in the keeping of a chieftain of our Anglii enemy. Aethelstan. Lord of the Red Hair." He saw the powerful man once more, the squawking babe who was Finn, incongruous in his mighty arms.

"Aethelstan gave you back to your father, telling him he was a warrior whose fight was only with men. King Casto told him they were bound in honour and the kinship could be claimed if ever Aethelstan needed it. He gave his royal ring as token of the pledge."

"Kinship with an Anglii chieftain." Finn spoke almost to himself.

"Those who heard were sworn by sacred oath to the Gods in secrecy."

"But kinship! Were such a tale told to me by anyone other than yourself I would not believe it."

"This man gave your father back that which he most prized when he could have so easily destroyed it."

Finn turned sharp eyes on Margem.

"I have not yet answered your question on how I came by this valuable trinket. It was draped around the neck of an Anglii slave who claims she is the daughter of Aethelstan."

"If this girl knows of the bond…."

"Know if it! She claimed it in full hearing of my entire hall, even as I bartered her price!"

Margem imagined the scene, reflecting on the bravery it must have taken to confront Finn, a bravery only bred in those of noble stock, a bravery worthy of the warrior Aethelstan.

"Then she is who she claims, for it was sworn it would be revealed only to the offspring of both men."

"Her captor has told me he kidnapped her for an Anglii Ealdorman called Girdar and received her as a reward. He knows nothing of her past, and why should he? She is a slave! But she is also beautiful and it would not have been impossible for her to have learnt of this bond in the bed of Aethelstan or his sons, or the whereabouts of the ring, which she could have stolen."

"My Lord King!" Margem was on his feet. "This was no ordinary event! This bond was between a true king and a man who prized honour above all else!"

Finn tapped his fingers on the chair arm, regarding his former father's battle-scarred retainer.

"You are telling me then that she whose body was to have been sold to the highest bidder, is, in fact, my sister?"

"I tell the royal son of Casto only what he already knows, that the sacred oath of noble warriors before their Gods are never broken. She who knows of this secret and possesses the proof of it can ONLY be the daughter of the Anglii chieftain who saved your life."

* * *

Averil entered the simple, but richly furnished chamber alone, the guard who had escorted her from her dark prison slamming the door behind him. A fire burned brightly, the only light in the dim surroundings. She saw a bulky figure sitting on one of the high backed chairs before the blaze, with a start she recognised the one eyed barbarian Margem. The former retainer of Casto. Her mind worked quickly as she moved towards him.....did he know of the bond?

"Sit."

Margem watched her obey him, her gown was ripped, the dirt which marked the pale face did not mar it's lovely delicacy, and her hair, dancing flames, the colour of Aethelstan's.

"You will tell me how it is she who claims to be the daughter of an Anglii Ealdorman and sister to a king is a slave."

"My name is Averil, and I do not claim to be any other than who I am Lord Margem.."

Averil answered the question before it could be asked. "I met you at your own hall. Hamund thought it better to pretend I was his pregnant woman, he sought to protect his valuable merchandise."

"Hamund's cunning is not unknown to me. Now speak."

Averil looked away from Margem, into the fire, recalling the leaping flames of another – that which had destroyed her home. Her voice broke through the heavy silence, she spoke slowly, almost to herself, words ebbing and flowing as she recalled the treachery and bloodshed which had brought her to the hall of the Frisian king. The ghosts of those who had died, Ranulph, Aethlestan, her mother and brothers, the serving girl Eglif, passed before her as she related their fates. When she had finally finished the fire was dying, casting only spurious blue flames from glowing logs.

"And what of the bond and the ring?"

"My father spoke of the bond of kinship sworn between himself and Casto once only to myself and my two older brothers. It was a long time ago, I was but a small child and cannot recall anything other than that. Perhaps he planned to speak of it to me when I was older. I managed to retrieve the ring from it's hiding place in the pommel of my father's sword before I was taken to Oswin's hall."

"The sword of Aethelstan and his forefathers" the name was on Margem's lips yet Averil spoke it, the word a melodic sigh as she saw once more her father holding the precious mark of their house.

"Elatha."

Their eyes touched, there was no doubt in Margem's mind about this noble girl's identity.

The sound of slow hand clapping came from the shadows as Finn emerged into full view."I venture to say Margem that here is a tale worthy of my finest storyteller."

"It is the truth." Averil protested.

"But what kind of truth?" Finn's appraisal was coolly calculating. "That of Averil, daughter of Aethelstan, or an opportunist slave who relies on her considerable charms and a quick mind and tongue?"

"My Lord King......" Margem's words were stilled by a wave of Finn's hand.

Averil saw Casto's former retainer was on her side. He MUST know about the bond! Only her identity was in doubt here.

She stood up to face Finn.

"The Frisian king does not look at a clever slave, no matter how much he wishes it to be so" her eyes were fierce as they locked onto Finn. "He looks at she who is bonded his sister before the Gods of both our peoples, whether he likes it or not."

For an instant there was utter silence as the two faced each other.

"Leave us Margem." Finn's eyes did not leave Averil's as he gave the command which left them alone in seconds.

A glittering object sailed through the air, landing at Averil's feet, she stooped to pick up the ring.

"I thank you."

"Save the words in prayers to our fathers. It was they who forged a bond between enemies." He poured a goblet of wine and sat down on the chair Margem had vacated, Averil took his lead, sitting across from him.

"It must have been something of great importance which prompted it."

"Aethelstan saved my life" he raised the goblet as if in salute before taking a deep drink.

"I should like to know the story of it."

"There is not much to tell. I was a newborn taken during battle with your people. Aethelstan slew my kidnappers and returned me."

Ah yes. It would be the way of her father, she saw him once more."My father was a great warrior, had my brothers survived him, they too would have been such as he."

"And been able to avenge him. Which is what you want of me."

Averil was startled for a moment, of course, he had reached the obvious conclusion from hearing what had happened when she explained all to Margem.

"It is not what I want but what duty demands."

"And what exactly does this duty of yours demand? A hearing before your king as your dead husband may have been planning? The payment of wergild?"

"Wergild! Do you think man price would repay what Girdar has done? I do not want his wealth. I want his life."

"At last! After so sweet a display of touching grief the vixen finally shows her teeth! She would have her newly found brother place his unborn sons at risk from vendetta by this Girdar's kin because she bays for blood."

"There is no risk of that! His death for the murder of my family would be within Anglii law. I accused him within the day of the slaying."

"The law cannot always control the hearts of men who believe themselves wronged."

"If such things were considered then honour would never be satisfied!"

"I think only of what could lie ahead. Though there is no question it will make any difference. He who has defiled the honour of the Frisian king could never be allowed to live."

Chapter Twenty One

Averil sat by Finn's side, her shimmering silver gown in keeping with her new status, now formerly declared before everyone. She should be happy, for her kin and Ranulph were to be avenged and would now be able to lie in honour. But it had been her thirst for revenge which had stemmed her grief and kept her going. Now she knew for sure that Girdar would receive his just reward all the sorrow and regret of the past kept coming back to haunt her.

She picked at her food, yet drank much of the heady red wine, each sip bringing back a flood of poignant memories of another evening when she had done much the same thing, the night of her wedding, the last time she and Ranulph had been together. His tender words that night to her, and the memory of their lovemaking all came flooding back. She tried to push the recollections away, making a determined effort to listen to the girl who was singing and playing the lyre. She heard Finn speaking to Margem of the song and found herself staring at his rugged profile. It was clean-shaven as Ranulph's had been, but there was no other resemblance, for Ranulph, even with his jagged facial scar, had been handsome, and Finn could never be described so, yet incongruously, there was an attractiveness in the very nature of this fact. The girl had finished, a sweet rendition rewarded by coins flung into the centre of the hall. A throbbing drumbeat marked the beginning of a dance by semi-clad slaves, their breasts easily discernable through the thin gauze material of their gowns, the same girls' Averil had seen on her arrival. Their inviting movements brought catcalls and salacious remarks from those around and eventually the physical attention of some of the audience – hands caressing swaying bodies, as Ranulph had once caressed her own.....she recalled the thrill of pleasure at his touch – and the horror of Girdar's – even if Ranulph had still been alive would she ever have been able to give herself freely to him again after her ordeal with Girdar? Yes. She would not have let him affect her love for Ranulph. Her thoughts ran in wild uncontrollable circles as she took another deep draught of wine.

"My sister enjoys the leisure of the Frisian?"

Averil blinked back a sudden dizziness as she answered Finn with a smile "Very much so." She had no intention of offending him, yet the wine would have it's say "Though I doubt the taste of entertainment from these sort of dancers when women of the household are still present."

"I did not know Anglii women were modest." An ironic laugh as his expression showed disbelief at the thought.

"We like to be treated with respect."

Finn raised an eyebrow. "As your brother-in-law Girdar has so boldly demonstrated."

Averil whitened. "You are determined to misunderstand your sister."

His hand came down on hers as she made to take another drink.

"I am determined to teach her to hold her tongue – and her wine."

Averil pulled her hand away.

"You can have no fear I shall disgrace you."

"Not me Lady" he leant towards her "Only yourself."

Averil picked up the goblet, saluted Finn with it and drank the entire contents before placing it back on the table.

"I would not want to order you to leave this hall" his calm tone gave lie to the violence of feeling beneath the surface.

She was up in a second, grasping the table to prevent herself swaying. "You do not have to. I am going."

Averil's gown rustled as she stalked out, down the long corridor which led to the chamber allotted her, slamming the door and leaning against it, clutching at her throat as the dam of pent up emotion broke within, finding relief as she threw goblets and a flagon of wine against the stone wall, smashing them to pieces before kicking over the table and the heavy chairs. A grip on her arm whirled her around.

"Stop this!"

She struggled as automatic reflex, Finn sought to bring her under control, catching her wrists in one hand to still her movements.

"Leave me alone! You cannot understand!"

"Understand what? The actions of an over-indulged child who cannot hold her drink!" The scornful accusation brought Averil up short.

"You....."

"What?" he wrenched at her wrists "What am I Averil?"

The room span as she looked up at Finn, she felt her madness whirl with it. What was she doing!

"You..." the ground beneath felt spongy, she groped for words as the alcohol worked on her brain...."You are all that is left to...." there was no colour in her surroundings, everything flashed grey and white and then nothing.....Finn caught her, lifting her in his arms and taking her to the bed, the only piece of furniture she had not tried to wreck. He threw her on it. Her copper hair trailed on the floor, he lifted a handful, the colour matched well the fearless temper and the dazzling loveliness married a reckless courage which he knew she didn't always need the help of wine to display. Physically fighting him by the Gods! What a slave she must have been! The Anglii Ealdorman Girdar must have thought on the idea of cutting out her tongue more than once, only the thought of perhaps marring her looks would have stopped him, and probably Ranulph too, after he had taken her from his brother. Ranulph. The husband who had bedded her only once. He let go of her hair, running a practised eye and hand down the length of her supple body. Averil stirred at his touch, a name a whisper on her lips. Ranulph. A ghost lover. While he, Finn, was very much alive.

* * *

The bulky figure paced the small guard room, the glow of torchlight highlighting the angry countenance..

"We should have killed him Hamund!" Colwarn rounded on his companion, who sat on a chair with his feet on the table.

"It is true the turn of events could put us in an awkward position."

"Awkward!" Colwarn snarled. "By Tiw! But you have a strange choice of words Hamund. Not only are we out of pocket we could be out of life! Or will our former captive who turns out to be bond sister of the Frisian king thank us for enslaving her noble husband!"

"You are too quick to jump to conclusions Colwarn. This can be twisted to our advantage. You are forgetting that we spared his life."

Colwarn turned away from Hamund, the atmosphere suddenly ice between them. "He is still alive?"

The other man shrugged. "He reacted badly to the lash."

Hamund was on his feet, grabbing Colwarn by the neck of his tunic in a powerful hold, leaving the thicker set man choking for breath. "Yes. He is alive. For now. But the wounds.....are.... not....healing as they should." he clutched his throat as Hamund let him go.

"So this is why you did not immediately sell him to Finn. You fool!"

"How in the name of all the Gods was I to know what was going to happen?"

"Where is he?"

"In the slave pens."

"Edred is there too?"

Colwarn gave a curt nod in reply.

"You are right Colwarn. It would indeed have been better to have killed him rather than now having him die through ill treatment at our hands!"

"If we finish him now no-one need know."

"It is not that simple Colwarn. Before he was an Anglii Ealdorman. Now he is brother in marriage to the Frisian king!"

Hamund sat down on this chair, rubbing his chin thoughtfully. "This must be handled properly. Otherwise we shall all be meeting our Gods sooner than expected."

* * *

Salt winds whipped Averil's hair as she sat astride the grey mare on the cliff, looking out at the glistening expanse of foaming sea. White birds flew high in a sharp blue winter sky, their cries filling the air. Her aching head had cleared but the memories of the night before, which had been just as painful, clung. To lose control was bad enough, but to do so in front of Finn was unforgivable. She turned the horse, it was time to return, she had been alone long enough, a lone rider was speeding towards her, she knew who it was before he reached her. Finn.

"It is not wise for the sister of the King to ride out unaccompanied."

"I wished to be alone."

"With your thoughts or your aching head?"

"Both."

"It is a good place to view the sea."

Averil wheeled her mount around to be by his side.

"I had only heard of it in songs and stories. Now I see for myself that it's beauty was not exaggerated."

"To look on the ocean is as nothing compared to riding a ship through it's waters, as I am soon to do once more. The new slaves for the markets should be arriving any day now."

"Soon? But what of...."

He cut her short. "Vengeance has the advantage of being able to wait, whereas trade does not."

"I cannot believe I am hearing such words from you. Trade more important than honour!"

"You think only with your heart. It is lucky for you that your royal brother thinks only with his head."

"I care nothing for what you think of me, only for your lack of judgement."

Finn's green eyes were stormy as he replied. "Of course, my sister would know about that. For did she not humiliate herself in front of the entire hall and then before her king by drinking too much wine?" in a swift move he caught the bridle of her mare, controlling the beast so she could not ride away.

"As I told you before you cannot understand."

"I understand more than you know sister" his gaze imprisoned her for long seconds, she felt heat rising to her face. "The time for grief for the dead is long over, now you must take your place with the living" he released her horse. "Come. We must return. I have much to do before my voyage."

"Finn" Averil caught his arm, it was the first time she had used his name. "I ask you to reconsider. Each day Girdar lives is an insult to our kin."

He looked down at the slender, cold hand on his sleeve, then into Averil's eyes.

"Perhaps I would be open to persuasion."

Averil removed her hand as though it touched fire. Finn galloped away without a second glance, she spurred the mare on to follow, her mind in fresh turmoil.

* * *

The Frisian horsemen thundered into the settlement, scattering livestock and people in their wake, their leader laughing at the chaos they caused and the waving fists and insults of the angry women at the disruption. Bringing up their rear were two carts carrying their frightened, tied captives, all of them women, and young and ripe, the hunting grounds of Elmet had been more than fruitful during this, the last haul until Ecre breathed fresh life in the spring. The carts rumbled into the courtyard as Averil and Finn arrived back, Finn made his way to the leader of the band, greeting him with a grasp on the shoulder before dismounting and striding into the fort. The contents of the carts spilled out, the women captives looked wretched, with barely enough clothes to keep out the cold. Averil rode over to the man Finn had greeted, he was stout and pale haired, and unlike his shivering captives warmly wrapped with brown bear fur, she felt like tearing it from his miserable hide!

"Are you in charge of this?" the voice was imperious, used to command.

The man's expression was incredulous as he looked at the beautiful redhead astride a grey horse who had addressed him.

"Well?" The sister of your king asks you a question!"

He found himself grinning, what sort of jest was this?

"Guards!" the woman's call was answered immediately, the Frisian Lord stared at them in confusion as they gave her a clenched fist salute across their chests, their expressions deadly serious.

"Lady" he spluttered, his face draining. "I have been away for many weeks and have received no news of the hall."

She waved away the guards.

"I thank you. I am Blanwar. It is an honour Lady."

"But not one which at the moment I share Lord Blanwar. What need is there to tie these women? Where do you think they will run to?"

"They are captives Lady."

"And what of their lack of warmth? Even the animals of the forest have protection from the cold!"

"They are well enough."

"I say not Lord Blanwar. These women will have their ropes removed immediately and warm food and clothes given to them. Do I make myself understood?"

Blanwar bowed his head. Satisfied, Averil rode over to a waiting stable boy.

"Lady!" the familiar voice.....Averil turned, a gaggle of ragged women, an arm lifted, Averil jumped from her mount, happiness spreading through every part of her as she ran over to the slaves until she embraced she who had called her, both of them laughing and crying at the same time. Ebba.

* * *

Ebba sipped the warmed wine slowly, savouring the glow it gave a body too long exposed to the cold. She had been seated in front of a roaring fire in Averil's chamber, and Averil herself had placed a fur around her razor-thin shoulders.

"Food shall be here soon Ebba." Averil sat across from her slave who was closer than any kin could be.

"I have prayed and prayed to our God for your safety Lady! I never thought to see you again."

Averil reached out to touch Ebba's hand. "Nor I you Ebba. Now tell me what has happened."

Ebba related her story in hushed tones, telling Averil all, the long terrible days of waiting after Ranulph's departure, then rumours Girdar was on his way which had led to a desperate flight to her homeland of Elmet, her journey for nothing when she was captured en route by Finn's men.

"And now here, in the hall of the devil, I find my Lady safe."

"The devil you speak of Ebba is Finn, and he is my bond brother."

Ebba's eyes widened in amazement as Averil poured out her own tale, speaking more openly that she ever could have to Margem, opening up the wounds, finding that doing so to she who was closer to her than anyone alive eased the pain. As she came to an end a servant arrived carrying a tray loaded with meat and bread which she set down beside the fire before leaving them alone once more.

"Let us break bread together Ebba and thank our Gods for this reunion."

"When will the king seek out Girdar?"

"He has said it will not be until the time of new life."

"That is many months away."

"He has also said that perhaps I could persuade him to change his mind."

Ebba stayed her mouth on a piece of warm bread, taking in the implications of the comment and seeing them only too clearly.

"Do you want to Lady?"

"No" Averil stared into the fire, the bread in her hand uneaten.

"Will you go with the king back to your lands?"

"Oh yes Ebba" her smile was hard as she regarded her former slave. "What is my duty will also be my pleasure."

Chapter Twenty-Two

The applause for the two sweating, semi-naked youths was deafening as they avoided the swords and spears of their tormentors with grace and skill. Averil ate and drank little as she watched from her seat at the head of the women's bench, Margem's sister Jarna next to her. This evening was a special one. The Feast of the Mothers. Earlier Finn and the priests had led a torch lit procession to a sacred place of stone on the cliffs where animal sacrifices had been made. A huge bonfire had been lit in the midst of the settlement and dancing and feasting were even now taking place alongside it, as well as that activity which marked the annual celebration of fertility. How long ago it was now that she had lain with her long dead youngest brother on the sun speckled grass in the woods and thought of such rites? A slave moved to refill her untouched goblet of wine. Averil waved her away, catching the sidelong gaze of Jarna, who had been watching her.

"Your thoughts are far away." Jarna smiled, Averil seeing that true beauty can never fade with age.

"The feast marks the end of a year which has changed my life."

"Forever Lady?"

"It can only be so. I am a widow who spent only one night with her husband."

"Were you not blessed with such beauty then your widowhood would always be assured. However, I am sure you will have another opportunity to marry and perhaps, this time, produce children."

"Perhaps Jarna. If it is what I want."

"I have been twice widowed and I can tell you that it is a stark choice between dwelling with the living or the dead."

Averil smiled faintly at her companion, a compelling urge to be alone taking a grip.

"You will excuse me Jarna. I wish for the peace of my chamber."

"But the feast has only just begun. The king will expect his sister to stay."

"The king expects much of his sister." Averil stood, the action bringing the rest of the company hurriedly to their feet until she left them, followed by Ebba. Jarna took her seat and glanced over at Finn, she saw his eyes followed Averil even as he conversed with the retainer at his side – she well recognised the look. So. Finn desired the Anglii woman. Jarna found herself amused. It was interesting to see him want that which was so obviously being denied him. It was by far the first time Finn had been in such a position.

* * *

Ebba brushed her mistress's long hair gently, Averil feeling little pressure as she gazed at her reflection in the shining brass hand mirror without really seeing it.

"Margem's sister told me in the hall that I must choose whether to take my place with the living or the dead."

"She has no knowledge of what has passed Lady."

"Just so. Though perhaps it is what Finn may be thinking. I do not believe I misinterpreted his meaning when he spoke of my persuading him to change his mind about when he should take vengeance on Girdar."

"Could you have been wrong my Lady?"

"I would wish it were so Ebba, but I think not." A banging on the door stayed Ebba's reply. At Averil's command to enter it was opened by a helmeted guard to admit he who they had spoken of seconds before. Ebba brought Averil a fur wrap to cover her thin linen nightdress without needing to be asked.

"Leave us." Finn's green gaze rested only briefly on Ebba.

"Go Ebba. Enjoy yourself."

As Ebba closed the door behind her, Finn poured himself a goblet of wine. "It seems you did not enjoy the same entertainments you have commended to your slave."

Averil got up to face him. "My family lie dishonoured in their graves. Would you have me dance on them?"

"You speak without sense. They will be avenged as soon as it is possible to do so."

"I speak only of duty, as I would if it were you who had been murdered."

"You have a way of twisting words to suit your own purpose."

"It is something I share with my royal brother."

The words hung in the air as Finn considered her.

"This then is the persuasion you offer me to change my mind? Talk of duty?"

"I still mourn my husband my Lord and duty is all that there can be between us."

Their eyes caught and held for an instant. Finn slammed down the half empty goblet and strode to the door, pausing to look back for a moment.

"We ride in two days. After Girdar is dead we shall speak again."

He was gone. Two days. Soon my dear Ranulph, my dear father, mother and brothers, Girdar would be dead.

* * *

Dawn was breaking as Ebba made her way up the twisting stone steps which led to the top of the fortress battlements. She had been unable to sleep, and was in need of the windswept solitude to think out Averil's request to join her on the journey back to the Anglii lands which would begin in just a few hours time. The thought of seeing Girdar once more made Ebba's blood run cold, and the other reflections, which she had tried to push aside, reared up to haunt, what would happen if Girdar were to evade justice as he had already done once before? Ebba had reached the third wooden landing and was about to climb to the top when she heard the voices above her, muffled at first, then concise, clear tones.

"Speak plainly Hamund of what is on your mind." Ebba stopped in her tracks at the sound of Finn's command as her mind dashed ahead. Hamund. He who had kidnapped Averil for Girdar and sought to sell her.

Hamund spoke. "My Lord, this is no easy thing for me to impart."

Finn's impatient reply. "Come to the point Hamund!"

"It concerns Ealdorman Ranulph, husband to your Lady sister."

Ebba caught her breath, Finn's voice again, this time imperious."You mean the DEAD husband of my Lady sister."

Nothing. Ebba could almost touch the excruciating tension in the strained silence. Footsteps above her moving.....to the stairs? She flew down them, her cloak billowing behind her as though chased by the devil himself, tripping down at the last, breathlessly dragging herself up and racing through the courtyard to the warm womb safety of the bustling kitchen, where her frantic entrance went unnoticed amongst the hard working slaves preparing foodstuffs for the king's journey. Leaning against one of the tables Ebba gathered her wits, she must tell Lady Averil! But tell her what? She had heard Hamund speak about Ranulph, for that was all she had heard, yet......something.....something in Finn's voice, it were as though he were TELLING Hamund Ranulph was dead – and Hamund – perhaps he had wished to say that Ranulph was alive!

"You wish warmed water for your Lady?" the question made her jump from her skin, as she accepted the offer she made up her mind. There was no point in raising the hopes of her mistress until she knew the truth. She must stay behind and solve this, for Averil's sake.

The morning was crisp, an unusually strong winter sun glinting on the boars head helmets and chain mail of the assembled warriors already astride their impatiently pawing horses in the courtyard. The two women embraced a fond farewell. Ebba watched as her mistress, muffled against the cold in a heavy, fur-lined cloak, mounted her horse and moved alongside Finn at the head of the group. Finn gave the order to move. Ebba watched them leave with a heavy heart, wishing now that she had chosen to go, that she had never gone to the tower just a few hours before and overheard the strange conversation between the king and Hamund. She wrapped her cloak closer, pulling up the hood, there was much to do, first she must go to the kitchens and then to the stockade which housed the male slaves.

* * *

Hamund and Colwarn stood together on the fortress battlements, eyes fixed on the departing column.

"He spoke to me in this place not a few hours ago Colwarn."

"Why should he wish his brother-in-law dead? Ranulph could save him the trouble of killing Girdar!"

"Aye. And Ranulph would also claim his wife."

The two traded glances, Hamund looked away, searching amongst the departing warriors, resting on the copper hair glinting in the morning sunlight.

"It was what I had already suspected. The Lady's beauty has perhaps also been her curse." Hamund spoke almost to himself.

"So. Lord Ranulph will join the Gods."

"No." Hamund grasped Colwarn's arm.

"Your command is without sense Hamund. The others will agree with me!"

"The others will follow my lead if they wish at last to get some reward for their work – as you will!"

"Perhaps Finn is not the only one whose head has been turned by the Lady Averil! Her Lord husband owes his life to you not once, but twice."

"This has nothing to do with the Anglii woman! Why should we obey the Frisian king? He has offered us no compensation for our loss. There are others who will willingly pay good money for an Anglii Ealdorman."

Colwarn regarded Hamund with narrowed eyes.

"Why is it that I do not believe you?"

"Because Colwarn. As I told you once before, you are a fool."

In an instant Colwarn had grasped the handle of his sword and would have released it from it's sheath had not Hamund pulled the hand which would draw it and held it in a bone-crunching grip.

"I am your leader Colwarn. Forget it at your peril." He let Colwarn go, leaving the man to rub his agonizingly painful hand, curses on his lips.

* * *

The settlement was already awake and the people going about their daily lives, fires had been lit and food prepared, the cooking smells mingling with peat in the cold air as Ebba went to the guarded stockade which enclosed the slaves. It was a good way away from the homes of the people, behind clumps of now bare trees whose foliage provided ample cover for it in the spring. She had volunteered to join a group of women taking foodstuffs to the male slave compound and carried a bundle of fresh baked breads on her back. The gates swung open to admit them, Ebba took in everything about the surroundings, storing it into her memory. There were a couple of huts near the slave pens which consisted of a long wooden building and opposite them were the guard's barracks.

"Take this to the slaves. Move yourself!" a surly order which Ebba was only too willing to obey. She moved along the pens which had doors similar to stables – the larger bottom half locked and the narrow top half bolted. It was through the top half of the door that the food was distributed. Shadowed by a guard, Ebba gave out the loaves, urgently scanning the dirt streaked faces of the men within the straw strewn pens. She had come to the end one when she saw the muscular, familiar figure leaning against the back wall. Her heart leapt. Edred. Their eyes met for a split second and then he came over to get some bread.

"I will get you out." Ebba's voice was barely a whisper as she gave him a loaf and then continued handing them out to his fellow prisoners as if nothing had happened.

***

Ebba sat in Averil's chamber, wrestling with plans to free Edred and Ranulph, for she knew now that he must be alive and in there somewhere The compound was heavily guarded, how in the name of Christ was she going to do it alone? And if she did manage it, how would they get away? She couldn't possibly steal horses from the stables, although they were in the settlement and within easier distance than the fort. Her head throbbed, the more she thought about it, the more impossible it seemed. If only Lady Averil were here with her, she would surely know of a way, aye, and would not baulk at seeing it through. Ebba looked into the empty, cold grate, no fire would be lit there until her mistress's return. Fire, the word swirled around in her mind, alongside another, water. Fire and water. She was on her feet in seconds. Yes. This was the answer she had been seeking. But first she must get her hands on a weapon to hide about her person.

***

The early hours of the morning, a dim half moon hardly illuminating the sky, bitter cold winds rustling the night shrouded trees from which a dark figure detached itself, moving towards the compound. Ebba kept her mind fixed on her goal, beneath her cloak she had a length of rope tied around her waist and tucked into it wrapped in hide a long, deadly edged carving knife, stolen with a cool, calm efficiency which had surprised her. Two torches burned in sconces on each side of the gate over which a couple of guards kept watch, taking it in turns at regular intervals to patrol the perimeter wall. Ebba went to the back, body shaking, her heart hammering, calling up courage from her God and praying for his protection. She looped the rope, taking a few heart stopping throws before finally getting it around the pointed top of one of the timbers, the noise it made horribly loud to her but not attracting any attention. She climbed up, willing her legs not to weaken, she'd made the move, now there was no going back and she must make it work. At the top she peeped over, all was in darkness, but she could make out the shadowy figure of a guard sitting idly playing dice by the far side of the slave pens which were lit at each side by a torch inside a sconce. She tugged at the rope and threw it over, clambering down the other side with great speed, praying she would not be seen. She hit the ground with a soft thud, crouching low as she dashed to the back of the building which housed Edred, pressing against the wall as she moved around it until she reached the edge. Thanking God he was in the pen at the end. Ebba kept her eyes firmly fixed on the back of the guard who was preoccupied with his solitary game as she came out of her hiding place and quietly drew back the bolt on the narrow top gate and opened it.

"Edred!" she called out his name as loudly as she could so the guard did not hear.

He was in front of her – she hurriedly gave him in the knife, closed and re-bolted the top gate and ran back to her hiding place.

The silence was suddenly torn by a loud moaning.

"Guard!" Edred called once and then again.

"Shut up you scum!" the guard replied.

Edred called out again. Cursing, the guard reluctantly got up and went to the pen.

"What in the name of Gods is going on!"

"There is a man here who is sick."

"He better be bloody dying for me to leave my dice !" The guard opened the top half of the pen a little, Edred grabbed him by the neck and stuck the knife in his throat before he could even utter a sound,.

"Ebba! Get over her and get the keys!"

Ebba dashed from her hiding place and did as she was bidden as swiftly as she could while Edred held the guard upright, cutting her mind off from the fact she was taking keys from a blood soaked corpse. She opened the pen and Edred dragged the lifeless guard inside, threw him to the ground and took his sword.

"Where is Lord Ranulph?" Ebba asked looking around at the men.

"In one of the huts – he is injured."

"Edred you have to set the barracks on fire to create a diversion."

"My thinking too little Briton." He turned to the men and threw the keys to one of them. "I'm going to burn this place down – when its alight open all the pens and get out of here." He turned to Ebba "Stay here. Do not fear. I will be back for you." He left swiftly.

The man Edred had given the keys to looked around at his fellow prisoners, his eyes fierce in his dirty face. "Freedom is waiting."

"Freedom! We'll never get out of here alive!" the protestation came from one of the prisoners skulking in the corner.

"You stay if you want. But I'd rather die fighting than die slowly in slavery! While the compound is burning we can fight our way out of here to the settlement where horses are waiting to be taken. Whose with me?"

Ebba breathed a sigh of relief at the clamour of voices in agreement. Now all they had to do was wait.

* * *

Shouting filled the night air, the sky was alight. Edred had started the fire. The men dashed out, running along, opening the gates, crying out to those inside to get out. Panic stricken voices were replaced by horrifying screams........ Ebba prayed, fighting to control her fear as she waited by the pen for Edred to come and get her. She saw a ball of flame stagger nearby, the stench of burning flesh almost too much to bear as what had been a man fell burning to the ground. She stumbled back retching, through the smoke she could see the men fighting, grappling with bare hands against the guards, overwhelming them by the sheer savagery of their urge to be free, snatching the weapons from the bloodied bodies, heady with their victory, eager to grasp freedom, ready to keep killing for it.

"Ebba!" Edred's cry brought her back from the abyss of horror, he gripped her arm, she saw he was carrying an unconscious man over his shoulder. "We have to get to the settlement."

"No. I have a boat. We can escape on the river. Come." She moved as though chased by the demons which were said to inhabit the Devil's hell, running until each breath became painful, out of the compound and into the enveloping darkness to the calm safety of the black water and the coracle of animal skin moored to one of the jetties, in which she had secreted supplies for an escape she had thought impossible.

Chapter Twenty-Three

Averil pulled her damp cloak tightly around her as she stood in the doorway of the bower at Halliwell's former hall where she had once been imprisoned by Girdar. She stepped into the empty room, unpleasant memories rushing back to how she had waited for Girdar to come to her and planned to escape, to warn Ranulph, she had almost made it – her eyes brimmed tears. Ranulph. Coming back had opened up still fresh wounds. She had escaped from this hall twice, the second time successfully with Hamund, successfully and too late, for Ranulph had already joined the Gods and she was being taken to another destiny. Finn. She saw the Frisian king in her mind's eye, he had left her in guarded safety in the forest before the dawn attack which had taken Girdar's men by complete surprise, telling her Girdar would be taken alive so she could witness his execution. There was never any doubt Finn and his warriors would subdue those there, and she had been right, for the Frisians had cut down Girdar's retainers with ferocious, enjoyable ease, more than ready for a fight they had travelled long and hard for, only to discover Girdar was not amongst them. Averil's heart had twisted at the news brought by a blood stained, battle weary retainer, the demons themselves must keep careful watch over that black hearted dog! She leant back against the wall, closing her eyes, raging against Girdar, anger and frustration at being thwarted welling up inside her.

"You are unwell?" she opened her eyes to see Finn standing before her.

Averil shook her head.

"There is food prepared in the hall." Finn said "It will be the last you shall have in comfort until we reach the Anglii King's hall."

"Oswin?"

"One of Girdar's men was....." he sought a suitable description, his cold smile savage "persuaded to talk. Girdar is with Oswin." Finn glanced around the bower, his tone casual. "He has gone there to marry the king's daughter."

"Princess Ingilda!"

"It seems King Oswin is not a good judge of men."

Averil's heart turned over as the implications of the weighty news sank in, Girdar could now be son-in-law to the king!

"The game has changed Averil. An Ealdorman may now be son to a royal house. I shall offer Oswin the chance through his law to rid himself of bad blood."

"And if the judgement goes against us?"

He shrugged. "Girdar will die just the same, and take most of his tribe with him."

"How so most of his tribe?"

"There will be war if Oswin chooses to deny my kin the right to lie in honour."

"But once Girdar is dead there will be no need to fight!"

"We shall see."

"Bringing death to the Anglii tribe...." she did not finish, for he had grabbed her right hand, lifting it to show the boar's head ring which had been altered to fit her.

"This token, as you have so often told me, marks you princess of the Frisian people. Your loyalty is to them! I do not ever wish to hear you forget it again!"

"The Frisian king does not have to remind the daughter of Aethelstan of where her loyalty lies! I have forgotten nothing!" she sought to pull away, her green eyes blazing angry fire.

"I am glad it is so. For revenge is a hard master Lady, once embarked on there is no going back. All you have to think on is that one way or another Girdar shall die. Slowly." He released his hold, she watched him as he strode out and then drew her cloak around her, looking around once more at her former prison before following him out.

* * *

Girdar stretched beneath the furs of the pallet, waking to the new morning. He had slept alone, a concession to Ingilda, which would, of course, change once he had made her his wife and got her with child. He had wanted the wedding ceremony to be held on the Feast of the Mothers, but the queen had opposed it with the excuse that she wished her only daughter to be married when the barren winter had given way to the spring, although he knew Ethelburga was merely delaying the inevitable because of her deep dislike and distrust of him. But, he would make Ingilda his wife, he had worked for it and would not be disappointed by anyone, not even the queen, which was why he would leave the hall again only with Ingilda at his side and the best wishes of the bitch Ethelburga ringing in his ears. The princess would provide some novelty for a while – Averil's beautiful face came to his mind, as it sometimes did in moments of reflection, he should have known the Frankish mercenary would want payment for what was, after all, a job well done. Ranulph well and truly dead. His story had been wonderfully plausible, his feigned grief at the telling of it something to be proud of. The hall which had once been Aethelstan's full of the dead and dying, Ranulph along with his new wife, already victims of the dread plague, their bodies long burnt by the time he and his men arrived. Girdar stretched out to pour a goblet of fresh water, recalling how badly Leofric had taken the news, his precious eldest son, the only one he ever cared for, now with the Gods, only Girdar left to carry on the line. Leofric's face had been ashen, drained, a look which had not left him, it were as though some of his youthful vigour had died along with his oldest son, he had aged since then. Girdar refreshed his mouth, recalling the masterly mourning of his mother, not overdone but dignified, as that of a step relation ought to be, her sacrifices to the Gods for her dear stepson and his lovely wife Averil. So beautiful, so spirited, he remembered how good it had been to take her in the forest, how she had fought him every inch of the way – what a victory that had been! There were many times when he hated Hamund for depriving him of her, for he would have found a way to have her all to himself. Suddenly, the agreeable picture of Ingilda dissolved, there was no comparison between the princess and Averil, making love to her would be like kneading a lump of dough. He banged the goblet down on the table, it would be best not to think of Averil, she was gone now as surely as if she were indeed dead and he, Girdar, had everything and would soon be acquiring more, which is what he had always wanted, and was what, after all, he deserved. The banging on the door broke his reverie, his father entered without announcement.

"Dress yourself. The king has need of his son-in-law to þe." Leofric picked up a crumpled linen shirt from the floor and threw it over to Girdar. "We have been honoured with an unexpected visitor. Oswin wishes us to accompany him to the meeting."

Girdar pulled on his shirt. "Who and where?"

"The Frisian king. We will meet him in the ruins."

"Finn! What brings him from his lands in the dead of winter? And why does he not come to the hall?"

"One visit cannot change the deep distrust which has always existed between our tribes."

"Do you trust this?"

"Finn has sent his ring of kingship as honour pledge of friendship."

"That was not my question."

Leofric's reply was considered – careful. "I think Finn can be trusted for this one meeting, Nevertheless Oswin shall ride with his best fighting men." A grin split Leofric's face, Girdar met it as he strapped his sword around his waist.

"Come then father. Let us go and meet this king."

* * *

Averil stood behind the wide main doorway of the villa concealed by the darkness within. Frost twinkled diamond like on the dilapidated stone courtyard before her as weak sunlight shone on the horsemen who had seconds ago charged into it's heart, the chain-mailed King Oswin, his gold crown gleaming, at their lead. Averil's hatred flamed as a living thing as she once more looked upon Girdar, his white blond hair twisted into a long pigtail, smoothed from the handsome face which denied the evil within. He looked about him, supremely confident, Leofric at his side. She was shocked to see how much Ranulph's father had aged, the flaxen hair, which had only been peppered with grey, was now nearly all so, and deep lines were etched into a countenance which has always seemed to deny the years. Oswin dismounted, he and Finn greeting each other as brothers while their respective retainers looked on with mutual suspicion. Finn had moved the bulk of his men out, he did not want Oswin to see his strength, and he had sent a man to watch Oswin's departure and report on how many he brought with him, and how many perhaps, followed on. The mistrust was almost palpable, despite the warmth of the meeting, as they both walked away from earshot of the others, speaking closely, their breath smoking in the cold. Averil caught a side view of Oswin, if only she could hear what exactly was being said. They talked for what seemed like a long time, the horses pawed the ground restlessly, Averil studied Girdar's profile, seeing Ranulph there, the brother he had murdered. Finn was calling for his sister. The time she had long awaited was now here, she had counted the hours until this day. The day when she wrought vengeance on Girdar.

"This is for you all, my dear loves." She uttered the affirmation in her mind as she stepped outside, eyes fixed on her prey, speaking their triumph without words as they homed in on Girdar, his face registering a potent mixture of stunned shock and disbelief as, almost in slow motion, Leofric turned to his son and then back again to Averil. She saw he knew there could be no mistake and wondered at the lies Girdar had told to conceal her own and Ranulph's disappearance.

"The Lady Averil. Princess of the Frisian." Finn's formal introduction, his hand taking her own, she tore her gaze away from Girdar, looked to King Oswin. His expression was closed, unreadable as he regarded her.

"Your presence here opens many questions Lady."

She felt the heat of Girdar's eyes, met them with a malevolent gaze, directing her next words to him. "And I call upon them to be tested before the Law."

Leofric dismounted and was beside Oswin in seconds.

"What in the name of the Gods is all this about!"

"Your son Girdar is a murderer. Not only has he killed my kin but also my husband. Your son, Leofric, Ranulph."

Leofric took a step backwards as though he had been struck. Girdar was at his father's side, his expression vicious. "Your lies should strike you dead Lady."

"Tell your Ealdorman I shall personally relieve him of his tongue if he cannot control it." Finn addressed Oswin, Girdar beneath his notice.

"Enough Lord Girdar! This matter can only be settled according to our law, a full hearing in front of your king and his highest ranking retainers before the next full moon."

"And I want it here Oswin, on neutral ground."

"So be it."

"And what of Girdar?"

"He will be kept under close guard."

"I trust it shall not be close enough to escape." Finn replied, the air immediately thick with threat at his words.

Oswin replied in formal tone. "We shall meet here in two days at the dawning of the sun."

A stiff bow between them before the three men went back to their horses. Oswin staying Leofric's questions with a wave of his hand before mounting and shouting his order to leave. Girdar turned to Averil before spurring his horse, his look murderous – then he was gone with the others, frost dust gleaming in their wake.

"We shall keep close watch on the hall." Finn moved nearer to her as they both watched the departure. "Girdar is as yet not married to Ingilda yet King Oswin has a hard decision to make. I know not if he is strong enough in power to risk the wrath of his Ealdormen by handing one of their number over to me."

"You think he will allow Girdar to escape?"

"Perhaps. Either way it will soon be at an end. And you shall be able to leave the dead and carry on living."

She looked away, yet stayed close, blotting out the sharp pain which darted through her heart as she thought of Ranulph.

* * *

"I cannot believe what I have heard!" Ingilda raged, her round face puffed into ugliness from angry tears. "The woman must be mad!"

Ethelburga's features puckered anxiety. "These are heavy accusations Ingilda."

"It's a pack of filthy lies! Girdar could never do what she has accused him of!"

"This situation could pose much trouble for your father."

"It is lies! All of it, vicious lies!" Ingilda hardly heard her mother, feeling rage choke her. Girdar locked away under guard as a common criminal, his men too under watch, his mother Lady Egwina, weeping her distress, pleading his innocence and Leofric, still as stone, not wishing to speak to anyone, alone in his chambers, away from the eyes of those around him.

"You will control yourself daughter. You are a royal princess! We must at least thank the Gods that Girdar is not your husband."

"You never wanted him to be! Now I see you are glad this has happened. Glad I am to lose the man I love!" Ingilda screeched, hysteria and imagination visualising Girdar's execution.

"Get to your chamber until you have proper command of yourself! I will not have you humiliate yourself or our kin in this way." Ethelburga was on her feet, formidable in her quick spurt of anger at Ingilda's behaviour, extremely worried about the turn of events, sensing danger in any path Oswin chose to take. Her daughter was out of the door, running to her apartment, fair hair streaming down her back, fresh tears stinging her cheeks. She reached her room, breathless and dishevelled, slamming the door purposefully shut, pressing her back against it as she wiped the tears, smearing her face with the back of her hand. Without Girdar she might as well be dead! And she would be soon, for her mother hated Girdar and could well persuade her father to give the Frisian king what he wanted ! Girdar's head. No!

"This Lady whom you once told me Girdar desired above all others will be his death!" she screamed at Brigid who was cowering in a corner, knowing tears were just as likely to produce a nasty whipping as a temper tantrum. Brigid tried to make sense of the statement, she had heard rumours of Girdar and his retainers being detained, that the Lady Averil was back, not dead of the plague at all, accusing him of horrible deeds -so it was true then! Ingilda suddenly stopped weeping, gulping for breath as she controlled herself.

"Give me your clothes Brigid."

The slave did as she was told, believing Ingilda demented with grief, undressing hurriedly and handing over her sack cloth tunic, shivering in her nudity as she hurried to get her cloak. Ingilda began dressing herself in Brigid's mean clothes, she was wonderfully calm, was she not a princess? Daughter of a Royal House? She was not going to lose the man she loved this way, soon it would be nightfall and did not desperate times call for desperate measures?

* * *

The three travellers took their rest for the night in the dubious shelter offered by the derelict, beehive shaped building amidst the denuded trees. They sat around a crackling fire which sent thin plumes of smoke into the black, icy air.

"We should reach Oswin's hall in two days." The big man spoke through mouthfuls of freshly scorched rabbit.

"I fear for what we might find." Ebba's small voice, her thin body shivering even beneath the fur cloak.

"I wish only one thing." Ranulph's dark eyes, now free of the fever which had wracked his body for many days during their journey, burned brighter than the fire as he turned to Ebba. "That my brother is alive."

"I should think my Lord that you would wish it otherwise." Ebba hardly dared match his gaze, a wolf howled in the distance, the urgent scurrying of a forest creature rustled nearby.

"Of course you do not understand." The smooth, relaxed half smile on the scarred face was more terrifying than hot anger.

"I wish him still living so that I may have the great pleasure of killing him."

Chapter Twenty-Four

The gloom of the ante-room lit by a single rush torch cast shadows on the two stern faced men.

"This turn of events must be carefully thought on Lord Leofric." Oswin's voice was troubled.

"I speak as both loyal Ealdorman and father when I say to you that I cannot believe the guilt of my own flesh and blood in these vile accusations."

"I could not have expected any other response from my most faithful and honourable retainer."

"Girdar believes Lady Averil must have been crazed by the plague which so obviously spared her."

"But it is madness which could sweep me in its tide. What loyalty do you think your king would inspire should he give up one of his own Ealdormen to the Frisian King for certain death?"

"If the case was proved then it would be I, Girdar's father, who would strike him down."

"And what king would allow his Ealdorman to kill his only son left living by believing the word of a Frisian against an Anglii!"

They tracked each other's path of thought in silence which Leofric broke.

"You think of escape. Finn has more men than he revealed. He will keep close watch on the hall."

"No matter. Girdar shall get out. But once away from this hall he must be on his own."

"I understand."

"By doing this I risk trouble between our tribes. But it is the only way open to me."

"I respect your decision Lord King. Nothing can alter what has happened. This way my son shall have fair chance. His fate will be with the Gods."

"So be it." Their hands clasped in a tight grip, sealing that which could not now be altered.

* * *

Ingilda, disguised in Brigid's clothes, trudged across the courtyard carrying a platter of bread and meat. Torches burning on the walls marked her progress yet there were no watchful eyes, this part of the compound was strangely silent, even as she steeled herself for confrontation with her father's guards she realised there were none about – her heart pumped wildly as she saw the hut where Girdar was imprisoned was without sentries, even as she walked towards it, the door creaked open and a cloaked figure emerged – Girdar! She dropped her burden, running over to him as fast as she could, unable to call his name, he drew his sword as she approached, she pulled down her hood, eyes glistening tears.

"My Lord! It is I, Ingilda. I came to set you free! See, I have a knife! Take me with you!" her plea desperate as she held onto his sleeve.

"Go back" he hissed the order as he pushed her from him and darted towards the stables. Undeterred, she chased at his heels, clutching at his cloak.

"Please. You cannot leave me." He looked at the imploring face, his mind working. This escape, who had arranged it? His father? Oswin? Whoever it had been it meant only one thing, that Oswin had not the courage to defy Finn, that he would have given him up to die. He saw Oswin's face in Ingilda's pathetically entreating expression. He had been forced to become an outlaw, outcast of his own people. Oswin knew he could not judge him guilty against his sworn oath and risk the wrath of the other Ealdormen, he had brought him to this for expediency. How rich it would be if he took Ingilda, his precious daughter, and married her. Let him then see Oswin lift sword against his own son-in-law!

"Come. Quickly." He took her arm, pulling her over to the horses, conveniently unguarded.

* * *

"My Lord King!" the banging on the door woke Oswin and Ethelburga from their peaceful slumber.

"Enter" Oswin sat up as he shouted the order, knowing he would be given the news of Girdar's escape. The two sentries ran inside, their leather tunics glistening wet from the rain.

"My Lord Girdar and his companion have escaped the hall!"

"Companion?" Oswin was on the alert, Ethelburga sat up next to her husband, foreboding gripping her.

"My Lord King" the sentry looked nervously at the man at his side who stared straight ahead, refusing to take the responsibility for the news.

"Well? Speak!" Oswin demanded.

"The Princess Ingilda"

A sharp intake of breath from Ethelburga.

"You let the princess ride out of here with Girdar!" Oswin's anger exploded as he jumped out of bed, throwing a fur-lined cloak around his shoulders. "You fools!"

"My Lord King, she rode side by side with Girdar of her own will, told us to tell you...." he faltered at the dark fury on Oswin's face.

"Tell me what?"

"Tell you that she sent you all the love in her heart for the last time for now it was all my Lord Girdar's. We thought....."

"Don't give me excuses for that which can have none. Call out the men and go after them! Now!"

They were gone in seconds, away from the fearful presence of their outraged liege who was pulling on his clothes.

"By Tiw! I'll have that bastard's head for this!"

"As your Ealdorman, you could outlaw Girdar and thus solve the problem with Finn, but as your son-in-law Girdar will be more difficult to shed."

"Marriage?" Oswin turned to his wife.

"She loves him beyond sense or reason. I read the message she gave the guards as you did not."

"I should have let Finn have him."

"No Oswin. Your decision was the right one for then, but now, Girdar has changed the stakes."

"He will not be free long enough to wed my daughter, and I promise my queen this. That if he should dare to, then Ingilda shall return to this hall a widow!"

* * *

Averil awoke from her nightmare with sweat pouring down her face, sitting up as thunder crashed it's raging anger while the rain played a heavy drumbeat against the villa walls. In the next room a fire burned, its glow casting shadows, she could hear the muffled conversation of Finn's men. She had dreamt of Girdar, riding through the night, cloak flying in the wind, rain plastering his white blond hair, he had come to a halt in front of her as she stood tied to a lifeless tree and thrown the bloodied body of Ranulph at her feet, then he had leapt from his horse, his face triumphant as he grabbed her throat and began to squeeze the life from her.....she shook her head........it had only been a dream....a dream of the blackest hours. A white lightening flash lit the small room, illuminating the cloaked figure standing in the doorway.

"He has escaped." Finn's voice "And it seems he has taken the king's daughter with him." A wry smile touched his lips. "Dress yourself Lady if you want to be in at the kill."

* * *

King Oswin drummed his fingers on the arm of his chair as he awaited the arrival of the stranger at his gates who had identified himself as Ranulph, son of Leofric. After all that had happened, he was unsurprised by this new turn of events which had also brought hope, for if anyone could track down that bastard Girdar it was Ranulph. The door opened, a black cloaked figure stepped inside and bowed to King Oswin before pushing back the hood to reveal the familiar scarred face.

"Lord Ranulph. You are welcome back from the pyre."

"And glad I am my Lord King to be so far from it" a glimmer of an ironic smile.

"Your half brother told us you and your Lady were dead of the plague."

"An interesting disease and one which I have never been unfortunate enough to contract."

"Your Lady told us it was so."

"My Lady. She is here?"

"Your half brother escaped this hall while awaiting a hearing of accusations of murder of yourself and her family by Lady Averil. She rides with the Frisian king in his pursuit."

"And my father?"

"Your father has gone to his own hall. He wished to be alone with the heavy burden of his grief."

Ranulph waited, there was something else, he felt the king's suppressed rage.

"Your father did not believe the Lady Averil and he spoke in defence of Girdar. It was...." he floundered as he searched for the correct way to present a decision which had been the wrong one, "expedient for me to allow him a chance and help his escape. Girdar saw fitting to take my daughter with him."

Ranulph stood still as death as he took in the gravity of the situation, his thoughts flying to his father and the terrible sorrow he must now be feeling. To lose one son and then for the other to betray the trust of himself and his king - if only he had arrived earlier!

"Come Lord Ranulph. Your journey has been a long one." Oswin motioned for him to sit down and summoned a slave from the corner of the room who poured warmed wine into two silver goblets by Oswin's side and handed one of them to Ranulph. "Drink and take your ease. There is much for us to speak of."

Ranulph sat, realising his legs were still stiffened from the arduous journey which had brought him to the hall days earlier than he had planned thanks to a punishing pace, yet he had still been too late to ease both Averil and his father's minds with the knowledge that he, Ranulph, was very much alive. The wine's heat refreshed him. He had expected to find much here. Averil. Leofric. And found nothing. The two men spoke in low tones, Edred, who leant against the wall outside the chamber waiting for his master, could hear nothing of the conversation though he knew that there was much to speak of between his Lord and their king. His eyes had been closed in a kind of half slumber for quite a while before Ranulph appeared and shook his retainer by the shoulder to wake him up.

"Come Edred. Tonight we eat and rest. Tomorrow we go after Girdar."

Edred gave his master a questioning look as they walked along the narrow corridor which led outside.

"Girdar escaped from here barely a day ago while awaiting a hearing before his peers about the death of Averil's family and myself - with the Princess Ingilda to keep him company."

"And you know where."

"Have you ever thrown the dice with the certainty that it will give you the numbers to win Edred?"

"I know not what dice has to do with this but I know you will enlighten me my Lord."

"Girdar is pursued by the Frisian king and Oswin's men and has a woman to think on. His best bet is to lie low for a while."

"And so?"

"There is a place. A secret place, known only to myself and to Girdar from our boyhood."

"Where is this?"

"On my father's lands, which is the last place anyone would think he would run to. We shall find him there, a rat caught in a trap of his own making."

* * *

Ingilda drooped astride the tired horse, Girdar had set a frantic pace and the cold had sliced into her during what had become a nightmare, torturous journey through inhospitable forest. Her stomach screamed it's protest at a lack of plentiful food, Girdar's rations had been well stocked for himself and his mount, sacks of horse fodder had been slung across his saddle along with dried meat, cheese and apples and pigskins full of mead and water, all of which had to be halved between them. She thought she would never again be full or warm as they picked their way through the trees, yet as she glanced at Girdar she knew it was worth it, for was she not with the man she loved above all else? What price was the comfort of a fire in exchange for the warmth of his arms? She shifted uncomfortably, for he had not offered any such closeness, barely touching her, little less talking, yet she told herself that his anxieties for their safety were to blame, and soon it would all change when they reached the place he had told her of, where he had assured her, no-one could possibly find them. They had been following a main path, Ingilda now realised they had been gradually going uphill, the nature of the landscape changing, the road becoming steeper, she saw rocks through the trees, they were climbing a valley, below them a thick carpet of trees, before them ragged cliffs. Girdar halted and dismounted, motioning her to do the same. She followed wordlessly, the road now almost impossibly sharp, until they reached the gaping mouth of a cave carved into the rocks. The clumps of trees at either side promised leafy shelter in the spring but now they stood as gaunt, statue guards.

"This will be our shelter and there will be enough food for our needs."

"How so?"

"This valley is peopled by a tribe whose Gods demand fresh food sacrifice at their shrines."

"Take that which was intended for their Gods?"

"They are barbarians, what use have we for those they worship? I know of their secret places and there will be good meats and black bread aplenty to keep us from hunger."

"How did you come to know of this place?"

"Ranulph discovered it. We played here as children, and it was known only to us. No-one will find us here." He drew her to him without ceremony, his lips hard against her own in a bruising kiss. "And now my princess we shall seal our bond." He spoke against her hair, his hand exploring her ample bosom, sending tremors of arousal along Ingilda's spine, how she had longed for this! She wanted to give into him but they were not yet married, it was not as it should be, with supreme willpower she tried to push him away, but he held her fast.

"Oh no Ingilda, you have chosen your path, now I claim what you offered." his breath was hot against her ear. " Do not worry. I will not use you and discard you. You will be my wife as soon as I can make it possible. Think on this as practise for your married state" His lips found her own once more, stifling any protest and wearing down any resistance.

Chapter Twenty-Five

Averil and Finn stood together by a crystal stream, running fast between clumps of white ice. The sky above them was sullen grey and there was a sharp taste of snow in the biting air.

"Our trail is as cold as death Lady."

Averil watched the rushing water, swollen by the downpours which had dogged and hampered their search.

"The heavy rains have helped play their part in wiping out any tracks." she said.

"If there ever were any." Finn turned from the water's edge, taking her arm as they walked.

"Tell me what is on your mind Finn."

"I think our quarry is in hiding with the princess."

"A good thought, but they could be anywhere."

"Perhaps Girdar chose to return to the bosom of his family."

"Leofric's lands?"

"He must know much of them and would be well able to find a good place to lay low for as long as possible."

Averil looked up at her companion. "Perhaps you are right. Though I wish our path did not lead to Leofric. I have caused him enough pain, my presence would only add to it."

"So." He brought her to a halt, tilting her chin to face him. "Beneath the stone there is some softness."

Averil brushed his hand aside, wishing to dispel the unexpected intimacy of the moment. "Leofric is still my father-in-law."

"Your husband is dead. There is no bond between you now."

"Except my love for Ranulph."

Finn took her arm in a tough grip as he led her forcefully through the trees.

"Come Lady. We must waste no more time. The shadow of your husband has been too long left undispelled." He quickened his step, she could almost reach out and touch his deep displeasure as they moved back to the camp where the men, their morning meal over, were busy preparing for their departure.

* * *

Ingilda grimaced her distaste as she bit into the black bread, she detested it and would be glad to be back in the comfort of a hall with fresh killed, succulent meat to devour and warmed mead in her belly instead of the sour, dry wine which was all the barbarians left for their Gods. She had half a mind to spit it out into the campfire but decided against it, a quicksilver fear at the possibility of inciting Girdar's wrath staying her actions. She shifted on the sacking which provided little protection from the rocky ground, eyes sliding to Girdar who stood at the cave mouth, looking out into the night. She saw he held the handle of his sword with the same strong fingers which had so expertly touched her own body. For a second her cheeks reddened as she recalled her own abandonment to the pleasure he gave, and then disquiet as she felt the freshness of the bruises he had inflicted during their lovemaking. She thought of how he would react if she refused him. Here in the wilderness of the forest, without the trappings of the royal hall, there was no need to be anyone but himself, and, there was a violence in his lovemaking which frightened her, although at first she had been loathe to admit it. A wolf howled in it the distance, Girdar came inside and sat beside her.

"You wish bread?" her smile was pleasant, it went unacknowledged as he merely shook his head without looking at her.

"The animals are noisy this night."

"Yes." Girdar's unease was plain. "More so than any other. Perhaps I shall have need of this." He drew his sword from it's sheath, the intricate silver work on the hilt shone in the firelight. Elatha. It was the first time Ingilda had seen the sword properly since Ranulph and Averil's wedding. It was very beautiful, the craftsmanship a work of art.

"The sword of Averil's father" she murmured that which was the first thing which had sprung to her mind.

"Is rightly mine now Ingilda." He flashed a covetous, satisfied smile "As are you. When the spring comes I will send word to your mother and she will arrange our marriage."

"My father would never hand over his son-in-law to Finn."

"Your noble father was not beyond handing over one of his most loyal Ealdorman to Finn " he sounded savage as he rounded on her. "And he may still think on killing me for taking you, his precious daughter. Unless of course, he should be otherwise tied." He reached out and grabbed her stomach. "By his grandson."

Ingilda struggled to be free of his painful grasp as she protested against the assault. "My Lord! You are hurting me! And possibly the baby you so wish for!"

His mouth twisted into a nasty smile as he dragged her over to him and forced her onto her back, reaching inside her tunic, roughly probing her thighs.

"If only your father could see you now princess, beneath Lord Girdar." He worked on her body as he stripped her. "We have until the spring to fill your belly Ingilda. Let us waste no more time. For in our baby lies the safety of your loving husband and, of course, your future."

* * *

Leofric strode past the snoring bodies of his retainers who slept on their straw pallets in his hall, amidst the debris of the evening meal. He was fully clothed, his sword clanking at his side as he walked out into the grey dawn. Today he could leave this place of melancholia and regret where his Lady languished, closeted away, unapproachable in her grief for Girdar. He could stomach none of it any longer, his sorrow was eating him away inside, his own hall bringing back memories of the sons he had lost. One of them. he could admit now, he had always favoured, long dead, and the other, lost to him as though dead, and that was only a matter of time. He mounted his horse, the flesh beneath him warm, amenable, waiting for his command. Today he would ride through his forest and forget, cast aside the untold humiliation and shame Girdar had brought by betraying their king, fling away the growing suspicion that Averil's accusations against Girdar were true. For his action in taking Ingilda had revealed a depth of treachery and a disregard for honour which may not be beyond the murder of the brother who, and Leofric could admit it to himself now, he had always despised. Yet had he not thrust this aside, blinded himself to the hatred he had often seen blazing in Girdar's eyes? Could he not have done something to dispel it? Leofric spurred the horse, galloping out of the stables, his startled, sleepy sentries moving quickly to open the gates to let him through. He felt the cool fresh air rush past him as he rode hard across the frigid ground, as one with his horse, in a bid to wipe out all bloodstained thoughts from his tortured mind.

***

Grey dawn broke to find Girdar by the cave mouth, sword drawn, body tense and alert. The wolves' howls had awakened him from a fitful sleep, bringing with them the unease he had experienced the night before. His eyes scanned the still landscape, the leafless trees stretched to the dip in the valley offering little hiding place for any who planned an ambush. He caught a glimmer of metal, a sword? He stepped out, the figure crouched on the cliffs above leapt, sending a shower of stones as he felled Girdar with a crunching thud, knocking Elatha from his hand. The two men rolled on the ground, both grappling for ascendancy, through blood mist Girdar saw the scarred face of his attacker. No! It was a ghost! A shadow....a trick of the Gods! His brother was dead! The ghost pinned a thrashing, twisting Girdar beneath him with his weight, hands clamping his throat in a death vice. Girdar bit into one of them, blood gushed from his mouth. Even as Ranulph's flesh ripped, he still retained his brutal grip.

"I've got you now you bastard!" the words were a growl through clenched teeth as Ranulph squeezed out the life. Girdar reached out, clawing for a rock, grasping it with superhuman strength born of desperation and smashing it against Ranulph's head, the dizzying blow momentarily weakening his grip, enough for Girdar to struggle free and run, gulping air, to the cave, to Ingilda. Cursing, head still reeling, Ranulph was after him, reaching the cave mouth to see Girdar, eyes blazing in his dirt-stained, bloodied face, holding Ingilda in front of him with a knife to her throat.

"I'll slit her throat if you come near me."

"Do it." Ranulph approached.

"Think you I do not have the guts to kill Oswin's daughter? What have I to lose?" Girdar dug in the knife tip, Ingilda screamed as blood trickled down his grazed fist. Ranulph stopped dead in his tracks, seeing Girdar meant it.

"That is better brother, you cannot let Oswin's much loved daughter came to harm. Now get out of here. Slowly. That's right."

All three moved out into the open, Girdar taking the now hysterically sobbing Ingilda over to his tethered horse, mounting the stallion and holding her in front of him.

"Once again your honour has cost you what you desire Ranulph." He squeezed Ingilda's breasts with vicious glee. "Oswin's daughter beds well and I would have been sorry to lose her, but she could never measure up to the pleasure your own Lady gave me" he pulled the horse around, kicking up dirt as he rode down the treacherous mountainside at breakneck speed.

Girdar looked behind him swiftly as he raced along, no sign of Ranulph. That treacherous dog Hamund had lied to him, and had taken Averil in payment for a job he hadn't even done. Ranulph alive meant that the only thing he, Girdar, had to concentrate on was getting out of this in one piece. Ingilda, whom he had knocked senseless to stop her pathetic crying and wailing, lay limp in front of him, perhaps he should dump her. No. She could still have her uses. He would cross the border into the wilderness of the northern lands, peopled by the strange barbarians who coloured their bodies. Spittle spumed from his heaving horse as he tugged at the reins, jerking him around to a new direction and catching a glimpse of the grey haired horseman from the corner of his eye, his heart recognising his father before his mind registered. He cursed as he sped away with fresh impetus, away from his brother, and now Tiw spare him, his bloody father, who could understand nothing except his precious honour and duty. Who would hand his own son over to the king for certain death should he catch him and justify his action as serving his liege! Leofric saw the lone rider, who appeared to have a sack of grain strewn across his saddle, the sunlight gleamed on the white blond hair......realisation hit him. He looked upon the man who had brought shame to his kinsmen, his renegade, traitorous son and the kings daughter. Without even thinking about it, Leofric spurred into action, dashing through the trees with consummate skill, his fresher horse diminishing the distance between them with each stride until they rode neck and neck.

"Girdar!" the order of father to son brought nothing as Girdar whipped his mount to increase the pace, lashing the animal to the limit.

Leofric sprang with surprisingly agility, sending himself and Girdar flying, the two of them hitting the ground with tremendous force which drove them apart. Girdar's riderless horse reared, the trampling hooves, barely missing the two men and Ingilda who had been thrown clear and was now regaining painful consciousness. Girdar was scrambling to his feet when a wrench on his ankles sent him thudding onto his stomach, as Leofric pulled him around, Girdar slid the dagger from his belt and struck out. Leofric moved swiftly to deflect the blade from his chest, it plunged deep into his shoulder, scraping bone, he fell back as the pain shot through, blood spurting from the wound, splattering Girdar's victorious face. Girdar raised the dagger once more, this time sure of hitting home, but Leofric stayed his hand, the two men fought to control the dagger, but Leofric was too weakened for such a contest, his strength failing him as with agonising slowness the blade turned towards him and was moving inexorably towards his heart ......the knife span away as the boot smashed into the arm which held it. Girdar turned. Ranulph!

"Get up you whore spawn!"

Girdar sprang to his feet, Ranulph had drawn his sword and stepped back.

"Ah, my noble brother! Why stick a knife in my back when honest combat will do? You are confident." He drew Elatha, lunging at Ranulph, who blocked the move.

Through his now debilitating pain Leofric saw Girdar and another man, as his eyes dimmed into darkness he recognised he who he had thought long dead, the name a whisper on his lips before he blacked out. For several minutes his sons fought, their swords ringing as they clashed again and again, glinting steel slicing with murderous intent as they moved back and forth amongst the skeletal trees. Ranulph lost his footing, Girdar taking swift advantage of the precious moment to slash at his brother's sword arm, slicing the flesh, the shock of agony causing Ranulph to step back and fall over a rock, he saw a dull flash of a sweeping sword blade as it whisked towards his unprotected head, his own blade came up to ward off the death blow and push his attacker away, giving him the precious seconds he needed to get up once more. The wound oozing blood down the hand which gripped his sword, Ranulph attacked with fresh ferocity, forcing Girdar backwards in a hacking onslaught, with a cry Ranulph thrust at him, Girdar parried the blade and the sword hilts locked as they fought to wrest control. Elatha clattered to the ground, Girdar was thrown back against an oak tree, with lightening movement, Ranuph threw away his own sword and picked up Elatha, lunging at his half brother's unprotected torso, skewering him to the oak and coming out of the body clean. There was a look of surprise in Girdar's blue eyes as he slithered lifeless to the ground.

* * *

Averil dismounted in the courtyard of Leofric's hall. Finn was by her side, taking her arm to lead her inside where Lady Egwina waited, sitting as still as a corpse in Leofric's chair at the main table. She was swathed in white, the colour of mourning, her face the only part of her visible. Her eyes were diamond hard as she bowed her head to Finn, looking only at him, never once touching or acknowledging Averil's presence.

"We welcome the Frisian King."

"The Frisian King thanks you Lady."

"My husband is unable to greet you in person. He has left us this day for the solace of the forest. His burden of grief at such a turn of events is weighty." The venom in her tone was expected.

"We do not wish to take advantage of your hospitality for any longer than we have Lady. We wish fresh supplies and rest for our horses."

"The hall of Leofric is now yours. You may take all for your needs." She stood up to take her leave, as they made their way for her a panting, wild eyed sentry bounded into the hall. "My Lady!" Averil's eyes were drawn beyond him to the gaping doorway. A blood splattered man stood within it, his chain mail tunic ripped, his black hair unbound, in his arms he carried a wounded old man. Averil fell back against the wall as she felt the ground beneath her began to yield, she was in danger of fainting as her shocked mind and pumping heart tried to come to terms with the reality before her eyes.

"Your husband is wounded Lady and needs tending" the voice was the same, she clutched her throat, closing her eyes to dizziness, this was a dream, it could not be happening! Ranulph was dead!

"Where is Girdar?" Egwina shimmered hatred.

"He is beyond your help Lady"

Egwina stiffened in a sudden, stunned silence."That you should dare touch your father with the blood of your own brother on your filthy, murdering hands!"

"Save your soft words for the mourning of he who deserves them."

"Where is he?"

"Outside." Ranulph strode past Egwina as she ran from the hall, resting his unconscious father upon the length of the long table. "Guard!" the sentry was instantly to attention "Get some women here to tend your Lord's wound."

"I have a skilled man within my company who will tend Ealdorman Leofric." The offer brought Ranulph around, as, for the first time, he noticed the flaxen haired stranger who stood as tall as himself.

"I thank you." The stranger moved to leave the hall, the other men behind him following, Ranulph too preoccupied with his father to ask questions. He looked once more to Leofric, knowing from his experience the wound was not fatal and once more thanking the Gods he had caught up with Girdar in time. Averil approached as if in a dream, her eyes fixed on his broad back, her body burning with longing to press against him, to be enfolded in his embrace. The touch on his arm was feather light, his name a whisper as he turned to look upon a face far more gorgeous that he had remembered it, he took her in his arms and they held each other as if they would never let go, after long moments they kissed, there was no need for any words between them. Averil matched the passion of his kiss with equal fervour as she clung to him, joy branding every part of her, after a long time he released her mouth, still holding her near.

"Ranulph." His name, almost a sigh as Averil's happiness flowed freely from within. "This is the work of the Gods. I believed you dead by Girdar's orders."

"I was better served. I have known you were alive since I escaped the Frisian. I planned to seek you out once I had dealt with Girdar. I should never have left it to others to guard you while I went to your father's hall"

Averil touched the jagged scar which marked his face, she wanted this moment to sear her mind forever, to remember the intimacy of his voice, how he had held her suffocatingly close.

"You were not to know Girdar would anticipate your plan to bring him to justice."

"My misjudgement could have cost your life."

"The past is dead my Lord, with Girdar."

Ranulph moved her from him and drew out Elatha from his scabbard, Averil's eyes drawn to the blood which smeared the burnished blade as he handed over her father's weapon.

"Your kin have been properly avenged Averil. Girdar was killed with the sword of the man he murdered."

"They now are for certain in the halls of Great Woden." The affirmation a whisper as she kissed the handle of the sword and placed it on the table. "The Gods grant Elatha may never be used in hatred again."

"Finn has been spared his task of revenge. Oh yes, I knew of his kinship to you and all that has happened."

"But how could...."

"Your Briton Ebba, remember how I once scorned the great love you bore for each other? Without it she would not have helped Edred and myself escape from Finn's slave pens."

"I do not understand"

"Hamund thought more of coin than he did of obeying his paymaster Girdar by murdering me. Edred and I were taken to Finn to be sold as slaves. Ebba discovered we were there after you had left."

Warm love and gratitude washed over Averil, soon would be time to thank Ebba for that which perhaps she could never properly thank her for – the life of the man she loved.

"But how could she have known?"

Ranulph stroked her luxurious flame hair. "Like the past Averil, the reason is now dead." As he spoke Finn came back into the hall, a stocky, brown haired retainer by his side, and a small band of women behind him carrying linen and pitchers of warmed water.

"This man, Lord Ranulph, will take care of your father's injury." The man bowed to the king and Ranulph before motioning to the women behind him to follow him over to the patient.

"Once more I am in the debt of the Frisian King." Ranulph fixed Finn in an unswerving gaze.

"Perhaps one day I shall call on you to account for it." Finn watched them both as Ranulph led Averil over to him.

"I shall await that time in honour Lord King. For you have both the unswerving loyalty and the sword of your Anglii brother." Ranulph held out his hand.

Finn glanced at Averil, whose happiness brought a translucent loveliness to her beautiful countenance, then back at Ranulph. Her husband. Alive against all the odds. It was the work of the Gods. Meant to be. The hands of the two men met in strength of equal match in the grasp of friendship. Averil put her own, slender hand upon theirs, it had a strength which did not surprise either of them, as all three sealed that which could never now be broken.

THE END

Printed in Great Britain
by Amazon.co.uk, Ltd.,
Marston Gate.